"ANXIOUS TO GET

Wynne asked as he pulled the car away from the curb. "We could stop at my place and listen to the crickets in the backyard."

Leila felt a thrill shoot through her. Wynne wasn't thinking of crickets any more than she was. "Sounds nice." She somehow managed to keep her voice even.

"Hey, loosen up," Wynne whispered as he parked in the driveway. "My crickets aren't going to eat you. Or are you afraid they'll spread rumors?"

"Well, they do an awful lot of chirping...."

Wynne smiled. "You're not irrevocably committed, you know. I still could take you home."

"No, this is what I want," Leila said, taking his hand.

Wynne kissed her sweetly, as though giving her a moment to change her mind. Then he leaped from the car, opened the passenger door with a flourish and literally swept Leila off her feet.

"Where are you taking me?" She laughed.

"Somewhere the crickets will never find us...."

ABOUT THE AUTHOR

Patricia Rosemoor is a prolific author, and it is
obvious she loves her chosen career. She is a
woman who embraces life and meets its challenges
head-on. Yet this Chicago-based writer recognizes
that many young women today are preoccupied
with image, which can be devastating to their self-
esteem. With warmth, compassion and a touch of
humor, this issue is addressed in *Working It Out*.
Patricia hopes readers will share her belief that a
person's true worth is on the inside . . . and always
shines through.

Books by Patricia Rosemoor

HARLEQUIN SUPERROMANCE
301–AGAINST ALL ODDS

HARLEQUIN INTRIGUE
38–DOUBLE IMAGES
55–DANGEROUS ILLUSIONS
74–DEATH SPIRAL
81–CRIMSON HOLIDAY
95–AMBUSHED

Patricia Rosemoor

WORKING IT OUT

Harlequin Books

TORONTO • NEW YORK • LONDON
AMSTERDAM • PARIS • SYDNEY • HAMBURG
STOCKHOLM • ATHENS • TOKYO • MILAN

Published December 1988

First printing October 1988

ISBN 0-373-70334-1

To every woman who has
ever tried to change herself
to meet someone else's standards
rather than her own....

And to Ursula, the original "hot body."

PROLOGUE

A MUSKY SCENT permeated the bedroom area of the
New York loft. Leila Forester lay back in her lover's
arms, content. What more could a nineteen-year-old
girl ask for than a loving relationship with a mature
man who had overwhelming good looks, charm and
sophistication?

"Let's do it now." His whisper was low and urgent, surprising her.

"Again?" she asked, her dark eyes wide. She'd
really prefer lying in his arms for a while so she could
savor the feeling of being loved.

He raised a golden blond brow. "That's not what I
meant." Disentangling himself, he left the water bed
and held out his hand to her. "We have an assignment to complete. Remember?"

"Now?"

"Now."

She gave Christian her hand just as she'd given him
her heart eight months before. Leila had never known
anyone like him. She'd never had the kind of approval he gave her—not from any of the guys she'd
dated, not from her family. She'd do just about anything to please Christian. He pulled her long lithe body
up and against his, then kissed her deeply.

"You're sure it's work you're interested in?" she asked with a gasp. When he nodded, she tried to move away.

"Where do you think you're going?"

"To the bathroom. I need a shower. And I have to do something with my makeup and hair."

"You don't have to do a thing. You're perfect as you are."

"Christian!" she protested, but he dragged her down the curved steps to the photo setup, a Victorian couch in cream watered silk backed by hangings of lace and red velvet.

He picked up the teddy she'd been posing in earlier, before he'd forgotten about work. "Here. Slip back into this."

Leila inspected the lace-trimmed red silk garment as she took it from him. At least he hadn't ripped the delicate fabric in his hurry to remove it.

"All right. But you'll have to give me a couple of minutes."

He was already turning on the lights. "No. Now."

"You're serious? You don't want me to fix myself up?"

"Honey, the way you look, no man could resist you. I'm having trouble myself."

Hiding behind the silky material, she laughed to cover her embarrassment. "The spread is for a woman's magazine."

"Probably a third of *Sophisticate*'s readers are men. They're the ones who are going to go out and buy that sexy little number for their lovers for Christmas, even though none of their women will have the hot body that you do."

He turned his back on her as he reached for a filter. She quickly stepped into the teddy. Shaking away the uneasiness that made her throat tighten, Leila pulled on her thigh-high lace stockings and secured them with mistletoe-adorned garters. She slipped into red satin high-heeled slippers and stretched out on the Victorian couch.

Christian studied her through the viewfinder, then stepped forward to slide back a strand of her long dark hair and to lower the strap of the teddy below her shoulder. "You're so perfect," he whispered, kissing her again, trailing his fingers down her bared skin.

Leila's healthy young body responded immediately. She felt the warmth spread from her belly to her thighs. Her breath came unevenly as Christian backed off.

"Perfect," he repeated. "Don't move. I want to capture you on film with that expression."

Even as Leila froze, the uneasy feeling returned. But there was no reason to be edgy with the man she adored. She trusted him completely, or she wouldn't be living with him. He was her lover, her mentor, her protector.

He would never do anything wrong....

CHAPTER ONE

LEILA FORESTER SWAYED and stretched to the soft pop music, losing herself for the moment to the rhythmic sounds. Doubling over, she slid her hands down the purple tights that matched her brief red-and-purple-striped leotard. She wrapped her fingers around her left ankle and pulled in until her forehead touched her knee.

"Stretch but don't strain," Leila told her class from the bent-over position. "Remember, no locked knees. We don't want any back injuries, so keep those knees flexed." The tip of her ponytail trailed the floor, and her dark hair splayed across the off-white carpeting. She used the mirror behind her to check the class. "Good. Now change and stretch!"

Midway to her right leg, two worn jogging shoes and frayed socks caught Leila's attention. Even with her topsy-turvy view, she recognized the hairy masculine legs and the running shorts that had seen better days. He was there again, watching her class.

No. Watching her.

She smiled tightly at the voyeur through the glass wall of the exercise room. Somehow, she thought she wasn't at her most intimidating when upside down and twisted like a pretzel. Keenly aware of the stranger's green eyes roaming the long length of her legs ex-

posed by the high cut of her leotard, she had a difficult time keeping her voice level.

"And up," she said as the taped music segued to
another piece with a faster beat. "Take a deep
breath...and reach." Shifting into the low-impact
aerobics portion of the class, Leila stretched to the
left, raising her right arm and lifting her right foot,
then switching directions. "Reach. And reach. Keep
one foot on the floor at all times. Come on ladies,
push yourselves a little. For inspiration, think of all
those cocktails and pieces of chocolate cake you're
going to work off today."

Involuntarily, she glanced at the man on the other
side of the glass. Six feet of lanky body was topped by
a full mop of reddish-brown hair, an unruly wave
spilling onto his forehead. A matching mustache accented full lips that curved into a friendly smile, while
a dimple popped into his right cheek. He didn't look
like a typical wolf, but then, was there such an animal?

She turned away from the stranger, determined to
concentrate on the individual members of her class.
"Remember, if you can't keep pace, slow down," she
said directly to Elizabeth, the heaviest woman in the
class. "Just make sure you keep moving." Her gaze
traveled to Grace Vanos, an overweight teenager who
was new to the club. "All right, let's kick. Get those
designer leggings in the air. Good, Grace. That's the
idea."

She drove the women, all the while warning them to
adapt the exercise to their own capabilities. As director of physical fitness education at The Total You, an
exclusive health club and luxury spa located in the
River North area of downtown Chicago, Leila felt a

responsibility to the members. Her philosophy of fitting the program to the individual included watching for potential injuries. Some enthusiastic members tended to overdo exercise as well as diet. Her goal was to keep the club's clients on a safe yet effective track in all phases of their programs.

The music shifted in tempo once more. "Everyone walk. Ready to take pulse...." She checked the second hand on the wall clock as the women felt for the arteries in their throats and began to circle the room. "Now!"

Passing the window, Leila came face-to-face with the stranger, who was still watching her. His wink and boyish smile distracted her. She didn't know why he made her tense. Plenty of other male clients sauntered past the exercise-room windows and stopped to watch the almost exclusively female classes. Perhaps this man bothered her because his perusal seemed so personal.

"You missed it!" Jane Radcliff protested loudly, her narrow face pinched into a triumphant expression. "You're supposed to pay attention to this class, aren't you?" she whined, stopping in the middle of the floor.

Aware that the woman was merely trying to draw attention to herself, Leila tried to circumvent further complaint by saying, "So I did. Sorry, Jane. Why don't we try again. Starting...now."

Jane moved with the others, muttering, "I have a mind to speak to Mike Kramer."

Since she normally had a terrific rapport with her ladies, Leila didn't think the executive director of the club would do more than pacify the client, who had a spa-wide reputation for rudeness. She wasn't sure what Jane would expect Mike to do. But the obviously unhappy woman was consistently unpleasant to the club's employees and was always ready to criticize.

Closely watching the sweep hand on the wall clock, Leila said, "Stop. That was ten seconds. Multiply by six. You should be working at 60 to 75 percent of your maximum heart rate. Check the chart to see what's best for your age, and make sure you're within those parameters." Though they'd all heard it before, she repeated the warning. "If you're working at too high a level, slow down until you're back in the correct range. I've never had to use my CPR training yet," she added with a thankful smile, "and I have no desire to ever do so. If any of you are working at less than sixty percent, put a little more effort into the exercise or you won't get the benefit you should from the class."

As she reclaimed her place at the front of the room, Leila sneaked a quick look at the window and immediately relaxed. The stranger was gone.

She continued with renewed enthusiasm.

Forty-five minutes later, after a tough aerobics session and relaxing cool down, she announced the end of class. "That's it, ladies. I've found some new recipes for low-calorie gourmet hors d'oeuvres that I think you'll like. Feel free to take copies as you leave."

The music was replaced by the sound of groans mixed with satisfied chatter. The women filed by the counter as Leila picked up a towel and dried the sweat from her neck and shoulders.

Lingering for a second, Fran Cantello whispered, "Don't let sourpuss Jane get to you. She's rude to other members, too. That woman is her own worst enemy."

"Is that the psychiatric nurse speaking?"

"No. It's the ticked-off human being."

Fran patted Leila's arm and continued on to the counter. About to turn off the stereo, Leila hesitated when she noticed Grace Vanos standing a few yards away, arms twisted behind her back.

"Can I help you with something?"

"I—I just wanted to tell you what a great class you run."

Folding a sheaf of recipes in half, Melanie Bricker joined them. "I told you Leila is the best."

Leila smiled at the teenagers, who seemed to have formed a close friendship in the two weeks since Grace joined the health club. "You girls are going to turn my head with all these compliments."

Grinning in return, they were a study in contrasts. Grace had large hazel eyes and interesting, if bold, features framed by a cloud of dark brown curls. She was an attractive girl in spite of the extra thirty pounds that added to her natural voluptuousness. With her delicate features in a classically pretty face, Mel was her companion's exact opposite. The success story of the club since it opened the year before, the blue-eyed blonde had lost seventy pounds.

Maybe more since her last official weigh-in, Leila thought, her gaze critically sweeping the taller girl's small-boned frame. Was Mel looking a little too thin? Perhaps not. Maybe she was being too sensitive.

"So," Leila said, looking from one to the other, "what's up?"

The girls glanced at each other, and Mel poked her friend. "Go on. Tell her."

"I, uh, lost five pounds," Grace said shyly.

"In your first two weeks—how wonderful! I thought I could see a difference." From a long conversation with the girl's concerned mother, Leila knew that Grace had tried several different diets since entering high school, but the fifteen-year-old hadn't been able to keep off the lost pounds. "As you take off weight, you'll have more energy in class, which will help you continue to lose more—hopefully forever. You were looking pretty good out there today."

"Thanks."

Grace flushed and backed away, but Leila could tell the teenager was pleased in spite of her seeming embarrassment.

"See you Friday," Mel said before throwing an arm around her friend's shoulder. "Come on, kid. I'll teach you how to play racquetball, if you want."

Kid. Melanie was only sixteen herself. Shaking her head, Leila popped out the tape from the stereo system and placed it in the well-stocked cabinet. She left the exercise room and headed for her office, where she'd check for messages before taking a much anticipated shower.

WYNNE DONEGAN WATCHED the voluptuous dark-haired woman rush toward the offices. Leila Forester. The name fit her, as did the classy surroundings.

Taking up most of the upper three floors of a downtown high rise, The Total You was the ultimate in modern health spas—from its restaurants, boutiques and beauty salon to its visual design. Glossy white walls were decorated with geometric shapes and stripes of red and purple, the club's official colors. The pattern was repeated in the plush carpeting underfoot.

He didn't belong here. He'd only come as a friend's guest. But once he'd seen her . . .

He'd been floored. No other way to put it. He'd had to come back for a second look, but that hadn't changed his mind. He had sworn she was Brenna McNeal.

That, of course, was impossible, and Wynne knew it. Still he couldn't help but make comparisons. Raven hair. Exotic features. Deep-set eyes. Luscious mouth with full upper lip. Long lush body. Expensive taste.

But this woman's name was Leila, not Brenna. And she seemed warm. Compassionate. Human. The kind of woman a man might fall in love with.

He couldn't help himself. He had to stick around, had to find out whether or not she was the woman he imagined. . . .

AFTER TAKING CARE OF BUSINESS, Leila left her office only to spot the stranger watching her from a distance. A sense of unease crept through her as she ignored him and strode toward the employee locker room. She almost ran into Gail Sommers, the director of cardiac rehabilitation and a good friend.

"Hey, you could watch where you're going," Gail protested.

"Sorry. I was distracted."

"I'll say." Gail looked over her shoulder as Leila opened the locker-room door. "Is that him?"

"Who?"

"The guy you told me about the other day—the one who was watching you. He fits the description. You didn't tell me how cute he was."

"A cute wolf, maybe."

"So what's wrong with that? You haven't had a wolf or any other really interesting male animal in your life since I've known you." Gail began undoing one of her short blond braids. "And that, my lovely Leila, has been a year, in case you've forgotten."

"Don't start coming on like a mother, okay?" Not that her own mother had shown the slightest interest in what she did with her life—professional or private—since Leila had left New York City and had returned to Illinois and the state university nearly a decade ago. She softened the warning with a teasing, "You're too short to be related to me, anyway."

Gail laughed. "That's it, avoid the issue by reminding me of my deficiencies."

The two women gathered towels, soap and shampoo from their lockers and headed for the showers.

"Sometimes you make it sound as if I don't date," Leila complained.

"Dating and having a significant other are not the same thing."

"Look who's talking."

"At least I can remember what my last significant other looked like."

And she could remember hers, too, Leila thought, entering a cubicle in front of one of the showers. As if she could ever forget the blond hair, blue eyes, chiseled profile and hot body of Christian Manley....

She hung her cotton jump suit on a wall peg, stripped off her work clothes and stepped into the narrow shower stall. Having given her friend an edited version of her long-finished but never-to-be-forgotten relationship with the well-known Manhattan photographer, she thought Gail might be more understanding about her cautious attitude.

"I'm not against finding someone to love," Leila insisted. "I'm waiting for Prince Charming to come along, as is every other living breathing female. Like I've told you before, I'd rather keep business and my personal life separate."

Gail merely grunted, "Christian again," as she turned on the shower.

But Leila didn't want to think about the dark-shadowed past. She merely wanted to enjoy the feeling of pulsating hot water beating down on the back of her neck and shoulders. She must have been tense throughout the aerobics class, even after the stranger had disappeared. Leila sighed. She hadn't meant to think about him. There was no point to it. Still, she couldn't help wondering why the man was so interested in her—other than the obvious.

When Leila stepped out of the shower and back into the dressing cubicle a few minutes later, Gail promptly asked, "So, are you going to go out with him or not?"

"Who?" As if she didn't know.

"Mr. Cute."

"You mean Mr. Wolf."

"Right. Him."

"No."

"You're nuts, Forester."

"First of all, he hasn't even spoken to me—"

"He will."

"Supposing he does—"

"You won't mix business with pleasure."

"Will you let me finish my own sentences?" Leila asked, running the towel over her arms.

"Sure. When you start making sense."

"If you're so hot on the guy, *you* go out with him."

"We haven't been introduced."

"Neither have we."

"Well, when he does approach you with the big come-on," Gail said, her tone sparked with amusement, "you could always let him down gently and tell him you have a friend who *is* interested."

"You're impossible."

"That's why you love me."

It was. Being impossible, if lovable, was part of Gail's appeal. Added to intelligence and compassion, the trait made her small friend a delight.

Leila wrapped her towel around her dripping hair before negotiating the jump suit. Deciding it was an impossible feat in the confined space, she opened the door and stepped out into the waiting area. In the middle of inserting her leg into the garment, she halted at the sound of a sigh, raised an eyebrow and asked, "What now?"

On her tiptoes, Gail was peering over the top of the door to her cubicle. "That was me getting real. What man would want me when he could have you?"

"First of all, I'd have something to say about who could or could not have me. Second, don't start. You know I hate that. Looks aren't everything."

"You can be flippant. You have them."

"And so do you."

"Yeah, if you like the girl-next-door type."

"Plenty of men do. Oh, forget it," Leila muttered, glaring at the other woman while climbing into the fire-engine-red jump suit. "You're not sucking me into this one."

For once Gail gave up gracefully—no doubt she was tired of hearing her friend lecture her. Leila was sure Gail didn't really believe her when she said that looks

in and of themselves were no guarantee of happiness,
fame, fortune... or a man's love.

ONCE HE'D MADE UP HIS MIND that he had to meet
Leila Forester, Wynne had settled in across from the
employee locker room to wait.

He had managed to pump a few staff members and
customers about her, had heard a lot about her
professionally, nothing about her personally—at least
no details that had to do with her life outside of the
club. Everyone agreed that she was a pretty nice human being. Obviously she kept the two areas of her life
separate.

Wynne wondered how she managed it, working at
a "people" job as she did. He himself had never been
able to make the separation, though he'd consciously
made the effort once or twice. He couldn't even count
the number of times he'd wound up more involved
than he'd meant to be in one way or another.

Not that he'd ever been sorry. If the truth be known,
he was superstitious—probably the legacy of his Irish
ancestors. He believed that a person should give
something of himself for every good that happened to
him. And so far, life had been very rewarding, indeed, at least in the ways that really counted.

Wynne wondered if his luck would hold in the case
of Leila Forester.

TYPICALLY IMPATIENT, Leila snapped off the blow-
dryer. Long and thick, her hair took forever to dry, so,
as usual, she left it hanging down her back and around
her shoulders in damp waves. A little gray smudged
around her eyes and a swipe of clear red across her
lips, and she was ready to go.

"Are you sure you don't want to see a movie?" Gail asked. She was poking through her cosmetics bag as though she couldn't make up her mind which of her myriad eye shadows to choose.

"Not tonight. I've got a date."

Pale gray eyes flew to meet hers in the mirror. "With who?"

"The laundry."

Gail grimaced. "I think I'll stick around here for a while, then. Maybe something interesting will turn up."

"Good luck," Leila said as she left the locker room and headed down the hall toward the elevators.

"In a hurry?"

She froze, intent on the deep voice with the pleasant, if slight, lilt. *His* voice, she was sure. When she whirled toward the stranger, he was smiling at her.

Something inside her quivered in response. "So we meet at last."

"I didn't expect you to get out of the showers so quickly. It's a good thing I didn't go anywhere, or I would have missed you."

He'd wedged a shoulder against one of the purple building supports and had crossed his arms over his chest. *It wouldn't hurt him to lift weights,* the professional in her assessed, while another part of her admitted his lanky body wasn't bad just as it was. Dressed in well-worn jeans and a short-sleeved pullover that was lacking an alligator or any other status symbol, he seemed out of place in the sleek surroundings. Obviously the man had confidence in himself.

A wolf in sheep's clothing, she thought with amusement.

"I already know you're Leila Forester," he went on. "So it's only fair to introduce myself. The name's Samuel Wynne Donegan III. Call me Wynne or I'll think you're talking to my father."

"How can you be sure I want to talk to you at all?"

He laughed outright and the skin around his green eyes crinkled. "I can be a pretty amusing person. Why don't we get to know each other better over a drink, and you can see for yourself?" Without losing eye contact, he nodded in the general direction of the open bar at the opposite end of the hall in the central lounge area.

"I don't think so. It's been a long day, and I'm anxious to get home." He needn't know that home was on one of the lower floors of the building. She took a single step away from him. "So, if that's all…"

Wynne's expression was curious. "Do you always discourage men who are interested in you before you give them a chance? Or is it me?"

Leila couldn't stop her lips from curving into a cynical smile. "And what about me interests you?"

"I know you care about your work. The clients like you. You're very personable with them, and they're eager for your approval. I suspect you might be a nice person."

His answer threw her; the compliment wasn't what she'd expected. She wondered if he was sincere, or if he was trying out a clever ploy. "I—I don't date clients."

"Well, then we don't have a problem, because I don't belong to the club." He lowered his voice conspiratorially. "And I promise I won't even consider joining if you agree to have a drink with me."

While trying to think of a reason to refuse, she noticed Gail lurking several yards away, out of Wynne's view.

With broad gestures Gail pointed from Leila to Wynne while nodding vigorously, then threaded her fingers together in mock pleading. Leila did her best not to laugh and tried to discourage her friend with a halfhearted glare. Wynne glanced over his shoulder toward the focus of her attention, but before he could catch the mischievous woman at her antics, Gail quickly headed down the hall for the bar.

She nodded. "Gail is both friend and co-worker."

"We could join her if that would make you feel safer."

"Safer? You think I'm afraid of you?"

Wynne shrugged. "Are you?"

Leila didn't answer. She was surprised that he remained warm and easygoing, and she experienced an unexpected flutter of nerves. An exaggerated check of her watch gave her the excuse to back off toward the elevators. The laundry was waiting, she told herself.

"Nice meeting you, Wynne, but I really must be running. Go ahead and have that drink before you find yourself facing this evening alone." Other women would be eager for Wynne's company, Leila knew.

"Until tomorrow."

"I'm sure you'll be seeing me."

Her flippant statement was punctuated by amused male laughter. Just then an elevator door opened to let out several arriving clients. Leila hurriedly took their place in the now empty car. As she pressed the button that would take her down, she wasn't surprised to see that Samuel Wynne Donegan III was still staring after her.

THE ELEVATOR DOORS closed with a shush of finality that might have discouraged a less determined man. Wynne had never been one to give up on anything he wanted. And he definitely wanted to know more about the mysterious Leila Forester. Brenna could take a few pointers from the intriguing woman.

His gaze strayed to the bar, where Leila's friend Gail sat talking to the bartender. It only took him a second to make up his mind.

CHAPTER TWO

LEILA KEPT A WARY EYE OUT for Wynne the next morning. Knowing he intended to make good his parting challenge, she expected him to show up on the other side of the classroom window. Rather than making her edgy, the idea pumped an extra shot of adrenaline through her system, giving her a boost of energy. She was actually looking forward to the encounter, even though she'd spent a restless evening in the building's laundry room concocting reasons to avoid Wynne.

When lunchtime arrived and Wynne hadn't, she felt a peculiar sense of disappointment. The energy drained from her, leaving Leila hungry and irritable. For some reason, she hadn't heard her alarm that morning and therefore had missed breakfast. Stomach rumbling, she wrapped a dance skirt around her waist and headed for Health Nuts, the club's fast-food vegetarian eatery, where she met Gail for lunch.

The two women quickly whipped through the cafeteria line and found seats at a small table in the corner.

As they set their trays down, Gail said, "I don't know why you wouldn't have a drink with Wynne, but I did. He came to the bar after you left. He's adorable."

"So are stray puppies."

"He's so amusing. I wish the evening had lasted longer. One drink and he had to go."

The women made themselves comfortable. Gail attacked her cheese enchiladas with gusto. Leila picked at her salad and pretended disinterest as long as she could before asking, "So, when is your big date?"

"Well, Wynne didn't exactly ask me out. As a matter of fact, we were talking about you."

"What?"

About to demand the details, Leila was put off by her friend's sudden groan and pained expression.

"Oh, no. Get ready for the Neanderthal Wit. He's heading this way."

Knowing her lunch was about to be ruined, Leila sighed deeply and took a quick look to her left. Jocko Gorski was moving toward them. She kept her features passive even when Jocko paused in the middle of the room and flexed his muscles for the benefit of some young women who were avidly watching him. An ex-football hero, he'd been snapped up by Mike Kramer at retirement. More than once, Gail had suggested that Jocko had quit football because he'd been kicked in the head one too many times.

"What do you think he wants?" Leila muttered, spearing some lettuce and a crouton with her fork.

"Who cares? You know, he reminds me of one of the great apes in Lincoln Park Zoo," Gail said in a low tone. "There's something about that protruding forehead... And have you ever noticed that his hands hang nearly to his knees?"

Privately, Leila thought the comparison a disservice to the zoo animals, who were better behaved. Jocko was bad news, and now he was heading straight for them. She crunched into her apple and steeled herself for the coming confrontation. Though she was normally easygoing, Leila tolerated the chauvinistic director of recreation only with concentrated effort.

Jocko stopped directly in front of their table and ceased his habitual gum chewing long enough to goad her. "So. How's the two beauties today?" His eyes were glued to Leila's cleavage, making it obvious that he wasn't inquiring about the two women.

Angry, feeling her skin flush, Leila did her best to stay calm. "Jocko, your vulgarity never ceases to amaze me."

"Thanks." He grinned and resumed chewing his gum.

"Is there a point to your disturbing our lunch, or did you come over here simply to annoy me?"

"Hey, what a kidder you are." He punched her lightly in the arm while drawing a chair from the next table. He flipped it around and straddled it.

"Pea brain," Gail muttered under her breath.

"Huh?"

"I was wondering if it was going to rain."

"Nah. Forecast is clear for the rest of the week."

Gail smothered a giggle and studied her lunch. Jocko continued to sit and chomp and stare.

Losing her patience, Leila dropped her apple. "Jocko, get to the point. Why are you here?"

"Oh, yeah. The boss wants you in his office right away."

"Fine. Now that you've delivered your message, why don't you flex your way back to Mike's office and tell him I'll be there as soon as I finish my lunch."

"Uh-uh. He said now."

"You had better be telling the truth," Leila warned him.

But Jocko was already ignoring her, his attention centering on a redhead two tables away. He flexed, the redhead smiled, and Leila wanted nothing more than to get away from him, lunch or no lunch.

"I'd better see what Mike wants," she told Gail as she stood.

"Hurry back. I won't let the busboy clear your food while I'm here. But you know how fast this tray will disappear if it's left alone for five seconds."

"Thanks. I'll do my best."

Curious, Leila thought as she set out for Mike's office, it wasn't like the executive director to single her out for a command appearance without an explanation. Then an unpleasant thought struck her, making Leila groan. Jane Radcliff. The woman must have complained about her as she'd threatened to do in class the day before. Worse, Mike must be taking her seriously.

At her boss's office door, Leila pasted a smile onto her stiff lips and took a deep breath before knocking.

"Come on in."

Stepping through the doorway, she was aware only of the executive director, whose rugged face was softened by a welcoming, if self-satisfied, smile. As usual he was dressed impeccably, today in an off-white suit and a butter-cream shirt that complemented his gray-streaked light brown hair and set off his carefully cultivated year-round tan.

"Jocko said you wanted to see me immediately."

Mike stood and held out his arm to her right. His sleeve lifted slightly, revealing a gold Rolex. "I have someone I want you to meet, Leila."

If ever her inner radar should have warned her, it should have been then. Relieved she wasn't in for a grim session with her no-nonsense boss, Leila turned to the other person in the room without suspicion.

"Leila Forester, meet Wynne Donegan."

His very appearance left her wide-eyed and speechless. She'd been ready and waiting for him to show all morning. She hadn't guessed it would be under these circumstances. She hadn't guessed he would be wearing perfectly creased brown trousers, a well-fitted tan blazer and a respectable-looking tie.

"A pleasure to meet you at last, Leila. I've heard nothing but praise about your work here."

Wynne greeted her as though they were strangers. As though their conversation the evening before had never taken place. As though he hadn't pumped Gail for who knew what information about her!

She forced her throat muscles to work. "Mr. Donegan."

Mike indicated a chair next to Wynne. She sat. Staring. Waiting.

"Mr. Donegan is a respected journalist," Mike explained. "Before going into business for himself, he was on the feature staff of the *Chicago Tribune*. In addition he has free-lanced for several national magazines for the past few years."

"Really. How fascinating." Instincts humming, Leila said, "And now you want to do a free-lance article on The Total You."

Wynne's quirky smile answered for him.

"For *Glitter* magazine," Mike told her. "And he wants to pick *your* brain for information and an approach."

Though Leila doubted picking her brain was what the reporter had in mind, she decided to be diplomatic and keep that observation to herself.

"You flatter me, Mr. Donegan, but perhaps you ought to work with one of the other directors who has more media experience. I'm sure you'll remember Jocko Gorski—"

"It's not Jocko I'm interested in."

He couldn't be more direct than that, Leila thought, refraining from responding to his unspoken meaning.

"What Mr. Donegan means is that *you* are the director of physical fitness education, and that's the area of expertise he's most interested in."

She knew exactly what Wynne Donegan meant. The question was, which had come first—his interest in the article or his interest in her? "Yes, but Jocko is so... flamboyant. In the public eye, I mean." She referred to Jocko's recent success on the football field. Her own short-lived shot at fame had been buried for a decade, so Wynne couldn't know, unless... No, Gail would never have told him.

When he merely said, "I'm sure the public would prefer to know about you—and your area of expertise," Leila was sure she was correct. Yet as he spoke, she was drawn to his sparkling eyes and the thick burnished lashes that framed them. She willed herself to ignore the attraction. Instinctively, her guard went up.

"So, I expect the two of you will work very well together," Mike said.

"I'd love to," she hastily assured her boss while deciding one last escape attempt was mandatory. "But I don't know when I'll have the time. You know how many classes I handle in addition to scheduling and supervising my staff, arranging individual client consultations, completing all the required paperwork—"

"Find time." It was an order, one Mike would not expect her to argue with. "Even if you have to schedule someone else overtime to cover for you, the corporation would be compensated quite generously by the publicity."

"Undoubtedly," Leila said.

But what did Wynne Donegan imagine was in it for him—other than his professional fee? Or was her past experience making her unduly suspicious?

"Good. Then you can start making arrangements immediately." Mike stood and held out his hand to Wynne, who also rose. "Well, Mr. Donegan, let me know if I can be of further assistance. I would appreciate your keeping me posted about the angle you intend to use...although I'm certain you'll display our best features in your article."

Wynne shook the executive director's hand. "I plan to do just that," he agreed, his voice warm, his intense gaze centered on Leila.

Preceding him out the door, she strode away from the office without a backward glance. She couldn't shake the feeling that she was the focal point of a smoothly executed setup. Within seconds, Wynne was at her side making his presence known.

"What's the rush?"

She continued to stare straight ahead. "I only have fifteen minutes to finish my lunch."

'I haven't eaten, either,' Wynne said agreeably. "Where are we going?"

"To Health Nuts. A vegetarian cafeteria."

"Sounds...great."

In spite of herself, Leila glanced at Wynne. His inability to hide his lack of enthusiasm made her grin. "I expect you're a regular meat-and-potatoes man."

"I've been known to eat an occasional piece of quiche. So far, it hasn't hurt my reputation."

Amused, Leila relaxed. Spending time in Wynne's company might not be too hard to take, even if it was in the line of duty. She'd been put off by the thought that he was trying to manipulate her into seeing him despite her wishes. No doubt it was the other way around; Wynne had decided to pursue a story on fitness, had come to the club to do research and had found himself inadvertently attracted to her.

When they entered the cafeteria, Leila promptly looked for Gail, but both her friend and her own barely touched lunch were gone. Figuring she'd just have time to eat something small if she rushed, she picked out another salad. Wynne bought three slices of vegetarian pizza and a chunk of cheesecake before following her to a nearby table.

Sprawling out across from her, he eyed her meager selection as he pulled a small notebook from an inner breast pocket. "Do you always eat like a rabbit?"

"Of course not. I'm not a vegetarian, nor do I have any desire to starve myself." Hearing her own sharpness, Leila told herself there was nothing to be defensive about. She cleared her throat and in a much more natural tone added, "I never eat much when I'm working. There's no pleasure in exercising on a full stomach."

He made a few scribbles in his notebook. "No heavy meals before exercise." When his green eyes met her dark ones, they were flashing with a wicked gleam. "Does that include *any* kind of exercise?"

Leila pretended to misunderstand. "I believe in a balanced diet. With all the exercise I get, I usually can eat what I want. The holidays are the only time I have to watch my intake."

After glancing at her watch, she split her concentration between eating and wondering about Wynne Donegan's motivations. He looked around at the blackboard with the daily fare, checked to see what selections other diners had chosen and made a few more entries in his notebook. He seemed to be taking this story seriously. Then he tried his vegetarian pizza.

Leila watched him bite through the thick gooey cheese. "So, what do you think?" she asked.

"Delicious," he mumbled with his mouth full.

"You sound surprised." She took one last bite of salad and chewed quickly. "Just because something is good for you, it doesn't have to be boring."

The wicked gleam returned to his eyes. This time, Leila laughed.

"Can you do that again?" he asked. "It was terrific."

But she was already pushing herself up and away from the table. "Sorry. No time. I have to leave for class, but I'm free afterward. Meet me in my office in an hour. We can work out a schedule for tomorrow if you spend some time now figuring out what you want to know."

"I want to know everything about you."

"That's not why we're working together."

His mustache twitched. "Are you sure about that?"

Leila stared suspiciously at Wynne. Had she been correct, after all? "Exactly when did you decide to do this feature on the club?"

"Hmm. I think it was when you ran off yesterday before giving me a chance to get to know you better."

Leila was about to respond when Wynne popped a piece of pizza into her open mouth. Leila just stood there, astonished.

"You'd better hurry or you'll be late. Don't worry, I'll find you."

GRACE VANOS WALKED BRISKLY down La Salle Street, wondering if she hadn't made a mistake in agreeing to meet Melanie Bricker at Rica's Café. Dieting was difficult enough without placing herself directly in temptation's path. She knew she ought to lock herself away from the places that contained any food that couldn't be found either in the produce section or at the fish counter of the local supermarket.

But if Mel could lose weight without sacrificing her social life, why couldn't she? It was a matter of developing willpower, Grace told herself. She would meet Mel as she had agreed to do and limit herself to a cup of espresso with noncaloric sweetener. The adult treat in itself could be enough to satisfy her so that she wouldn't be tempted to cheat.

She would not cheat.

Grace repeated the silent promise to herself over and over like a litany. She had lost five pounds in two weeks. She had to remember that and to keep in mind her goal of twenty-five more. This time, she would succeed in losing all of the weight—and she would keep it off. She knew she could do it. Leila had said so, and Mel was living proof the impossible could happen. The other girl had lost seventy pounds since she'd joined The Total You.

Turning on Superior, Grace spotted Rica's Café tucked between two art galleries. She hesitated only a moment before peering into the restaurant to make sure Mel was there. If she hadn't arrived yet, Grace would wait outside. She'd feel weird in a sophisticated place like that, all by herself. People would watch her, maybe feel sorry for her.

But the first thing her startled eyes encountered was Mel near the window at a small table on which sat a large piece of chocolate torte and half of another on a single plate. Grace hesitated in the doorway, expecting Mel to be embarrassed or maybe even try to hide the desserts. She considered leaving and giving the other girl time to cheat in private.

Before she could back out, Mel spotted her and waved her over as if nothing in the world was wrong. "Hi, Gracie. I got here early, so I ordered. I hope you don't mind."

"N-no, of course not."

Grace tried not to look at the torte, but she couldn't help herself. Chocolate was her favorite thing in the entire world. It was the only thing that could make her feel good when everything else was rotten. Of course, that feeling only lasted as far as the bathroom scale, she reminded herself.

She sat across from Mel, wondering what had happened to make her go off her diet so drastically. "You must have had a bad day, huh?"

"Not particularly. You want some of this?"

"No."

"So what would you like?" asked a young waitress in jeans and a fancy sweatshirt who stopped at their table. "We have mocha and Black Forest—"

"No dessert!" Grace said quickly. "A cup of espresso with noncaloric sweetener, please."

"Back in a minute," the waitress promised.

"You don't know what you're missing." Mel stuffed an extralarge chunk of torte in her mouth.

"Oh, yes I do. But let's talk about something more exciting. Like what did you do last night?"

"Hung around. Walked over to Oak Street Beach with a couple of friends. Met a new guy."

"A guy?" Grace echoed with interest. "What's he like? Did he ask you out?"

The question was hardly out of her mouth before Grace felt foolish. Any guy who didn't try to put the make on a gorgeous thin blue-eyed blonde was crazy.

"Luke is an absolute hunk, and we're going to a party at his friend's Lake Shore Drive high rise on Saturday. His parents are out of town. Radical, huh? Want to come?"

"Nah. I'd be in the way."

"Ask a guy."

"What guy?"

"Oh, right." Mel's brow puckered. "I could fix you up with one of my friends. Or maybe Luke—"

"No fix ups, please."

Grace shuddered. She'd had a blind date once when she'd doubled with a friend. At least the guy had wished he'd been blind so he wouldn't have to look at her. He'd told her friend's date who'd told her friend who'd told her.

"Maybe you're right," Mel said. "After all, I don't really know Luke yet." She pointed to her plate, which was almost empty. Only a third of a piece of torte was left. "Are you sure you don't want a taste of this before it's gone?"

Grace swallowed hard. "I'd love to, but no thanks."

Mel whipped into the piece and took the last bite just as the waitress brought the espresso.

"Listen," Mel said after she'd barely taken her last swallow, "I have to go to the ladies' room. Keep an eye on my purse, would you?"

"No problem."

While Mel was gone, Grace sipped at her espresso and tried not to think about guys, an almost impossible task considering she had a perfect view of the dark-haired hunk at the table in the corner. The gorgeous redhead with him leaned over for a kiss. Not a light smack but the serious kind. Grace could see his leg rub against hers under the table. Embarrassed by the public display, she looked away, out to the street and the passersby.

Another couple stopped in front of the window and looked in. The well-dressed man had a possessive hand on the woman's hip. There was nothing out of the ordinary about her looks. Her features were average, her medium brown hair spiked in a current style. But her legs . . . She had long *thin* legs, which were displayed by a miniskirt. Grace knew she'd rather be dead than wear something so revealing, but this woman obviously liked the exposure.

Would she ever have that confidence? Grace wondered. Annoyed with herself, she concentrated on her espresso, but her mind didn't stop churning. Would she ever have a guy who looked at her with longing? Who wanted to kiss her intimately?

Suddenly she realized her coffee had gone cold. What was taking Mel so long? She checked her watch. Almost ten minutes. She forced herself to make the tiny cup last. Finally, a couple of minutes later, Mel came back to the table, rummaged through her purse and found a breath spray, which she promptly used.

Clearing her throat, she asked, "You want to go look through the galleries or have another cup of espresso?"

"We could have another cup after we tour the galleries," Grace suggested.

"Great." Mel waved to the waitress and dug in her purse. She pulled out a wallet and a package of gum. "Want a piece?" she asked, sticking two of them into her own mouth.

Glancing at the package, Grace frowned. "But it's not sugarless."

"Yeah, I know."

"I don't understand. How can you eat chocolate cake and chew gum with sugar and keep your weight down?"

"The exercise, mostly. And I don't eat chocolate all the time. But I cheat if I feel like it, and I don't care who knows. Rules are made to be broken, Gracie. You have to know how to get around them."

"I wish you would tell me how."

"Maybe I will. What are friends for, anyway?" Mel winked at her just as the waitress brought the check. "My treat."

"Thanks."

Grace felt a rush of happiness shoot through her. She still couldn't believe Mel had decided to befriend her. Not that she didn't have friends, but none of the girls at school understood how difficult it was to be fifteen and a "porker." A couple of the guys had called her that after a coed gym class last spring. When they realized she'd heard their nasty comment, they hadn't even seemed sorry. They'd snickered and walked right past her.

Well, she wouldn't be a porker for long. She would spend the entire summer changing her image. She was willing to diet and work out three or four afternoons a week at The Total You. More, if necessary.

She would do whatever she had to do to look like Mel, Grace decided, even if it killed her!

HE'D HAVE TO FIND an appropriate way to thank his old friend, Harry Benton, Wynne thought as he followed Leila into her office. Maybe he'd send the man a bottle of cognac.

When Wynne had called him the night before, the managing editor of *Glitter* had jumped on the idea of an article about an exclusive health club built expressly as part of a new high-rise complex. He'd promised to make room in an upcoming issue less than a month away. Privately, Wynne was sure some other reporter hadn't come through with a promised story and Harry needed a fill-in, but he didn't care about the editor's reasons. Whatever they were, he had his opportunity to get to know Leila better, and that was what mattered.

Wynne knew Leila had been upset that he'd decided to do the article after she'd turned him down. Maybe he shouldn't have told her. Though he didn't mind being manipulative when the occasion called for such covert action, lying or hiding the facts wasn't his style.

Still, he didn't think she appreciated his honesty, and he was sure there was a definite chill in the air as they made themselves comfortable, she behind her desk, he facing her. Silent and a little grim around the edges, she was obviously waiting for him to speak.

"I was thinking about what you said over lunch, and it's given me an idea." Wynne pulled out his notebook.

"What was that?" she asked coolly.

"That you don't have to watch the calories except at the holidays because of all the exercise you get. Maybe we could use 'exercise instead of diet to manage weight' as our angle."

"That would be misleading. Most people have to balance exercise with diet to stay fit. Not everyone has the same metabolism. Not everyone is able to get the same amount of exercise. As a matter of fact, not everyone is meant to be equally thin."

"Are you saying some people shouldn't lose weight even though they're not within what's considered the acceptable range?" Wynne asked.

"Exactly."

"I wouldn't go spreading that around. You might forfeit customers. I mean, you are in the glamour business."

He practically felt her bristle when she stated, "Pardon me, but I'm in the fitness business."

"The Total You ads sell glamour."

"I'm not in charge of the club's advertising campaign."

"If you were, would you change it?"

She stared at him. Silent. Suspicious. He wasn't getting to first base with her.

"Okay. I don't really care about the ads," he admitted. "I'm merely trying to figure out what makes you tick. Professionally," he quickly added before she had the chance to misinterpret him. He could wait a while longer to explore her personal side.

Leila seemed to relax a little. "I wasn't suggesting anyone should remain grossly overweight and not try to do something about it. That wouldn't be healthy. However, I personally believe that treating these so-called charts like the word of God is ridiculous. Individuals should be treated as such. A person might easily carry five, even ten pounds or more than what is considered 'acceptable' and still look good—and more importantly *feel* good."

Wynne could tell that was important to her. Leila cared, and her concern showed as she warmed to her subject. He had trouble keeping up with his notes as she continued.

"The type of regimen a person should follow must be determined by a variety of factors, the most important of which is general health, including any glandular problems. Then there's body structure, type of work, type of life-style. I help clients formulate nutritionally sound diets and safe exercise programs that not only help them get and stay fit but that they can live with and enjoy."

Still scribbling, Wynne stated, "The Total You concept."

Leila nodded. "That's why I took the job. As director of physical fitness education, I've done my best to make the concept a reality. The psychological factor is very important when dealing with people."

"Psychologically speaking, doesn't every woman who walks through your doors want to be gorgeous, every man a hunk?"

"Perhaps they do. My personal goal is to help them be healthy and physically fit and happy about who they are. Society's concept of beauty is an artificial one, anyway," Leila said with vehemence. "It changes constantly. Fifty years ago, thin was not in as it is to-day."

She was touchy about something, Wynne thought, trying to read her intense expression. Had she been overweight herself once? Her negative attitude toward society's concept of beauty was at odds with her own appearance. He found it hard to believe that she hadn't always been perfect looking.

Perfect. She would probably debate that. He could hear her now: "Perfect for whom and by whose standards?" Leila Forester was turning out to be even more intelligent and intriguingly complex than he'd hoped.

Wynne quickly scanned his notes. "Interesting," he finally said. "What is beauty? Beauty versus health. Developing the individual. I think we're onto something."

He could sense that he had Leila's reluctant approval and that she was trying to hide it from him. For some reason, he thought her distrust ran deeper than his having tricked her into working with him.

"How would you suggest we begin?" he asked.

"By your getting a feel for the various exercise classes and activities, as well as the kinds of counseling sessions and nutritional guidance we offer our clients. Talk to them so you get a better idea of how we individualize programs. I think you should spend a few days observing my classes, perhaps some of the other instructors' classes, as well."

"I'll be here tomorrow morning, ready to start observing."

Wynne noticed the momentary flicker of surprise that crossed her features before she schooled them into a more passive expression.

"Good. Then if there's nothing else . . ."

He ignored her attempt to end the session. "I would like to get some pertinent background here. You do have a somewhat different view of your role than many other professionals in your position. What kind of training do you have, and where did you get it?"

"I have a master's degree in exercise physiology from the University of Illinois."

"Was your personal philosophy formed by that training—" he watched her closely for any involuntary response "—or by personal experience?"

Her gaze locked with his for a heartbeat before she glanced down at her watch. "You'll have to forgive me, but I have an appointment in twenty minutes. I need to prepare for it."

Wynne was a man who knew when to yield. Temporarily, that was. Leila Forester wasn't going to open up to him at this point no matter how long or hard he probed. He'd only alienate her further if he continued to try. And alienating Leila was the last thing in the world he wanted to do. It would ruin everything.

"I can take a hint," he said, rising. "I'll meet you here in the morning at . . . ?"

"Eight-thirty would be fine."

The cool reply was meant to chill him. He countered it with what he hoped was a warm smile.

"See you then."

He left Leila's office without looking back. He had tomorrow and the day after and the day after that to chip away at her icy reserve. Eventually he was going to find out what made that lady tick.

CHAPTER THREE

LEILA CHECKED HER WATCH and hurried down the hall. Seven minutes until class. She'd been tied up in the monthly planning meeting with Mike and the other directors longer than she'd expected. Before entering the empty exercise room, she looked around for Wynne. He'd spent at least part of the past hour interviewing a client. No sign of the reporter. She went inside and searched the cabinet for the audio tape she planned to use for the next hour.

Leila had been more than a little surprised when Wynne hadn't objected to her suggestion that he spend several days observing not only her classes but those of other instructors, as well. He'd sailed through most of this first day with flying colors. She had to give him credit: he seemed to be taking this article on fitness seriously, even if he was using the opportunity to get to know her.

She supposed she should be flattered that he'd gone to so much trouble. In a way she was.

Still, she'd had plenty of experience with just such a determined man in the past. An ambitious photographer, Christian had manipulated her and then had used her for his own purposes. Wynne worked in a related field. While living in New York, Leila had met reporters who weren't any more reluctant about furthering their own careers at the expense of others than

Christian had been. Leila knew she'd better be careful around the tricky Wynne Donegan.

That's why she'd been on her guard when Wynne had started delving into her past the day before. Afraid he'd been after a "hot lead," she'd decided to be careful about what she said around him. She didn't want to read about her past as a model—and her reasons for quitting—in a national magazine. Only a few people knew the real story, and she was determined to keep it that way.

Though the wounds had healed years ago, Leila suspected they could be reopened with little effort.

She found the tape and popped it into the stereo system just as Grace Vanos entered and moved toward the back of the room, where she began some stretching exercises. Good. Leila had been hoping for the opportunity to approach the shy teenager without an audience.

"Grace, can I talk to you a minute?"

"Uh, sure, Leila." Her brow furrowed, Grace bounced up from the floor immediately. "Is something wrong?"

"No. Not at all. I was wondering if you'd like to make an appointment with me to go over your program. You might want to consider some adjustments now that you've become more familiar with the club and our offerings." Leila smiled reassuringly. "I would also like to discuss your diet. You really ought to be attending a nutrition class."

Grace shrugged. "That's not necessary. I have things under control."

"I hope so." Leila tried to put her concerns delicately so as not to offend the girl. "I know that in the past you've had some difficulty keeping off weight you've lost. Many people have misconceptions about what diets can and cannot do for you. In the nutrition class, we closely examine the food groups and think in terms of lifelong guides.''

"None of that is necessary. I'm doing fine now. I've lost another pound.''

"Well, that's wonderful, but—''

"I'm planning on increasing my aerobic activities so I don't have to worry about what I eat every moment.'' Grace crossed her arms over her chest and stared at a spot on the floor. "Mel's helping me. I just have to keep doing what she does, and I'll be fine.''

Temporarily taken aback by the girl's uncharacteristic attitude, Leila tried to regroup. Then, when several other students including Mel wandered into the room, she knew she'd lost her chance for the moment. She would like to speak to Grace further—and to Mel, who really was beginning to look too thin—but she would wait for another day.

"All right, Grace. Why don't we let this go for now. Maybe we can arrange an appointment after you've been here a while longer.''

Rather than answering, the teenager went back to her stretching exercises, and Wynne's immediate entrance distracted Leila from dwelling further on Grace's unusual disposition. Though merely observing, Wynne was dressed as though he were ready to participate in the aerobics class. His neon-orange shorts clashed with his bright green sweatshirt, which had once had sleeves. That morning he'd told her he'd dressed to be inconspicuous, yet she doubted many of their male clients would wear such a disreputable outfit. Somehow, though, he looked more natural than he had in the trousers, jacket and tie he'd worn the day before.

Turning her thoughts to his interview with the client, she asked, "Did you get what you needed?"

"A real testimonial to your whole operation," Wynne admitted. "Impressive. If I didn't know better, I would say you set me up."

"That's not fair. You chose your own subject."

"True, but if I had my real choice..."

Green eyes sparkling with good humor, Wynne let the sentence go unfinished—leaving Leila with no doubt that he'd have chosen her. An odd feeling curled through her stomach, leaving her speechless and uncomfortable. If she didn't know better, she would conclude that she was attracted to Wynne Donegan.

"What in the world is going on here?" Jane Radcliff's shrill voice made them both jump as she strode into the room, pinched face indignant. Pointing at Wynne, she demanded, "Who is this man?"

"The name's Donegan, ma'am."

Leila noticed that Wynne recovered from his initial surprise quickly. He smiled at the woman. Jane shifted uncomfortably, drew her brows together and tightened her lips as she inspected his outfit from his cut-off sweatshirt to his scruffy jogging shoes.

"What is he doing here?" she asked Leila, as though Wynne couldn't speak for himself. "Are you using class time to further your social life?"

Only Jane Radcliff could jump to such a conclusion, Leila thought wryly. "Mr. Donegan is a feature writer on assignment."

"A writer?"

"I'm doing a story on fitness for *Glitter* magazine," Wynne volunteered. "I'm in the research stage

right now. That's why I'm here. I was hoping you and
the other lovely ladies in Ms Forester's aerobics class
might help me out with my article. For example, you
obviously don't need to lose weight, so I would like to
know what benefits you feel you get from this class
and the club in general.''

Preening at his compliment, her sour expression
dissolving rapidly, Jane murmured, ''I see, an article
for *Glitter*. Well, I guess you would have to observe
some of the classes and talk to the students. I, personally, would be happy to discuss anything you like.''

''Wonderful.''

Was that a smile turning up Jane's lips? Leila wondered in amazement. The woman blinked rapidly. If
Leila didn't know better, she might actually believe
Jane was flirting with Wynne. She gave the reporter a
sidelong glance.

''Well,'' she said to Jane, ''I hope everyone in the
class welcomes Mr. Donegan with equal enthusiasm.''

Her open smile was met with the familiar frown and
pucker that were Jane's trademarks. The client opened
her mouth as if she were about to utter another protest. Before she could do so, several more students entered, whispering among themselves. All eyes were
focused on Wynne.

''I'll introduce you to the others, Mr. Donegan,''
Jane said, quickly staking her claim and acting as if
the reporter were there at her invitation.

''I would appreciate that.''

Leila watched as Jane corralled Wynne and marched
him toward the other women. His ability to make
conquests was amazing. A few introductions and a
lopsided smile later, he'd won the group over. Several

of the students were trying to get his attention at once. She wondered whether the promised article was the cause—or if it was the man himself.

"Class time, ladies," Leila called over the din. "Spread out. Let's concentrate on the music, get in the mood and warm up our muscles."

The women reluctantly took their places while Wynne moved to the counter, where he leaned back. Aware of him watching her, Leila started the music and led the slow stretches that would allow the participants to limber up. Only with effort was she able to ignore him and concentrate on helping individual class members.

The music changed to a faster-paced number, and she began the aerobics routine. Noticing how much harder than usual her ladies were working—and no one was complaining—Leila realized she'd seen this amazing improvement in each of her classes that day. Then she noted several women turning their heads in Wynne's direction, as though they wanted to see whether or not he noticed how well they were doing. She couldn't believe it. The women were showing off for him.

Honestly, the way they were reacting to Wynne's presence, he might have been another Arnold Schwarzenegger. Amused, Leila contemplated bringing a man into class more often—great for some instant "inspiration."

When Leila announced the end of the session, several enthusiastic women immediately surrounded the reporter. Others took their time filing out of the room, all the while giving him covert glances.

"So when are you going to start these interviews?" one woman asked.

"Next week, between classes."

"I'll volunteer."

"So will I," said another.

"He's interviewing me first," Jane stated.

Leila put away the music tape and turned off the amplifier. Still surrounded and held captive, Wynne was looking a little harried.

"I'm delighted to see you have plenty to keep you busy, Mr. Donegan." Leila kept a straight face with difficulty. After all, he'd brought this on himself. "So I'll meet you Monday morning, same time, same place."

Wynne merely winked good-naturedly in response. Before turning away, Leila caught the dour expression Jane aimed at her. She bit her lip to keep from laughing and headed for her office. If nothing else, having Wynne Donegan around for a while might prove to be an interesting experience.

"I HOPE LEILA speaks to me after this," Gail said, her tone uncertain.

"What are you doing that's so terrible? I just want to talk to her, and you're making that possible."

Wynne smiled at his coconspirator as they left the apartment complex elevator on the seventeenth floor. Gail's expression was dubious.

"Right. I'm only using the extra set of keys she gave me to let you onto her floor. It's not like I'm letting you into her apartment."

"I won't even tell her how I got this far," Wynne promised. "I'll keep her guessing."

"Don't underestimate her. Leila has even more brains than beauty. She'll figure it out. Well, I'd better get going." Gail pushed the call button for the elevator. "Her apartment number is 1711."

About to head down the hall, Wynne hesitated. "Why did you agree to help me, anyway?"

"Leila usually takes excellent care of herself... I mean outwardly. But every woman needs someone else to care about, as well." Gail shrugged and aimed an impish smile at him. "I think you'd be good for her."

A reminder of his real reason for talking Gail into helping him brought with it a stab of guilt. He was sure she'd be furious if she knew the truth.

"Thanks," he muttered, turning away from her as a ding signaled an arriving elevator car.

"Good luck."

Wynne waved and went on down the luxuriously decorated hallway that might have intimidated a modestly impoverished man with less brass. But he'd been in plenty of places where he didn't exactly fit in, and it had never stopped him before.

His steps slowed as it occurred to him that this time was different. He wasn't hot on the trail of a story. Not exactly. This was far more personal. And he wasn't merely after "a name." He was after a flesh-and-blood woman who had so many positive qualities that he couldn't help liking her.

Wasn't that what this whole thing was about?

Stopping short, he tensed and tightly gripped the handle of his gym bag. His determination wavered. Was he being unfair to Leila? The thought hadn't struck him before. Then again, what would he ask of her but to let him get to know her better? They might even become friends. Wynne smiled—the idea gave him a warm glow—and he continued down the corridor. When he found 1711, he rapped on the door and settled his shoulder against the jamb to wait.

"Who is it?"

"Wynne Donegan."

He listened intently. Nothing at first. Then he heard Leila stir. Soft footsteps approached the other side of the door.

Wynne smiled at the peephole. Somehow—maybe because it took her so long to respond—he knew she was glaring at him through the thing. Finally, the door gave way. Framed in the opening, she presented a wonderfully sexy picture with her silky turquoise jump suit clinging to every curve. Wynne repressed the urge to whistle.

"What can I do for you?" she asked.

Her suspicious expression wasn't unexpected, yet he wondered why she drew on it so easily and so often when smiles and laughter suited her far better. That she didn't trust him was obvious. Because he was a reporter? Or because he was a mildly aggressive man who had managed to get what he wanted?

"You disappeared after class," Wynne said. "We didn't have a chance to wind the day up properly."

"I didn't see any reason to wait around. You were busy. We have all next week to—"

"But I'm not busy now," he cut in smoothly. "Can I come in? I need to ask you a few things."

Her deep-set dark eyes were expressionless, hiding her thoughts. "Can't your questions wait until Monday?"

"Actually, I need some answers before then."

A single brow arched. "First, I have a question for you—like how did you get on this floor?"

"I took the elevator, of course." Wynne pretended to misunderstand her meaning. "Seventeen floors is a tough haul, even for someone in the best condition. And I'm nowhere near that prepped."

Though Leila didn't pursue the topic, he had the feeling Gail had been correct; Leila knew exactly how he'd managed to get past the locked door at street level and into that elevator. Guiltily, he hoped this wouldn't cause a rift between the friends. Leila took so long to make up her mind that he was almost surprised when she moved out of the way and indicated that he might enter.

"Come on in."

What didn't surprise him at all was her apartment. The long open space that served both as living and dining room might have been a layout for a glossy magazine. Wynne stopped in the middle of the seating area, and, setting down his gym bag, took mental inventory.

The warm gray tones in the couches and carpeting were set off by vivid splashes of hot color—predominantly reds and yellows—in throw pillows, accent area rugs, framed prints and ceramic pieces. Neither cluttered nor austere. A perfect balance. The decor was classy, expensive, colorful, warm—reflecting the woman who lived there.

Brenna preferred off-white with cool pastels, which said something significant about *her* personality.

Leila cleared her throat. "You can sit down. The furniture won't bite you."

He made himself at home on one of the two large sofas, not a difficult task. The piece of furniture was plush and made for comfort. He patted the cushion next to him, but Leila ignored the invitation. Her arms crossed over her chest, she stood barely a yard away. If she meant to be intimidating, she was failing admirably. All Wynne could think of was that she was far more desirable than Brenna. He could imagine taking Leila in his arms and feeling her melt against him.

But that wasn't what he'd come for.

Impatiently, she demanded, "So what did you want to discuss?"

"Tomorrow."

"Tomorrow is Saturday."

"I know. Saturday usually comes after Friday."

"I'm not scheduled to work."

"Good."

Noticing the way her long hair fell loose and gently curved over one shoulder, Wynne was distracted from his purpose. She wore it in a ponytail or single braid at the club, but he preferred it like this. Soft. Elegant. Tempting.

He suddenly wanted to know what the heavy strands would feel like falling through his fingers...how those raven tresses would look spread across a white satin pillow.

Her scowl set him back on track.

"I was wondering if you were free tomorrow afternoon. If you have nothing else planned—"

"Free for what?"

"We could do something outdoors. The weather is supposed to be great. Not too hot."

"Whoa! Wait a minute. You mean the question you need an answer to is whether or not I'll go on a date with you?" Though Leila sounded indignant, she didn't look too surprised.

"Something like that."

He hadn't thought of it as a date, exactly—the word *research* had crossed his mind—but *date* wasn't sounding too bad at the moment. Wynne shifted uncomfortably when he remembered his recent pleasure at the idea of being friends. His thoughts were racing in much more intimate circles as though, away from the more businesslike atmosphere of the club, his imagination had been set loose.

"It'll give us a chance to talk," he went on quickly before his imagination could run away with him. Talking—getting to know the real woman beneath the stunning exterior—*that* was his motive for pursuing Leila. "The club has too many distractions and interruptions."

"I told you I don't mix business with pleasure."

"Not exactly. What you told me is that you don't date clients. And as you know, I'm not a client, so we don't have to face that problem." He could see that she wasn't allowing herself to be convinced so easily. "Let's make a deal. You think of our get-together as business, and I'll think of it as pleasure."

Leila sat down on the sofa opposite him. She was trying to look cool and relaxed, but Wynne recognized the underlying tension in the way her foot bobbed when she crossed her legs. And her fingers were busy picking at the material on the arm of the couch.

"Besides," he went on, "we'll be in a public place. How much safer could you be?"

"There you go with that 'safe' business again. Why do you keep intimating that I'm afraid of you?"

"Aren't you?" He couldn't help teasing her. He loved the way her delicate nostrils flared when she got indignant. "You never answered me last time."

"Because it was a silly question."

Wynne decided to let her off the hook. "Come on, Leila, give it a chance. I may be silly sometimes, but basically I'm a good guy. Upright. Honest." He gave her his most charming smile when he added, "And I can provide some very excellent references, if necessary."

The smile was contagious. It turned up the corners of her mouth. "Where is this public place?"

"Lincoln Park Zoo. I haven't been there since last summer. The park district has completed more of the renovations."

Even as he made the suggestion, Wynne knew the proposition was ridiculous. No wonder she was reluctant to agree. A woman who lounged in silk jump suits in a decorator's dream of an apartment wouldn't be interested in a freebie. Undoubtedly the men she dated spent fortunes on her. Well, he didn't have a fortune yet, probably never would. Not that he was broke. He'd merely learned to stretch the money he'd saved for this year of freedom he'd given himself.

And what he was proposing wasn't exactly a date, he reminded himself. Of course, she didn't know that.

"Hmm, the zoo can be a pretty dangerous place," Leila was saying. "It's full of predators...like wolves, for instance."

Now why did he get the feeling she was talking about the two-footed kind? "You don't like wolves?"

Her gaze was so direct he couldn't miss her message. "I don't mind them as long as they keep their distance."

"I don't think you have to worry. You're not as innocent of the ways of the world as Little Red Riding

Hood was when she set out for Grandma's house in the woods."

Leila laughingly complained, "I'm not sure that's a compliment."

"Believe me, it is. I have great respect for women with savvy."

"What time shall I meet you and where?"

Startled by her sudden agreement, Wynne blurted, "The seal pond at one."

"I'll see you tomorrow then."

Indicating the end of their discussion, Leila rose and held out her hand. Wynne followed suit. Her handshake was solid, her gaze steady.

"Tomorrow," he echoed.

Picking up his gym bag, he followed her to the door. He had to force himself to keep his eyes from her lush hips, which strained the turquoise silk. He was interested in the interior woman, he reminded himself, even as he continued to admire her outer attributes.

"By the way," she said as he passed her to enter the hall. "I'm a woman who's always on time."

"I'll remember that."

Swinging the gym bag to an inner tune, Wynne headed for the elevator. His spirits couldn't be better. He would get to know Leila just as he'd hoped. Then all of his problems would be solved.

As she was now, Brenna McNeal made a poor showing as the heroine of a popular novel. She had the looks, the dialogue, but not the in-depth guts that made a character. And characters were what sold books. He'd been having a helluva time making Brenna come to life, making her a woman a man could love. A woman *he* could love, at any rate.

Wynne had to admit he hadn't felt that all-encompassing emotion since shortly after his college days. He'd been disillusioned when it seemed that his longtime girlfriend had been more interested in his possible future as a reporter than she had been in him personally. The relationship had been disillusioning, and he'd thrown himself into his work.

Since then, he hadn't lived the life of a monk, but emotionally his relationships with women never seemed to progress past the warm friendship stage. And he always put his work first. Sometimes it seemed as if he'd been career-building forever. Almost fourteen years, anyway. His dedication had paid off; he'd made his mark as a successful reporter.

And soon, if he was very lucky, he would sell his first novel . . . assuming he ever finished it to his satisfaction. Brenna had been making writing torture.

Perhaps someday in the near future he would have time to look for love and a woman with whom he could spend the rest of his life.

A good plan.

All he had to do to assure its success was to keep his mind on his work and stop thinking of the upcoming excursion with Leila as a real date.

LEILA'S MOOD SHIFTED subtly after Wynne left.

She felt unsettled. Suddenly the one-bedroom apartment she'd decorated herself seemed to lack warmth in spite of the brilliant clear colors that surrounded her. She had that sensation again—as if she were waiting in suspended animation for the right man to waken her. Kind of like Sleeping Beauty.

Too bad life wasn't as simple as a fairy tale. Too bad Wynne Donegan wasn't Prince Charming. No self-respecting prince would wear worn jogging shoes and frayed socks, she thought with a smile. But then, she'd already classified Wynne as a wolf.

Crossing to the windowed wall, Leila studied Chicago's downtown area and, a short distance away, Grant Park and the lake. The view that was normally soothing made her even more restless. It made her want to explore the city environment and to experience its scenic wonders with someone she cared about. With a special man.

Images of her ex-lover, Christian, appeared on the plate glass before her. Leila closed her eyes and pressed her forehead against the window, willing the unhealthy memories away. She'd made a new life for herself, she thought with pride, and somehow, even her sense of humor had survived.

And now, for the first time in years, Leila realized something else in her had survived, as well. As crazy as it sounded, Wynne's pursuit had added to Gail's badgering and made her face the truth. She was tired of the easygoing, emotionally undemanding relationships with men she'd learned to perfect. She wanted more.

Opening her eyes, she stared at her faint reflection, hoping to see from Wynne's perspective. Her looks were obvious, but what about more important things that defined who she was as a person? Had he been serious that first day they'd spoken when he'd intimated he wanted to know her better because she was a nice person?

She was too suspicious of men's motives. Christian had done that to her. She'd fixed everything else that had been wrong with her life. Why couldn't she take that final step?

If she and Wynne hit it off the next day, maybe she would try giving her suspicions a long-overdue rest.

CHAPTER FOUR

"ON THE RUN. Wynne speaking." The silence at the other end of the line was palpable. "Is this your first time calling our hot line?" Wynne guessed. "You can talk to me. I want to help you if I can."

"You aren't going to tell me I have to go home, are you?"

The boy's voice cracked, making Wynne think the caller might be in his early teens.

"I can't force you to do anything you don't want to do, so don't worry. You're safe." Wynne only hoped that was true. Inevitably runaways landed on the streets. The majority of Chicago's streets weren't all that safe—not for kids who were alone and penniless. "Would you tell me your name?" *Click.*

Wynne sighed as he, too, hung up. He should have played the boy out and let him offer a name when he was ready. Usually he was more sensitive to the ones who needed that initial anonymity. What had he been thinking of this morning before taking his first call? Leila. Fantasizing about their upcoming "nondate" had distracted him.

He took a quick look around at the small dismal office decorated by every version of the poster that advertised their organization. On the Run? appeared in bold print above shots of frightened youngsters— black, white, Native American, Hispanic, Oriental, a girl as young as seven, a male as old as seventeen. They were all covered. At the bottom ran the copy, Want to Talk? Call 1-800-555-TALK.

So a kid in trouble had called, and he had blown it. Damn! He glanced at the five other volunteers, all of whom were tied up on the phones at their booths. Disgusted with himself, Wynne was about to get a cup of coffee when his telephone rang again. He picked up the receiver.

"On the Run—"

"Perry. My name is Perry." The teenager's voice cracked. "I don't have to tell you my last name, do I?"

Wynne took a deep breath and offered silent thanks for the second chance. "No, Perry is fine. And you can call me Wynne."

"You don't have a tracer on this line, do you?" the kid asked suspiciously.

"No tracer. No one else listening in. Only you and me. What would you like to talk about?"

"I—I don't know. I'm just..."

Lonely, Wynne supplied silently. *And scared.* "When did you leave home?"

"Last night. But I bet they haven't even noticed I'm gone."

Wynne knew Perry was talking about his parents. "How can you be so sure?"

"The only thing my parents are interested in is how much money they're making compared to their North Shore friends. I never see them, anyway. If they're not working, they're going to some dinner party or fund-raiser."

It didn't surprise Wynne that the teen had well-to-do parents. Runaways came from all walks of life; they ran for all kinds of reasons. Most home situations, in truth, were far more serious than this one sounded, but the streets and the people who preyed on these unhappy kids didn't distinguish between their motivations or backgrounds.

"What about brothers or sisters? Do you have any?"

"A ten-year-old sister."

"Don't you think she'll miss you?"

"I don't know. Yeah, I guess."

"And I'll bet you'll miss her."

"Nah, Tracy's a pain in the butt."

There was a vulnerability beneath the stinging words.

"Maybe Tracy feels just as alone and neglected as you do."

"You mean she might run, too?" Voice cracking on every other word, Perry sounded horrified. "She can't. Tracy's just a kid."

As if Perry were grown up himself. "Age doesn't matter," Wynne said gently, wondering if he should pursue the possibility of Tracy following his example. He decided to go in a more positive direction. "I'm sure your sister would like to hear from you."

"I'm not calling home. I don't want to speak to *them*."

Wynne heard the truth through the boy's anger. He not only wanted to speak to his parents, he wanted to hear that they loved him. "Doesn't she ever answer the phone?"

"Sometimes."

"You could take a chance. Then you could assure her you're all right."

"Maybe."

"Tracy would feel much better." A stubborn silence made Wynne think quickly. He didn't want to push too far or lose the teenager. This one could be talked home—he was sure of it. "Well, just think about it. In the meantime, I can help you find a place to stay."

"No. I don't need one," Perry said, quickly adding, "I have to go now."

"There's nothing else you want to talk about?"

"I...no. But later, maybe I could talk to you later."

"I'd like that. I'll be here for a few more hours, until noon. If I don't answer, ask for me. If I'm gone, someone else will be happy to talk to you, Perry. Just remember, you're not alone."

Wynne could have sworn the kid was starting to cry when he squeaked out, "Thanks."

Then the line went dead.

LEILA ROSE EARLY Saturday morning, her thoughts immediately turning to her projected afternoon. While she was stimulated by the prospect of seeing Wynne, doubts were starting to surface, making her wonder why she'd agreed to go out with him. Because he'd found a way to manipulate her once more, she told herself, not at all pleased by his intimating she was afraid of him. Of course she wasn't, and she didn't need to prove it.

"I'm not going."

That settled, she decided to call Wynne to tell him the date was off. After flipping the switch on the automatic coffee maker, which she'd prepared before going to bed, she found his number in the directory and dialed. No answer. Well, she would try again in a little while.

As she went through her usual morning routine—taking a shower, brushing out her hair, applying a light coat of moisturizer to her face, sipping a cup of black coffee—she changed her mind a dozen times about whether or not she would meet Wynne as promised.

She called again, but was no more successful at reaching him than she'd been the first time. It wasn't even nine o'clock. Either Wynne was a sound sleeper or he wasn't home.

She tried to keep her mind off the date she intended to break, but with little success. The blue sky on the other side of her windows beckoned invitingly. A perfect day for the zoo.

Leila finally decided to make her weekly call to her parents. She couldn't help her lack of enthusiasm about something she saw as a duty—not that she didn't love Myrna and Jim Forester. But nearly a decade had passed since she'd made a mess of her life in New York, and she'd never managed to recapture the closeness they'd once shared.

Knowing wishes were a dime a dozen and wouldn't change anything, Leila dialed their number.

Her decision to live in New York and tackle the glamorous world of modeling with Christian as her mentor had drawn mixed reactions from her parents. Her father had been angry and disapproving. Good girls didn't live with men, even if they were in love; worse, only one kind of girl became a model. Her mother, more romantic and ambitious for her daughter—perhaps because she'd once dreamed of being a famous movie star—had given Leila her blessings.

No one was answering the telephone at their place, either. She would wait a few more rings in case her parents were outside.

A year after moving to New York, heartbroken and disillusioned, recovering from the lowest point in her life, Leila had returned to Illinois, determined to start over. Her mother had been outspokenly disappointed in Leila's failure to succeed at modeling; her father hadn't let her forget her mistake in trying. In response, Leila had refused to tell either of them the truth—not about Christian, not about anything she'd gone through. Sad how their relationship had deteriorated further through the years. But that wasn't her fault, she thought defensively.

About to hang up, she heard a click at the other end.

"Hello?"

"Hi, Dad."

"Oh, Leila. Your mother went over to the Jewel to pick up some groceries."

Leila was silent for a second, wondering if that was supposed to be her cue to say she would call back later. Of course her father would deny the claim and tell her she was making something out of nothing as usual. But she knew that wasn't true. Biting back the hurt that quickly surfaced, she refused to be put off.

"What are you up to this morning? Working in the yard?"

"No. I was stretched out on the couch watching television. I paid the Anderson kid to mow the lawn and trim the hedges the other day."

How odd. The yard was her father's self-proclaimed domain. "Is your mower on the fritz?"

"My mower's fine, thank you. I'm just tired of tending to the lawn and the hedges and the rose-bushes. Let someone else do the dirty work for a change."

Leila frowned. Her father had always loved doing those things. He wasn't getting any younger, she guessed. Sometimes she felt pretty old herself.

"You're feeling all right, aren't you, Dad?"

"Good as ever." She didn't quite know what to believe, however, when he added, "So when are we gonna see you?"

Usually her mother demanded her presence; her father never seemed to care.

"I, uh, don't know."

Leila rarely traveled to the far south suburb where she had grown up; her visits with her parents were usually too demoralizing. And her parents had turned that reluctance against her, refusing to come to visit her in the city. It was a standoff, one that depressed Leila, but she'd just about given up hope that things would get better.

"Anything wrong with this afternoon?" he asked.

"This afternoon?" Even though she told herself she had every intention of canceling, Leila said, "I have a date."

Silence at the other end.

"Listen, Dad, what about tomorrow?" Perhaps her father really did want to see her. "Why don't you and Mom come up north, and I'll take you out to brunch at the Marriott. You would love the food."

"You know we don't go in for that fancy stuff. We're simple people, Leila. We don't put on airs."

Steeling herself for a familiar argument, Leila tried to be reasonable. "Dad, simple people have brunch in the city every weekend."

"We don't."

"Maybe it's time you tried it. My treat."

"I pay my own way—"

"Then you'll come?"

"No. You know your mother doesn't like the city. And I don't want to have to get dressed up. Suits are for weddings and funerals. Why don't you come out here? Places on the South Side have brunch, too, you know."

Her stubborn streak rose to the fore. "But I don't have a car, and you know the transportation to your place is almost nonexistent on Sundays."

"What's the matter? Afraid you'll get stuck spending some time with your parents?" Her father's voice rose. "That you won't be able to run in the door and out again so you can get back to your glamorous lifestyle?"

Leila took a deep breath. *What glamorous lifestyle?* she wanted to shout. For a good part of her job, she was covered with sweat, and she enjoyed little in the way of nightlife except on an occasional date. But explaining would do no good.

"Listen, Dad, I have to go now." Leila fought back the lump in her throat. "Give Mom my love, okay? Tell her to call me."

"Yeah, sure," he grumbled. "I'll tell her."

Setting down the receiver, Leila stared at the telephone. The argument had been a variation of many they'd had in the past, so why was she so upset? She shouldn't dwell on it or on her father's disapproval of her living "the high life" in the city—she guessed her apartment in a high rise might qualify her for that one. She was sure he considered her a disappointment, especially in comparison to her brother, Allen, who was vice president of a company and married with two kids. She, on the other hand, was still unmarried and childless. Even her mother praised her son every

chance she had, while she took equally as many op-
portunities to mourn her daughter's failure.

Leila looked out the window longingly. She had to
get out of the apartment. If she didn't breathe in some
fresh air soon, she would go bonkers. Climbing into
her short-sleeved short-legged red jump-suit and
matching high-top Reeboks, she decided to walk down
to Lake Michigan. Spending time along the water
would be chilly, so she pulled her red zip-up sweatshirt from the closet and tied the sleeves loosely
around her neck. Before leaving the apartment, she
copied Wynne's phone number on a scrap of paper,
which she placed in her wallet.

And yet, remembering Wynne's quirky smile, the
way his right cheek dimpled, the way he sometimes
made her feel inside, Leila wasn't sure she would use
the information, after all.

"HEY, MISTER, what time is it?" a little girl asked as
a sleek dark seal slid from the rock pile into the water.

Wynne checked his watch. "Five after one."

"Shoot! I wanna see them feed the seals."

"You'll have to be patient."

Just as he was trying to be, Wynne thought as the
little blonde walked away in disgust. Leila had claimed
she was a woman who was always on time. Did that
mean she didn't intend to show at all? he wondered,
watching two seals play tag in the water. His good
mood over his success with Perry began to evaporate
like the water that occasionally splashed the seal
pond's growing audience.

The teenage boy had called home to talk to his sister. His mother had grabbed the phone from Tracy,

told Perry they were scared stiff that something had happened to him and begged him to tell her where he was. He had. And then he'd called Wynne to say he was going home.

Most shifts at the volunteer center didn't end on such a high note. But now the tune was going sour.

He glanced at his watch: it was 1:10. How much longer should he wait?

"Worried that I wouldn't show?"

Wynne whipped around to see Leila behind him. Though her legs were bared, she wore a sweatshirt, hood raised, and her hands were tucked into the pockets. The clear red of her outfit made him wonder if she'd chosen what she was wearing as carefully as he had. He couldn't hide a grin. So she'd remembered their conversation of the day before.

"Little Red Riding Hood, I presume?"

Her dark brows rose when she got a good look at the picture on his T-shirt through his open jacket. "Big Bad Wolf, huh?" She only hesitated a second before adding, "My, my, what big eyes you have."

Wynne realized he was staring at her long, lightly muscled legs. He raised his gaze to her amused expression and purposely widened his eyes. "The better to see you with, my dear."

They both burst into laughter.

"I swear I didn't wear this outfit on purpose," Leila said.

"I confess I did, though this guy isn't exactly a wolf," Wynne admitted, looking down at the picture on his T-shirt. "More like a husky. I figured he was close enough."

"You really are silly."

"Sometimes."

"I guess it's part of your charm."

"Charm?" His eyebrows rose in surprise. "You think I'm charming?"

"A real prince of a guy."

"Hmm, I'd rather be the Big Bad Wolf than Prince Charming. More fun."

"Remember what I said about wolves yesterday," Leila warned him, though she was still smiling.

Wynne zipped up his jacket, hiding the picture of the husky. "I'll be whatever you want me to be."

"How about a tour guide?" Leila moved up to the iron railing and peered at the rock formation. She slid her hood back, and her long dark hair spilled freely around her shoulders. She leaned on folded arms, her stance relaxed. "I haven't visited the zoo in years. This seal pond is one of the few familiar-looking areas."

"The renovation work is almost finished. The park district has done a helluva job transforming this place into an animal paradise."

"If you can call an unnatural home like a zoo a paradise. Think they're happy?"

He heard an odd catch to her voice, almost as if she herself weren't. "The animals?"

She nodded as a lumbering sea lion flipped into the water, splashing them both with a fine spray.

"He seems to be in pretty good spirits," Wynne said, turning to study her fascinating profile and to probe beyond. There was so much about her that he didn't know, so much that he was anxious to explore.

As if Leila sensed his interest, she faced him squarely. "So, where shall we go from here?"

Wynne used a finger to brush a few drops of water from her deep-set eyes, and his blood began to pulse in an unexpected, if not unwelcome, rhythm. Then, reminding himself of his purpose for being with Leila, Wynne whipped his hand away and stepped back slightly, leaving some distance between them.

"My favorite is the polar bear enclosure." Having broken the fine thread of tension that had bound them for a moment, he indicated the north end of the zoo. "And on the way, we can say hi to the giraffes and elephants."

"Personal friends of yours?"

Wynne grinned. "We've shared a peanut or two in the past. Speaking of food, I hope you're hungry. I brought lunch. It's in the car. I thought we could have a picnic by one of the lagoons a little later."

"Sounds wonderful. I worked up an appetite walking here."

"You walked?"

"Along the lake," she said. "One of my favorite things to do on a beautiful day." As if sensing he was startled by the information, Leila added, "It was only about four miles."

"Only. Right." Wynne took her arm and led her up the path. "Let's tell the polar bears all about it."

"You talk to animals, do you?"

"Why not? They're terrific listeners."

Leila turned out to be a good listener, herself. While strolling past the new environments and then stopping to watch the giraffes alternate between exercising their long legs and seeming to pose for photographs, Wynne told her about his morning at On the Run. Although a small victory, he wanted to share his success.

"Perry probably would have gone home on his own," Wynne said, "but I can't help feeling good that

I might have nudged him in the right direction before he got himself into trouble."

Something akin to admiration made Leila's dark eyes sparkle. Or so Wynne thought.

"Don't underestimate your influence," she told him. "I'm speaking from personal experience when I say you can be pretty persuasive."

"Thanks. I wish that were true in more cases. There's one kid in particular who badly needs to go home. Vincent Caputo is a smart ass who got himself into some hot water a couple of months back. He left home voluntarily after his mother threatened to kick him out. He's learned how tough living on his own is and says he wants to straighten out. His current associates are not exactly the cream of Chicago's crop. He's afraid his mother would rather see him in some juvenile home than let him back into the house."

"Do you think she would?"

"I volunteered to call her for him. Mrs. Caputo is willing to talk. She was at the end of her rope when she threatened to make him leave. No father in the house. Three younger kids. She was worried about Vincent's influence on them. But he is her son, and she loves him. He promised to call me for her answer this morning."

"But he didn't?"

Wynne shrugged. "Maybe he lost track of time and will get my message from someone else this afternoon...or maybe he was indisposed." He didn't care to explain further. With a light hand in the middle of her back, he guided Leila away from the enclosure. "The polar bears await."

"You sound as if you feel personally responsible for Vincent."

"I'm not supposed to feel that way. I'm supposed to be professional, understanding and helpful. Not personally involved." He repeated that part of the training all volunteers heard over and over. "Sometimes you can't help it. Know what I mean?"

"Considering what I do for a living, how could I not?"

"True enough. At least we have something in common."

In their own ways, they each tried to help others find the right path. Wynne realized they weren't so different below the surface. He also realized Leila had moved in closer to his side. His arm naturally wrapped around her back as he inhaled her sultry scent. God, she smelled good. Felt good, too.

"So how did you get hooked up with On the Run?" Leila asked.

"A couple of years ago I did a series of stories on runaways that won me both recognition and respect in the industry. I guess volunteering Saturday mornings to help was my way of saying thanks."

"For the recognition?"

"And for being lucky enough to grow up as part of a family that could have come straight out of a Walt Disney movie."

"Walt Disney, huh? No wonder you're predisposed to fairy tales. You'll have to tell me more."

"Maybe later. If you make me do all the talking, how will I ever learn anything about you?"

"Look, the polar bears!" Leila said, taking his hand and pulling him to the large windows that gave visitors to the zoo an underwater view of their antics. "Isn't he cute?"

"A ton or so worth of adorable," Wynne admitted as one of the bears performed for his audience.

The large gray-white beast did a circling dive that allowed him to slip up the side of the window. Then he placed his paws on the glass, pushed off like a racer would at the side of a swimming pool and arched backward, circled and repeated the maneuver.

Wynne was entertained, but he realized Leila had distracted him to avoid any personal questions. At least he wasn't kidding himself any longer. He didn't want to know more about her only for Brenna's sake, but for his own, as well.

He observed Leila as she watched the bear go through its paces. Everything about her fascinated him. Wynne decided to forget about his research and to start thinking about the rest of the afternoon in terms of a real date.

LEILA WAS STUFFED. Seeing that Wynne had finished eating, too, she began returning the food containers to his basket. They had picnicked under a weeping willow on a grassy hillside overlooking one of the park's lagoons. They'd overdosed on healthy foods and fresh air and a carefree atmosphere.

Only a few yards away, children and adults alike splashed around in rented boats in the lagoon. Happy laughter and raucous screeches pierced the summer air. In the other direction, on an old bridle trail that city runners now claimed as theirs, a mounted policeman patrolled the park. And beyond horse and rider was the seemingly endless lake, its horizon dotted with boats, white sails snapping in the wind.

What came next? Leila wondered.

Wynne, it seemed, was content to relax. He sprawled his lanky body on the ground under the umbrella of the willow, stretched out his long legs and tucked his arms under his head. Leila wanted to talk, to learn more about this mild-mannered man who'd eased his way into her life.

Curious, she asked, "Why were you playing voyeur at The Total You? Honestly."

"I wanted to get to know you. You, uh, reminded me of someone."

That was the last thing she'd expected to hear. Leila's pulse surged as she quickly wondered if he could possibly remember seeing her in a magazine spread after all these years—or could he have done more recent research and found out about her modeling days?

"So who do I remind you of?"

"Her name is Brenna McNeal. She's tall and leggy and has dark hair and eyes...and an exotic quality unique to only a handful of women I've ever seen."

"You thought I was someone else?" she asked suspiciously.

He shook his head and enigmatically said, "That would have been impossible, but I was startled by the resemblance and couldn't help but be mesmerized that first day. I had to come back so I could meet you."

Even though she was relieved that he knew nothing about her time in New York, thinking Wynne might see her as a substitute for another woman left Leila with a peculiar feeling. To hide her uneasiness, she finished cleaning up, taking their small trash bag to the nearest container. Why would it have been impossible for him to think she was Brenna? Was the other woman dead, or merely someone out of his deep dark past? Although Wynne could be a bit manipulative, she couldn't imagine him hiding secrets.

"This Brenna..." She looked down at him. "Um, is she your ex-wife? Or girlfriend?"

Wynne laughed, making Leila wonder what she'd said that was so funny. Her question had sounded reasonable enough to her. He reached up, caught her wrist and tugged. She kneeled on the grass next to him and settled back on her heels.

"Neither. I don't even like her much. She may be physically attractive, but her character would have to be a lot better developed before I would think of her as any kind of personal love interest," Wynne told her enigmatically. "Unfortunately for Brenna, she lacks your warmth. Sense of humor. Human concern." He seemed thoughtful before adding, "I never could quite figure out what was wrong with her until I met you."

The peculiar feeling returned, muted this time by Wynne's compliments. He spoke of warmth, humor and concern as being more important than looks.

A man after her own heart.

Was he?

Leila blinked and felt heat rise up her neck as she realized Wynne was using the break in conversation to study her. A funny bubbly sensation spiraled in her stomach. She felt very young—yet ancient at the same time. Christian had been the last man who had made her so uncertain of herself. When she'd met him, she'd been green, not quite ripe for the picking. He'd changed all that. By the time she'd left New York, she'd been emotionally older than Lady Liberty herself.

"What are you thinking about," Wynne asked, "with such a serious expression?"

Leila shifted her weight so that she was sitting on the ground and crossed her legs at the calves. No way was she about to open up to a virtual stranger. Instead, she asked, "Why do people call you Wynne instead of Sam?"

A brief glimpse of his frustration told her that Wynne knew she was avoiding talking about herself again. Even so, he answered.

"Saved a lot of confusion in the family since there were three Samuels living in the same house."

"An extended family. Sounds nice."

Wynne snapped a long strand of grass and used it to tickle her knee. "Granda is Sam and Da is Samuel, so I'm Wynne."

"Granda and Da?"

"We're Irish, remember," he explained. " 'Pop' would sound kind of funny in our household. Anyway, I have three sisters and two brothers. And of course, various aunts, uncles and cousins were always in and out of the house."

"You loved it," she guessed, moving a tad out of tickling range before she started giggling.

"That I did. And now there are more of us. Our numbers are getting out of hand when we get together around the holidays." He chuckled. "We'll have to rent a hall soon. My sister Megan has four kids of her own. Sean has six—uh, let me warn you, we have twins in our family."

Why did he warn her? Did he expect her to meet them soon?

"Doreen has three and Katy is expecting her first. And don't let me forget all the new little cousins."

"Whew! You have a lot of relatives, all right."

A little envious, Leila had often yearned for a large warm close family, but she wasn't sure she could deal with so many people at once. At least not on a personal level. With a job like hers, she found the one-on-one conversation she was having with Wynne a nice change.

"Grady's not married and neither he nor I have any children," he assured her with a mock seriousness that made her smile.

"Why haven't you married? It sounds as if you would love having your own family."

"I would some day...when I'm not so busy with my career."

Leila wondered at his evasiveness—and at the note of surprising vulnerability in his words. Not wanting to embarrass him, she changed the subject. "I like the way you say all those names with a slight lilt."

"My mother Kathleen's influence. She came over from the old sod when she was a teenager." He switched into a more prominent Irish accent. "There's never any doubt when she's miffed with one of us. We can tell exactly how badly by the intensity of her Irish brogue," he ended, rolling his *r*'s as if the sound came naturally to him.

"She only has a brogue when she's annoyed with one of you?"

"Believe me, that's often enough when you consider she has six children, every one of whom gives her good cause at some time or other. What about you? How many kids in your family?"

"I have an older brother." Before he could ask any more questions, Leila rose. "Why don't we put the picnic basket back in the car and go rent one of those boats?"

"Haven't you ever heard of R and R?" Wynne complained from his grassy bed.

"Sorry, but that definition doesn't seem to be in my personal dictionary." She poked his hip with the toe of her Reebok. "Come on. It'll be fun."

Groaning and grumbling, Wynne rose and snatched up the picnic basket. "You need to have your personal dictionary expanded."

"By you?"

"I might be up to the challenge." His lips quirked, dimpling his cheek. "What about you?"

"Competitive by nature," she admitted.

"This may be a very interesting relationship."

Relationship. The word echoed softly through her mind. Leila was enjoying herself so much the idea began to appeal to her.

She even enjoyed Wynne's exaggerated complaints, of which there were plenty once they'd stored the picnic basket in the car and Leila dragged him to the concession stand, where she insisted they rent one of the paddleboats. The boxy-looking boat had two separated seats and sets of pedals and worked much like a bicycle.

Despite his grumbling, Wynne paid the concessionaire and helped Leila into her seat before hopping across onto his own. Pedaling hard and steering the awkward vehicle, he headed it toward the middle of the lagoon.

"You need to build up to this kind of exercise," he muttered as his long legs kept working. "I haven't been on a bike in years."

"We can fix that," she teased, pedaling also. "There's a bike rental concession not too far from here."

Wynne's stricken expression made Leila laugh.

"Okay, okay," he said. "I'll keep my complaints to myself if you promise not to threaten me with any more exercise this afternoon."

"Deal." Leila hesitated only a second before adding, "We can bike ride next time we're in the park."

That he didn't disagree made her smile with pleasure and wonder how soon that might be. They spent the next half hour dodging kids, who seemed to be more adept at this particular sport than the adults. Finally their time was up, and they brought the boat back to shore.

"I'm ready to throw in the towel," Wynne said. "I'm pooped."

"Maybe you ought to join The Total You. I can guarantee you'll be in shape in no time at all."

His brow furrowed. "I wouldn't want to do that. It would ruin everything."

"Getting into shape?"

"Joining your club," he clarified. "You don't date clients. Remember?"

Wynne circled her back with his arm. He was warm and sweaty and wonderfully appealing. Leila found herself melting into his side and realizing how happy she was. As they walked back to the car, she wished the afternoon could have stretched on endlessly. Though all good things came to an end, that didn't mean there wouldn't be more waiting for her right around the corner, Leila told herself. She smiled when Wynne helped her into the passenger seat.

She was still smiling when they arrived at her building. There was no legal parking available within blocks of the place. Ignoring her suggestion that he let her off at the door, Wynne left his car in the No Parking zone directly in front of the building. He slipped the doorman a tip so the guy would wave the cops on if necessary.

"What if you get ticketed anyway?" she murmured as they swept past the front guard desk and into the hall to the apartment elevators.

"I'll ask the doorman for a refund."

"And I'm sure he'll be delighted to oblige." Leila snorted. "Wynne, you really don't have to see me up. Do you realize how expensive parking tickets are in this city?"

His brow furrowed. "Don't worry about the money."

Leila wasn't worried about the money. If he wanted to throw his money away, that was his business. She was nervous at the prospect of being alone with him in her apartment. Wynne would probably expect to kiss her, and, although she was wishing the day hadn't ended, she was feeling unsettled and experiencing that bubbly sensation again.

She didn't know what she wanted.

And she didn't have long to decide, because they arrived at her floor before she knew it. Leila tried busying herself sorting through her half-dozen keys, but Wynne took the ring from her hand.

"Allow me."

With unerring accuracy, he chose the correct key and unlocked the door. She'd barely entered when he took her arm and turned her to face him. One hand raised to the jamb, he sprawled his long body in the doorway.

"I hate leaving, but I have work to do."

"On Saturday night?" she asked before catching herself. It sounded as if she wanted him to stay. Part of her did. She glanced at the husky, who seemed to grin at her from his T-shirt, before she looked up to find a grin on Wynne's lips. "Sorry, I don't mean I doubt you."

"Don't start apologizing and ruining everything. Your protest sounded pretty flattering."

Wynne was so close to her, he blotted all else from Leila's view. Using a single finger, he traced the outline of her cheek. She inhaled sharply, breathing in his pleasant scent. Her skin seemed to flush everywhere at once. Suddenly, there was nothing to decide.

Leila swayed toward him and lifted her face expectantly. Wynne slipped his hand under the mass of her hair and wrapped his fingers around the back of her neck. She could feel each tip, each tiny pulse against her sensitive skin. Tingles were already working their way along her nerve ends. She closed her eyes. He drew her head closer until she was holding her breath.

And then he gently pressed his lips...to her forehead!

Startled, she froze for a second. And then her eyes popped open. He was already backing off.

"Like I said, I have work to do, Little Red Riding Hood. Being with you has inspired me. Now get inside and don't open that door to any other Big Bad Wolf. See you Monday."

"Right. Monday," she echoed.

Leila stood in the doorway and watched Wynne walk away. Her eyes narrowed when she noticed a jaunt to his step that hadn't been there before. Unless she was crazy, there was something wrong here. They had just spent several terrific hours together. She had expected a kiss, perhaps a protest about leaving, maybe even a more seriously issued pass.

But being told that she had inspired a man to go home and work was a little more than even the healthiest ego could take!

CHAPTER FIVE

"Fixed up, this would be the perfect fairy-tale castle."

Brenna slowed her pace as James led the way up the path to the two-story gray-stone building with beveled glass windows and a hand-carved glass-trimmed door. He'd bought the handyman's special a couple of years before. Though the building was the disgrace of the neighborhood, he neither seemed to find the time nor the enthusiasm necessary to begin its transformation. Sometimes he thought he avoided what could be a labor of love because he felt the need to share the experience.

James merely said, "We could both use a woman's touch."

If she got his drift, Brenna didn't comment. She followed him up the steps. The middle plank creaked as it always did.

"When I was a kid, I would have given anything to live in a place like this."

"And now?"

Leaving barely a foot between them, she stopped and made direct eye contact. "Now I'm

all grown-up, and I don't believe in fairy tales
anymore.''

''Pity,'' James said, keeping his tone light.

He could see the truth within her fathomless
dark eyes, beneath the tough, if beautiful, fa-
cade. Brenna was aching to believe in fairy tales
again, and he had a sudden urge to become her
fountain of youth.

WYNNE PUNCHED IN the Save command and stared at
his computer display as his words were stored in a new
file. He had a handle on Brenna at last. The scene was
sentimental, but there was nothing wrong with that.

Fairy tales! He wondered what Leila would say. His
having turned their exchange about the Big Bad Wolf
versus Prince Charming into a thread of fiction would
probably amuse her. It would be a long time before he
knew for sure. Only his agent had read an early draft
of *Hot Bodies*. Now that his characters were fleshed
out more to Wynne's satisfaction, he was about ready
to send several revised chapters back to New York.
That's what this year off from a steady job was all
about—to see if he had what it took to write entertaining fiction that would sell.

He'd always had stories in his head, ever since he'd
been a kid. And being a reporter had taken him
through the gamut of experiences and familiarized him
with every level of humanity. He had a good eye for
details, a good sense of what a person was really like.
He'd learned to dig deep, below the surface. Now all
he had to do was translate that ability to fiction.
Brenna had stymied him for a while, but he felt he was

making progress at last, and all because of a fascinating woman he'd met by accident.

Wynne checked his watch. Almost midnight. He'd been writing like a demon since he left Leila at her apartment door the day before, breaking only for a few hours of sleep. He'd eaten his meals, such as they were, in front of the computer. He'd meant to call Leila earlier, to tell her what a great time he'd had with her, to ask her if she wanted to see him again outside of the club.

But she would be in bed by now.

Shutting down his equipment, Wynne tried to curb his disappointment as well as to control his overworked imagination. He could picture Leila in something silky and skimpy...and if he kept this up, he would never get to sleep.

"LADIES, THAT WAS a terrific class! Give yourselves a big round of applause."

The women laughed and clapped as they broke up into small groups, some rushing out the door, others lingering behind to chat. Mel continued to stretch her long thin body as Grace stopped at the scale to weigh herself. Leila saw her opportunity. She approached the teenager.

"Another three pounds!" Grace told Mel, who gave her the thumbs-up sign.

Although that was quite a bit of weight to drop in as many days, large losses were common at the beginning of a diet.

"How in the world did you do it?" Leila teased as Grace got off the scale.

Expecting an enthusiastic reply, she was taken aback by the girl's scowl. "How do you think? Diet and exercise. Isn't that why I'm here?"

"Absolutely." Leila studied the normally good-natured, if shy, teen. Something was obviously bothering Grace, but Leila couldn't put off this discussion forever. "Speaking of diet, don't you think it's time we got you into one of our nutrition classes? We want to make sure you stay healthy and—"

"I told you before, I've got things under control."

But Leila could see that Grace wasn't at all in control. She was tense, irritable . . . and she had a difficult time meeting Leila's eyes.

"Grace, I know how stressful dieting is—"

"No you don't!" Grace said, cutting her off again. "You don't have to do anything to be perfect."

It was Leila's turn to tense. "I'm not perfect, Grace, and I have no desire to be." Take it easy, she told herself, forcing her fingers to unclench from the unconscious fists she'd made. The teenager couldn't know she'd struck a nerve. "I try to be the best person I can be and a healthy one. That's what I wish for every one of my students."

"Look, just get off my back!"

Before Leila's startled eyes, the teenager ran into the hallway. "Grace, wait a minute."

"Leave her alone, would you?" Expression defiant, Mel cut across the room, pausing near the doorway. "Everyone's always bugging us about what we eat. What does it matter as long as we lose weight?"

Before Leila could reply, Mel shot out the doorway, calling after her friend. What in the world had she said to upset the two girls so? Leila thought hard, wondering if she could have inadvertently said something the teenagers might have taken as an insult or criticism. She didn't think so. Their reactions worried her. Stereo system and lights off, she headed for the locker room.

Immersed in uneasy thoughts, Leila didn't see Wynne until she almost ran into him. He wrapped both hands around her upper arms to steady her. The warm touch made her insides flutter, irritating her. She didn't need to be attracted to a man who preferred work over her company on a Saturday night, one who hadn't been interested enough to call all day Sunday, a man who'd seemed distracted the few times their paths had crossed that day in-between his interviews with clients.

"Going to a fire?" he asked.

"No. To the showers."

"Sounds like fun." His easy grin set her insides roiling. "Can I join in?"

She moved around him and continued walking, but his long-legged stride allowed him to catch up easily.

"You know where to find the men's locker room," she said.

"Uh-oh. Someone's in a testy mood."

"Sorry." Leila tried to smile naturally, but she had never been a good actress without the right inspiration. Realizing she'd forgotten to check her In box before coming to class, she veered off toward her office. "First, I have to check my mail."

"Care to tell me about it?"

"The junk stuff or the memos?"

"Neither. Tell me what's bothering you?"

"Not at the moment."

"How about later? At my place?"

"Your place?"

"My house. I could throw some burgers on the grill." He opened her office door and let her enter before him. "This is where you're supposed to jump in with a 'sounds wonderful,'" Wynne prompted.

"I'm tired. Maybe some other time."

"What other time?"

"I don't know."

Leila gave him her back as she quickly sorted through her mail—a fitness magazine, a couple of equipment advertisements and a memo from Mike Kramer about the plans for The Total You's first anniversary celebration, which was less than two weeks away. Wooden chair legs scraped the floor behind her, informing her that Wynne was making himself comfortable just as she was ready to leave.

"What about tomorrow?" he continued, as if there hadn't been a break in the conversation.

"I—"

"Probably have an excuse for then, too."

She turned to face Wynne, who leaned back in the chair as though he owned the place.

"I'm not giving you any excuses," she insisted.

"Good. Then you'll come."

"I didn't say that."

"But will you?"

"I'll think about it."

"You can lecture me on the harmful effects of red meat on the human body. I'll even take notes."

Leila stepped closer and peered down at him curiously, noting his endearingly boyish expression. "Have you always had this way with words? Verbally beating down a person until you turn objections to your favor?"

He grinned, his raised mustache showing straight white teeth. "Part of my profession, ma'am. A way with words and not taking no for an answer are two of a reporter's most valuable weapons."

"I didn't realize we were engaging in battle."

"That's up to you, although I would rather make love than war."

Leila's lips twitched. "You can't take credit for that slogan."

Wynne reached out, his long fingers circling her wrist as securely as a handcuff. "I'm not above a little plagiarism if it gets me what I want." He gave a sharp tug, and she went flying right into his waiting arms.

The chair swayed precariously, and Leila grabbed on to Wynne's knit shirtfront for support even as she realized he wanted her. The evidence was obvious against her Lycra-covered thigh. She tried to stop her own natural response to the eroticism of their position, but somehow the man was managing to get through her defenses. Her pulse picked up when he slid his free hand around the back of her neck. Made breathless by the contact, she shook her head in exasperation.

"I don't get it."

"Which part?"

"Any of it," she muttered as he put pressure on her neck until the distance between their mouths closed.

His was not the kiss of a disinterested man. The brush of his mustache followed by the touch of his tongue reminded her of the uncertainty she'd been feeling since Wynne had left her to her own devices on Saturday night. While one hand kept her head prisoner, the other roamed down and across her back to settle on the curve of her hip. The feelings that stirred within her were stimulating... but inappropriate for the setting. This was her workplace, where anyone might enter and see them.

She couldn't relax.

Rather than allowing the kiss to play out its course, Leila levered her palms against Wynne's chest, though to be truthful, she'd been ready for the embrace for nearly forty-eight hours. Wynne released her neck. She raised her head and met his smiling green Irish eyes. Her heart seemed to bump against her ribs. Part of her responded to him so naturally that it surprised her... and frightened her, as well.

"So what do you say?" he asked.

She thought about saying no, but the word refused to pass her lips. Admitting she wanted to see Wynne away from work, Leila relented. Their sparring was nothing more than verbal exercise, anyway.

"All right. You win. Tomorrow, your place, burgers on the grill."

"I was hoping you would see it my way."

Had he ever doubted that she would? Leila wondered as he released her and she rose a bit awkwardly. Wynne Donegan was certainly one determined persistent man! A sense of unease washed through her at the thought. Those traits had been part of Christian's makeup, also. The comparison disturbed her, and Leila was quick to assure herself that Wynne was nothing like her former lover.

A FEW MINUTES LATER, Leila waved before disappearing into the women's locker room. Wynne tried not to think of her capitulation as a hollow victory, something she'd agreed to do to get him off her back.

She liked him; he sensed that. But she kept trying to erect barriers.

Why?

The most obvious possible reason was his cash flow problem. First he'd offered her the zoo and a picnic, now burgers on a grill. Leila was a class act, the kind of woman who probably expected to be wined, dined and danced around the most exclusive restaurant floors in Chicago. He'd met women like her before, had even fallen in love with one. No, Leila was in a class all her own, he told himself. Yet he couldn't give her the very things he thought she might want, and that bothered him. Someday maybe he could, but would she be patient enough to wait for them?

Startled, Wynne realized he was thinking in terms of the future when he should be concentrating on the now—like getting home and straightening up. That got him moving toward the elevators. His place was a mess.

He had to be crazy to invite Leila to a house that was in an ongoing state of renovation. He'd bought the building before quitting his job, while he could still get a mortgage. His house was a handyman's special, like the one he'd designed for James. But unlike the hero of *Hot Bodies*, Wynne worked continuously on getting his home into shape, not that it yet reflected all the time and sweat he'd invested. Restoration and remodeling was slow going, but the final results would be well worth his energies.

Wouldn't it be nice, Wynne thought, if he had someone with whom he could share his labor of love?

LATE THE NEXT AFTERNOON, as they drove away from the downtown area, Leila recognized the pride in

Wynne's voice when he said, "My house is in Andersonville, a pretty nice midnorth neighborhood that was originally Scandinavian."

"I've been to a restaurant there. The area is lovely."

"The neighborhood is, but don't expect too much from my place just yet. I've been working on it, but it's still a shambles."

Realizing he was worried about her reaction, Leila was quick to reassure him. "It always takes a while to get a home the way you want it."

The late-afternoon sun was bright, the sky azure as they merged with the rush-hour Lake Shore Drive traffic. People milled along the cement walkways and played volleyball or lay on the beaches that lined the shore. They passed several such areas before Wynne turned off the expressway and headed west on Foster.

A few minutes and half a mile later, he pulled in front of a two-story turreted charcoal-gray stucco building with a large side yard that was actually a second lot. The house and garden could use work—a fresh paint job on the window trim, a firm hand pruning the rosebushes and weeding the perennials—but the place was charming nonetheless.

"I think your house is wonderful."

"You haven't seen the inside yet," Wynne said, sliding out of the car.

By the time he got around to her side, Leila had helped herself out and was taking in minor details like the huge white planters of brilliant red geraniums on either side of the front porch and the cozy setting under a maple tree—a curved white bench and matching low round table.

"Is that where we're going to have dinner?" she asked as he closed the car door and took her arm.

"I was planning on it—unless you would rather eat inside.

"No, not at all. Being surrounded by greenery instead of plaster and glass will be a real treat. It's been years since I've had a backyard dinner."

And it had been years since she'd been so comfortable with a man. Leila leaned into Wynne and smiled at him as he led her up the path toward the front porch.

"The downstairs is barely livable, so don't be shocked," he warned her. "I just had some new wiring put in, and I'm in the process of patching cracked plaster, so the place looks pretty grim."

"Will you stop apologizing!" Leila gave him a look of exasperation. "I like your place, so don't try to talk me out of it. Okay?"

He grinned. "Okay."

"I know that renovations don't get done overnight," she added as they mounted the steps. "I still remember how much work it took to redo my family's house. But I guess it was worth it considering my parents still live there."

"Where? In the city?"

Tempted to change the subject, Leila decided it wouldn't hurt to talk about that part of her past. "No. They bought an older home in the south suburbs when my brother and I were in grammar school. Actually, the house was built when the area was still farmland."

Wynne let go of her at the door, on either side of which were stained glass insets with a geometric design. Even before stepping into the small foyer, Leila sensed that she was going to like Wynne's house, mess or no.

"So, do you see your parents and brother often?" Wynne asked.

"Not very." Now it *was* time to change the subject. "So, when do I get the grand tour?"

A scowl flitted across Wynne's features before he answered. "After we eat. I'm trying to get the living and dining rooms in shape. So far, I've only finished part of the second floor—my bedroom and office."

"Your office is in the turret, no doubt?"

"Isn't that where all starving writers work?"

"Hmm, a romantic streak. Next you'll be telling me you secretly write poetry up there."

But Wynne didn't say any such thing.

Leila wandered through the living room with its ceramic tile gas-burning fireplace. The graying green walls were scarred with plastered cracks, but the barren oak floor was in near-prime condition. The spartan furniture consisted of a couch, floor lamp and coffee table. Natural woodwork spanned the double doorway between the living room and the empty dining room. There, a built-in hutch filled one entire wall.

"How beautiful. This won't take much to restore, either," she said, crossing the room to get a better look at the carved pattern in the wood and the beveled leaded-glass doors.

"You like old pieces like that one?" Wynne asked doubtfully.

"I love them."

"I got the distinct impression your taste was modern."

"Because of my apartment? The furniture goes with a high-rise image. It's okay, I guess."

"So why did you move there instead of finding a place more to your liking?"

Leila shrugged. "There's something to be said for the convenience. And the management company swung a substantial discount for employees of the health club—fewer apartments to stand vacant. I must admit I'm hooked on the view of the lake." Following Wynne past the swinging door into the large old-fashioned kitchen, she asked, "So, what can I do to help?"

"Pull up a chair and keep me entertained while I take care of the food."

"You'll spoil me."

"Believe me, I'd like to."

The warm way he was looking at her made Leila smile. For a few seconds, something special passed between them, a surprising closeness that almost made her hurt inside. Then, reluctantly, she thought, he turned away and opened the old refrigerator. The feeling passed as quickly as it had sparked.

"Do you cook much?" Leila asked, making herself comfortable on one of the chairs that surrounded a scarred oval oak table with a wide pedestal base.

"Cooking is my only hobby, although you won't get a proper idea of what I can do from burgers, corn and a salad." Wynne brought a package of ground beef and a bag of fresh ears of corn to the table. "I'm leaving the kitchen until last, because I don't want to rush it. I want to design the space right. Not just paint on the walls and tile on the floor, but cabinets and counter space, an island with a built-in grill. An eating area with larger windows overlooking the garden. The works."

"How ambitious. You're planning to do all that on your own?"

"Unfortunately, that's the only way I can afford to do it at the moment," he admitted on his way back to the open refrigerator, where he pulled out lettuce, tomatoes, a purple onion and a box of mushrooms. "Grady did offer to help, but my brother's superactive social life always seems to have priority almost every time I need him."

Was he trying to tell her something? Leila wondered. That his own social life was less hectic or that he had different priorities? She preferred the first thought, because it would mean Wynne wasn't busy with a lot of other women.

"If you ever want help, let me know." Leila offered before she realized she was making the assumption that he intended to continue seeing her.

But Wynne sounded pleased when he said, "You aren't really serious."

"Of course I am," she said, suddenly nervous. She reached for the plastic bag of corn to keep her hands busy. "Only don't expect an expert. I would probably be better at keeping you company and making coffee than plastering and painting. Want me to do the corn?" she asked. "I might as well make myself useful."

Wynne studied her thoughtfully as he spoke. "You could strip two ears."

She concentrated on her task and was relieved when he turned his attention away from her and to the food. He split the ground beef into four patties, seasoned them, then took the burgers out to the gas grill on the back porch. When he returned, he salted and buttered the ears of corn, wrapped them in aluminum foil and added a little water before twisting the ends closed. He put them on the grill, as well.

"What was bothering you yesterday, anyway?" Wynne asked as he placed a chopping board and large bowl on the table. "If you don't mind telling me, that is."

Not wanting to admit the part about having been disappointed because he'd seemed disinterested in her, Leila decided to tell him about the other problem that was still on her mind.

"I've been trying to get Grace into a nutrition class since she started at The Total You. Yesterday, I hardly had a sentence out of my mouth before she blew up and told me to get off her back."

"Is that so unusual—someone dieting having a short temper?" Wynne gave her a challenging glare. "I would be impossible if anyone tried to take away my food."

"Don't worry. You're safe. I promise I won't try." Though she had to laugh at his comical expression, she didn't want to abandon the serious subject. "Everyone reacts differently to changes in life-style, especially those that seem like some form of deprivation. Still, I don't really understand Grace's problem. It's only been a couple of weeks, and she's successfully losing weight. The reward is there every time she steps on the scale. Maybe her state of mind has something to do with her comment about being perfect."

"Perfect by whose standards?"

"Exactly, though perfection by anyone's standards is an unrealistic expectation, something always tantalizingly out of reach. As much weight as Grace loses, she may not be satisfied. It's a familiar theme. 'If only I could lose another half inch on my thighs, I would be perfect.' Or, 'If I could get rid of this tummy, I would be perfect.'"

Wynne was busy chopping vegetables for the salad. "Sounds like you've had a lot of experience with people who set unattainable goals for themselves."

She'd had personal experience with the problem, but Leila didn't feel comfortable explaining that to Wynne. Since returning from New York City, she'd never told anyone what she'd gone through during the year she'd been a fast-rising model. She'd left the reality behind her with her therapist and the members of her group counseling sessions. But even though she had recovered and had managed to stay both physically and mentally healthy for nearly ten years, the horror of what she'd gone through—of what she'd done to herself because of Christian and because of her own deeply buried insecurities—was clearly etched in her memory.

"Unfortunately, conditioning starts young," Leila said ruefully. "It's the fault of a society that erects exacting standards without taking the individual into account. It's so easy to fall into the trap of feeling you must live up to the expectations of others rather than setting realistic goals for yourself and being happy doing your best."

"Like an athlete who works for his coach rather than for himself." Wynne dumped the chopped mushrooms and sliced onions into the salad bowl. "Grady was really into that kind of thinking when he played football in high school and college. He took too many chances. He's lucky his injuries weren't the permanent kind."

"Exactly," Leila said, rescuing a stray mushroom half that tumbled off the cutting board. "Praise addiction taken to the extreme can be as psychologically harmful as alcohol or drugs. Too many people thrive on kudos, become depressed when they don't measure up. Teenagers especially buy into that kind of psychological conditioning."

Leila knew what she was talking about, because she'd bought into the mental manipulation herself. The memories would always remain vivid.

"Teenagers are an insecure bunch, all right," Wynne agreed. "I've had kids on the hot line admit they've run away because, no matter how hard they try, they can never live up to their parents' expectations."

"A sad commentary on family communications," Leila murmured, thinking of her own situation. "The parents probably don't even recognize what they're doing to their own kids."

Leila couldn't believe she felt so at ease discussing the uncomfortable subject with Wynne. But he was that kind of a guy. Comfortable. Sympathetic. Nice.

And not bad to look at.

She enjoyed watching him as he moved around the kitchen, cleaning up, gathering plates and utensils. His lanky body had an easy grace so different from many of the muscled specimens around the club. While the studs strutted, Wynne glided...in his own masculine way, of course.

"I'd better turn the burgers."

"Go ahead." Leila rose and picked up the plates, forks and knives. "I'll set the table."

"Deal."

He brushed his hand across her hip as he passed her. Leila caught her breath and looked up to catch Wynne winking at her. She had difficulty tearing her gaze from him, even when the screen door swung shut between them.

The ringing telephone made her start. "Want me to get that?" she yelled.

"Would you? I'll be right in."

The phone shrilled again. Leila juggled everything to one arm as she reached toward the wall to pick up the receiver. "Donegan residence."

The female voice on the other end held a breathless urgency. "Is Wynne there?"

Assuring herself that this undoubtedly was one of Wynne's sisters or cousins rather than another girl-friend, Leila said, "Yes. One second...here he is now."

She handed Wynne the telephone as the screen door banged behind him.

"Thanks." He winked again before speaking into the receiver. "Hello."

A frown quickly etched his forehead, making Leila uncomfortable. She mouthed the words, "I'll take these outside," but was sure he didn't notice. She hesitated at the door.

"Okay, calm down," Wynne was saying. "Tell David to keep him talking. I'll be there as soon as I can." He paused for only a second. "Five minutes, I promise." When he hung up, he seemed to realize Leila was standing there, staring at him. "Leila, my God, I'm sorry." His expression was frantic. "The burgers will have to wait for another day."

He quickly moved around her and through the door to turn off the grill, then came back into the house and locked the back door. Leila set the plates on the table.

"What's wrong?"

She had to jog through the house to keep up with him. He didn't stop, not for a second.

"Remember that kid I told you about? Vincent? He's on the line with one of the volunteers at the center...threatening to commit suicide."

CHAPTER SIX

"DO YOU KNOW where Vincent is?" Leila asked as they got to the front door.

"No, but he called the center looking for me. That's where I'm going now."

Following him onto the porch, Leila watched Wynne lock the door, his hand shaking. She'd never seen him so jumpy. "I'll go with you."

"No. This might not end well."

Leila swallowed hard. "Then *you'll* need someone to talk to. I'd like to be that person."

Wynne took a deep breath and touched her cheek. "That means a lot to me. But I really have to go alone." His brow furrowed. "Wait a minute—I've got to get you home."

"Don't worry about me." Leila took Wynne's arm, drew him down the steps and steered him toward his car. Although she was disappointed at the way her date had ended so abruptly, she was impressed by Wynne's sense of responsibility and didn't want to do anything to distract him. "I can walk over to Broadway and flag a taxi. The last thing you need is to have something else on your mind."

"You're sure?" he asked as he opened the car door and climbed in.

"Positive. Hurry."

"I'll call you."

"No matter what time it is—I'll wait up until I hear from you," she promised.

With a final glance at her, Wynne started the engine and drove off with a squeal of tires.

TWO HOURS LATER, Leila paced the length of her living room, then stopped to stare out into the darkening skies. She wondered if Wynne had made it to the center on time...if he'd been successful in saving the life of a mixed-up kid. His commitment went so deep. He really cared what happened to a fledgling hoodlum named Vincent Caputo.

So why didn't he call? She was worried—about the kid she didn't know and even more about the man who had been in a panic to save him.

When the phone rang, her throat tightened. *Let it be good news.* Her hand shook as she raised the receiver.

"Miss Forester," began the guard from the front desk. "You have a visitor, a Mr. Donegan."

"Send him up."

Leila wondered how long it would take Wynne to knock at her door, and why he'd come to see her in person when he could have called. Did that mean he'd been unsuccessful and needed a sympathetic shoulder? Good thing she was of sturdy stock, she silently joked, though she couldn't make herself smile. Adrenaline pumping, she paced the floor.

The expected knock finally came, and she rushed across the room and flung open the door. Wynne was leaning against her doorjamb. He looked exhausted. The backs of Leila's eyelids stung as she searched the normally boyish face that seemed to have aged in only a few hours.

"Wynne...?"

"I did it, Leila. At least I think I did."

"Thank God." Her eyelids fluttered closed for a second. She knew what it was like to be on the brink of despair. Thank God someone had been there for her. Thank God Wynne had been there for Vincent. "Come in. You look—"

"Awful." He pushed an unruly strand of reddish-brown hair from his forehead. "You don't have to tell me."

She closed the door and followed him into the living area. "I was going to say tired."

"I'm exhausted." He sank back into the couch as if his legs would no longer hold him. "And I guess I'm still worried." His expression one of a man in shock, he asked, "What if I'm not around the next time?"

"Maybe there won't be a next time." She sat beside him and put a comforting hand on his thigh. "Did you tell Vincent his mother was willing to talk?"

"I told him."

"And?"

"He promised he'd call her. But he promised he would call me Saturday, and he didn't." His hand found hers and squeezed, the pressure expressing his anxiety better than words. "Damn, Leila, this was a close one. Sometimes they bluff. *Usually* they bluff, and you can tell they're making threats to get attention. Vincent wasn't bluffing. I'm sure of it."

He was getting too close, too involved. Leila wanted to tell him to remember his training, to pull back emotionally, but she couldn't. She knew he wouldn't. Wynne was obviously an involved kind of guy; it wouldn't be in his nature to change.

"Let me get you a drink. Cognac?"

"Sounds great."

Reluctant to break the closeness, Leila rose and opened the drop lid on the wall unit revealing a few bottles of liquor. She poured a small cognac for herself and a more generous portion for Wynne. When she turned toward him, his head was tilted, resting on the couch back, his eyes closed. Approaching him, Leila cleared her throat.

His eyelids whipped open and he sat up with a start. "Sorry."

"Don't be." She handed him the snifter. "Why don't you sip on this and make yourself comfortable, and I'll find something edible. Not having dinner can't be helping your energy level."

"I don't want to put you to any trouble."

"No trouble. I haven't had anything to eat, either. Go ahead and stretch out," she urged.

"Don't mind if I do."

He took a healthy swig of the cognac, kicked off his shoes and stretched out on the couch, which was barely long enough for him. On the way into her tiny kitchen, Leila turned on the radio and set it to a New Age station. The soothing music would help Wynne relax. Luckily she had some chicken breasts and fresh asparagus in the refrigerator. Seasoning two breasts and drenching them with lemon juice, she placed the chicken in the countertop broiler. Next, she steamed the asparagus, intending to add salt, pepper and just enough butter to flavor it. In the meantime, she searched the refrigerator for a bowl of tabbouleh that she'd made the day before. A smile curved her lips as she anticipated Wynne's expression of horror when she explained the salad was largely cracked wheat and parsley.

She never had the chance to see that expression, however. By the time she carried the tray of food into the living room, Wynne was fast asleep on the couch, chest down, arm hanging over the edge, his breathing deep and steady. She set one plate on his side of the coffee table and walked around it to the couch opposite.

She studied him as she ate. Relief and the cognac had knocked the tension right out of Wynne. The years had fallen away from his face, and once more he looked boyishly handsome. Only the small laugh lines around his eyes belied that agelessness. Leila knew that Wynne was in his mid-thirties, but she was glad he'd retained that Peter Pan quality that made him see life through perhaps too idealistic eyes. The world could use fewer cynics and more caring individuals.

By the time Leila finished eating, darkness had cloaked the room, yet Wynne hadn't stirred. His food would be cold by now. Still, Leila couldn't bear to disturb him. Instead, she left his plate where it was and covered him with a light afghan. Returning to the kitchen, she swallowed the last of her cognac and washed her few dishes.

Though Wynne had succumbed to exhaustion, Leila wasn't sleepy. Her mind was spinning around and around, not from the liquor, but from thinking about the lack of communication between Vincent and Mrs. Caputo. Hadn't she experienced the same problem with her parents since she had been old enough to form her own opinions? Thinking about the rift that had widened between them saddened her. Her mother hadn't even taken the time to return her call in three days.

Maybe she should try again. She might even suggest they do something together to celebrate the coming Fourth of July holiday. She remembered the way she, her parents and her brother used to barbecue with neighbors or have a picnic in the nearby forest preserve. And at night, they would attend the fireworks presentation at a local high school football field.

Leila reentered the living area, flicking off lights as she went. The moon silvered Wynne's sleeping form, and Leila couldn't resist the temptation to brush the lock of hair off his forehead. His breathing changed at her touch and, for a second, she thought he might awaken. Her pulse gave an odd little surge, then settled back down as his breathing returned to that steady rhythm.

Leila continued on to her bedroom and closed the door before turning on the nightstand lamp and dialing her parents' number. Her mother answered after the second ring.

"Hello. Forester residence."

"Hi, Mom. How are things with you?"

"Fine, honey." The older woman's voice held a trace of puzzlement. "Is something wrong?"

Because she'd called in the middle of the week? Sad that her mother might think that was the only reason she would call. But Leila's determination to recapture some of the closeness that she and her parents once had was renewed.

"No, nothing wrong. I just wanted to talk."

"About anything special?"

"Well, I thought we might spend the Fourth together like we used to," she suggested, her enthusiasm for the outing now high. "I could rent a car for a few days and stay over. We could barbecue and go to the high school—''

"Leila, I'm sorry," her mother interrupted. "Your father and I already have plans."

"Oh." Leila felt instantly deflated, like a pin-pricked balloon.

"Your brother invited us to come to Peoria more than a week ago," Myrna explained. "The president of Allen's company is having a big party for all the executives and their families. It's going to be held at the local country club! I've been so busy buying new clothes and getting ready that I completely forgot about returning your call."

Despite her own interpretation—that her mother had been too busy for *her*—Leila tried to remain positive. "It sounds like something you would enjoy, Mom."

"I'm certain I will. The affair is going to be catered by Peoria's best chef. Allen's company has hired professional entertainers to perform. And there will be organized games. The children will have the chance to win some lovely prizes. Your father and I are very excited about going. Your brother was so thoughtful to have invited us."

"Yes, Mom, he was."

Leila tempered her resentment of her brother, but only with difficulty. It wasn't Allen's fault if he had succeeded in their parents' eyes while she hadn't. But then whose fault was it that her brother hadn't included her in his plans for a family outing? The least he could have done was asked.

As if her mother could read her mind, Myrna broke the uncomfortable silence. "You wouldn't want to go along with us, would you, dear?"

"That's okay, Mom. Really. I think I'll just stay in Chicago." If Allen had wanted her there, he would have issued the invitation himself. Besides, her mother probably felt obligated to ask because Leila had called. If she went with them, she would feel like an intruder. "You and Dad enjoy yourselves."

"Oh, we will," her mother assured her with renewed enthusiasm. "It'll be just like taking one of those long-weekend vacations." Another pause, shorter this time. "Was there anything else you wanted?"

"No, nothing else," Leila said. "I'll let you get back to your packing or whatever it was that you were doing."

"You do understand how important this visit with your brother is to us, don't you?"

Her mother sounded apologetic, Leila thought, but that didn't make her feel any better. "I understand. Have a good time. Talk to you soon."

Leila hung up and stared at the phone for a moment. Why had she been foolish enough to think she could draw her family closer just because she wanted to? She couldn't do it alone. She was sure her parents loved her in their own way, but in her mother's eyes she was a failure because she didn't have what Myrna considered a successful career or a successful husband who could invite them to country club events. Her mother's biggest complaint was that Allen and his family lived so far away, but Leila suspected her parents saw her brother more often than they did her.

Without thinking about the reason, she opened the living room door to seek out Wynne. Her hopes to find him awake were dashed even as she approached the couch. His breathing was as deep and rhythmic as it had been earlier. Disappointed, she returned to the bedroom and flung herself onto the bed.

She lay back against the pillows, lonelier than she had been in a long time. Even Wynne's presence in the next room couldn't change that.

As Leila stared up at the shadows playing across the ceiling, her feeling of isolation grew and threatened to engulf her.

THE NEXT MORNING, Leila woke to find she'd fallen asleep fully dressed and on top of the spread. Confusion cleared; she remembered the demoralizing phone conversation with her mother. And she remembered Wynne.

She rose immediately, wondering if he could still possibly be sleeping. When she checked the living room, the empty couch gave evidence that he'd already left. A note lay next to the plate he'd cleared.

Leila,
Thanks for the comforting words, the couch and the food. (It was delicious, even cold.) I owe you one, and I always pay my debts. Maybe we can make some plans later. I'm heading home to clean up. I figure I'd better look respectable since the photographer is scheduled for today.

Wynne

The photographer! She'd forgotten that this was the day, not that Leila was looking forward to the experience. If she had her choice, she wouldn't be photographed at all. She hadn't objected previously, because she was sure that Wynne would insist she participate.

Then, again, Wynne owed her one, didn't he?

"LETTING YOU OFF THE HOOK wasn't exactly what I had in mind when I said I pay my debts," Wynne complained when he found Leila in her office later that morning.

"You didn't specify the type of payment."

"What do you have against being photographed?"

"It makes me uncomfortable." That was the truth. Being photographed was part of the past, one that Leila would like to keep buried and not have to think about ever again.

"Why? Have you been photographed professionally before?"

"Yes. My mother had an entire series of professional photos taken of me every six months from the time I was a baby until I started high school." That, too, was the truth, even if an evasive one.

Wynne's expression was filled with suspicion. "And the experience was so bad that you're going to try to get out of being photographed now?"

"The clients are the important ones here," Leila hedged.

Wynne placed his hands flat on her desk and leaned toward her. "You know my angle on the story."

"Exactly. Individualization. Look around," she told him, waving a pencil. "You have plenty of individuals to choose from."

Wynne took the pencil from her hand and pointed it at her. "But you're the one who has made the program work. I'll be writing about your ideas, using direct quotes."

Leila rose and circled the desk, her arms crossed. "I don't want to be the center of attention."

"All right," Wynne said, flipping the pencil into the air. It landed with a plop in the middle of her desk.

"How about a compromise? I'll instruct the photographer only to take shots of you interacting with your students."

From Wynne's stubborn expression, Leila figured he could keep up the argument as long as she could. He might even complain to Mike Kramer if she refused to go along with the idea. And she knew what the executive director would tell her to do. Irritated more with the situation than she was with Wynne himself, she gave in.

"Okay, I'll agree on one condition—I want approval on any shots you plan to use that I'm in."

"What's the matter? Afraid I'll pick an unflattering angle?"

Actually, she was afraid of the exact opposite, but if she told him that, he would demand a fuller explanation—one she was unwilling to give.

"I assume that means yes." She headed for the door. "If so, let's get started."

"Of course it's yes, but wait a minute."

Wynne caught her arm in a light grip and swung her around so that her back was to the closed door. He placed his flattened palms on either side of her shoulders, effectively trapping her. Leila felt her pulse surge at his nearness. His eyebrows rose, giving his face an innocent expression while his tone was anything but.

"What about this tremendous debt I still owe you? Can't we figure some other way of squaring it?"

Her lightly issued, "Consider yourself squared," was actually difficult to manage when her heart was pounding with such vigor.

"I'm not sure I like the sound of that." He furrowed his brow, tempting her to smooth the wrinkles away. "Is this a brush-off?"

She hesitated, wondering if she should give him a hard time. He deserved as good as he dished out. Still, she couldn't quite manage to make him think she wasn't interested.

"Brush-off?" she echoed. "Not that I know of."

"Then how about spending tomorrow evening with me?"

"Your place, burgers on the grill?"

"I was thinking of something else. As usual, the city has scheduled its Fourth of July celebration on the third. Makes a lot of sense, right? Anyway, I thought we could make it over to Grant Park after you finish work. We could stuff ourselves silly at Taste of Chicago, recover by lying on the lawn in front of the band shell and listening to the concert, then end the evening by watching the fireworks display over the lake. What do you say?"

"I say...yes."

His smile was immediate and quirky, making the dimple in his cheek pop. "Great."

Wynne started to move away, but Leila used both hands to catch him by the shirtfront. "Whoa. You still owe me grilled burgers. What are you eating tonight?"

"Actually, I was going to stop at a fast-food joint since I planned on spending the evening patching cracks in my living room wall." One brow rose and his green eyes sparkled in challenge. "But I suppose I could be seduced into more interesting activities."

She ignored the last statement. "Need a plastering assistant?"

"You really are serious about helping me?"

"Well, first you have to understand that I've never in my life plastered before. But even if I can't handle the job, I can offer you inspiration and company."

"I'll take whatever I can get."

So would she, Leila thought. Before she could think of a clever retort, someone tried opening the door. It bounced off her back and closed again.

"Hey!" Gail's indignant cry came from the hall. "What's going on in there?"

They both jumped away from the door as Gail tried again. The door gave way and the small woman came flying into the room. She stopped herself from falling by catching onto Wynne's arm. Her gray eyes swept over Wynne then Leila, her expression going from confused to delighted. Leila felt a guilty flush creep up her neck into her cheeks.

"I hate to break up a good thing," Gail said, "but I have to talk to Leila about the anniversary party."

Wynne circled Gail to get at the door. "I'll go find the photographer and get him started." He looked straight at Leila, his expression serious, only his eyes giving away his amusement at their being caught at play. "Will you be long?"

"That depends on how difficult it will be to pound some brains into the Neanderthal Wit," Gail stated dryly. "There's not much room left in that skull, since his ego is only exceeded by the size of his biceps."

At Wynne's perplexed expression, Leila offered a one-word explanation. "Jocko."

"Oh. Well, try to make it quick anyway." With that, Wynne left.

Gail waited only a second before pouncing. "A wolf, huh?"

"I thought you wanted to complain about Jocko."

"I can do that anytime. He always gives me something to complain about. But at the moment, I want to hear about you and Wynne."

"There's nothing to hear."

"Leila!"

"Gail!"

"C'mon. I'm your best buddy, aren't I? You can tell me all the yummy juicy details."

"There aren't any."

Gail studied her through narrowed eyes. "That's why you looked so guilty and turned red when I practically had to break down the door to get into the room, I suppose?"

"Yet," Leila added when her friend stopped for a breath.

"Does that mean there's hope?"

"Maybe."

"Whoopee! Promise me you'll take notes so you don't forget anything. I want a play-by-play—"

"Gail, you're impossible."

"We've already established that." Gail stepped back and crossed her arms over her chest. "At least I don't plan on decorating my cardiac rehab lab with giant blowups of me in action for the clientele to admire."

Leila groaned. "Jocko."

"Our ambassador of bad taste," Gail agreed. "He brought in almost two hundred photos of himself, most of them from his football days, others from something called the Mr. Chicago contest he entered a couple of years ago. He actually walked down a ramp in a bathing suit. Can you believe it? You think he preens in the cafeteria? Wait till you get a load of these mug shots."

"And he wants to use them to decorate the recreation areas for the party?"

Gail nodded. "Revolting, isn't it? He brought the photos in only to get our opinions on which to have blown up. Leila, you have to talk to him. He just got up and left when I started laughing."

"Gail, you didn't."

"I couldn't help myself. So sue me."

Leila was almost tempted to feel sorry for Jocko, but she hadn't yet forgotten the "two beauties" comment. Usually he caused others embarrassment. She guessed it was fit justice that, for once, he brought embarrassment on himself.

"Let's go find him and get this over with," Leila said wearily.

Just what she needed. A confrontation with Jocko Gorski about his photographs, followed by having to pose for some of her own. She dreaded doing either.

As Leila followed Gail out of her office, she only hoped her evening had a better chance of success than her morning.

"YOU TOLD ME you never did this before," Wynne said after critically inspecting the cracks Leila had carefully cleaned out and plastered.

"I haven't," she insisted from her perch on the ladder.

"Then why does your work look better than mine?"

"Maybe because you patched three times as many cracks as I did in the same amount of time."

He tried to sound indignant. "That's no excuse."

"I can't think of a better one," Leila said, laughing.

Hands on hips, Wynne stared up at her. The view of her long legs at eye level distracted him for a moment. A blob of plaster decorated a spot just above her knee. He had to still the urge to remove it himself.

"Are you sure your father didn't teach you how to do this?" he asked, lifting his gaze from the immediate temptation.

"Positive. Our old house needed plastering, all right. The place was a lot more run-down than this one—it was all my parents could afford on my dad's salary. Anyway, he wasn't interested in teaching me anything that might be interpreted as 'men's work.' He and Allen did those things."

Wynne hesitated only for a second before asking, "What does your father do for a living?"

"He's a factory worker. His job can be grueling, but he's proud of what he does."

"He sounds like a man with old-fashioned values."

"He is."

"And it sounds like you take after him. The two of you must be very close."

A shadow flitted across her features. "Not really. Certainly not as close as when I was a kid." Feeling she had to explain, Leila added, "I sold my car when I moved into the downtown building. Not having my own transportation makes it difficult to get out to Crestview."

She turned her back on him and gave her full attention to her work. Wynne decided that was his signal to change the subject, not that he was about to forget it. She had revealed so little about herself other than her connection with The Total You. Knowing that Crestview was an industrial area, the housing mostly older frame homes or tracts of small bungalows built in the fifties, he wondered if Leila could possibly be embarrassed by her background or by her parents, who were obviously far from wealthy.

The idea unsettled him. He would hate to think he was correct. Glancing at her as he dampened the last crack in the living room, Wynne told himself he had to be wrong. If Leila was so concerned with material values, she would hardly be willing to settle for a simple date at the zoo—and she would never have volunteered to help fix up his place.

"So, how's your work coming?" Leila asked as she looked down the ladder.

Having filled in the shallow hole with plaster, Wynne set down his taping knife. "All done." He indicated his handiwork. "Take a look and tell me what you think."

Leila turned toward him. "Looks great. But I didn't mean the plaster. I was referring to the article."

"The article is coming along right on schedule. I've completed the rough draft, and I was planning on rewriting tomorrow. My editor needs it Friday morning."

"What about the pictures? Remember, I get to check them."

"The photographer will drop by in the morning with contact sheets. I'll pick out which photos I want, and he'll go back to his lab to print them. You can give me your stamp of approval on my selections before we leave for Grant Park."

"Think I'm easy, huh?"

Wynne almost wished she were—and he meant it in a far more personal context than she. Then again, he was equally aware that the challenge of wooing Leila was part of her appeal. She didn't make anything easy for him.

"Not at all," he told her. "I'm merely confident of my good taste."

Which included women, Wynne decided, trying to read the thoughts behind her dark eyes. He realized that Leila was studying him with equal interest. She looked away first, and he noticed the smudge of plaster on her cheek. She must have swiped at a stray strand of hair. He reached out and brushed the caked white powder away with his thumb.

Leila froze as if mesmerized by the touch, and Wynne felt a spark ignite between them. He trailed his thumb lower and found the pulse in her throat. Then, before he knew his own intentions, he was pulling Leila into his arms, his mouth finding hers.

"Wynne..."

His name was a silky whisper almost lost by their sudden embrace. Leila opened to him and returned his kiss. He'd been wanting to kiss her again for so long. Mere days had turned into an eternity.

Wynne probed Leila's mouth with a delicious laziness that belied the urgency of his hunger. She tasted so sweet, he ached to explore the rest of her. With difficulty, he held himself in check. He wanted to know Leila with a special intimacy that he'd never shared with another woman. He had no intention of rushing things between them.

When Leila stroked the back of his neck and snuggled closer, Wynne had to force himself to remember that. His all-too-human body responded to her touch with an eagerness difficult to control. His lips never leaving hers, he wrapped one arm around her waist and pulled her tightly into his arousal. They swayed together when his knees went weak. Needing support, Wynne pressed Leila backward into the ladder.

Suddenly, the ladder gave against their combined weight, the legs scraping the floor with a sharp bounce that seemed to punctuate the end of their kiss. Wynne pulled Leila upright as the ladder settled in place, but not before everything went flying from the top. Tools scattered. A putty knife clanked against the wall. The plaster bucket toppled and bounced off a ladder leg scattering semidry plaster across the floor in crumbled lumps.

Their romantic mood broken, they both began to laugh.

"We'd better clean up this mess," Leila said, stooping to pick up plaster chunks and drop them into the bucket.

Wynne joined her on the floor. "Did anyone ever tell you that you're a very special lady?"

"Not lately."

"Consider yourself told."

Leila seemed embarrassed. Or was the flush in her cheeks the remnant of their kiss? The idea that his effect on her was lasting pleased Wynne no end, but he ignored the urge to tease her. This particular silence was indeed golden, wrapping him in a cocoon of happiness and warmth.

Cleanup took only a few minutes, and Wynne was disappointed when Leila said, "I should be getting home."

He didn't want the evening to end just yet. "I'll drive you."

"That's okay. I can take a taxi."

"Don't be silly. You had to do that last night. The least I can do is see that you get home safely."

"I'll be fine. I'm a big girl."

Flicking his eyes along the length of her bared legs, he said, "I've noticed."

Leila's lips curved into a responding smile. "Besides, you're spoiling our doorman with too many bribes."

Wondering if she was making an observation about his finances, Wynne was about to protest.

"And," she added, "you can use the time to write."

He knew Leila meant the article. But his mind was far from The Total You. After that kiss, Brenna was much, much closer. His imagination already taking off, Wynne wondered if Brenna would be acting out of character if she helped James get his castle in shape.

"My writing can wait another hour, especially when I have good reason to skip out on it for a while. I'm driving you home. No arguments."

Leila smiled. "No arguments," she echoed.

CHAPTER SEVEN

THE NEXT DAY, Leila found herself daydreaming about Wynne at the strangest times—like in the midst of the weekly staff meeting.

"Before we break up, I have one last item on the agenda," Mike Kramer said, sitting on the edge of his desk. He looked directly at Gail. "I expect all the members of my staff to make the utmost effort to get along with each other. No exceptions. Your attitudes have a direct effect on the prosperity of this organization."

Leila could sense that her friend was squirming inside, but Gail kept her expression straight as she always did around their boss. Despite the outrageous things she sometimes said, Gail was a dedicated professional when it came to her work.

"Is there a specific problem?" Gail had the temerity to ask.

"Yeah," Jocko broke in. "I don't get any respect around here."

Leila glanced at the director of recreation, who sat alone opposite the two women. He was glowering at them both, though heaven knew how he had the nerve to be angry at her, Leila thought. She'd been the one who had smoothed things over the day before when Jocko had been acting self-centered and Gail had made things worse by giving him a hard time.

Now Gail's expression remained innocent when she told Mike, "I can truly say that, from now on, Jocko will get every ounce of respect he deserves."

Jocko seemed somewhat appeased by the conciliatory-sounding statement, but Mike studied Gail suspiciously.

"Good," the executive director said. "Then, at your next planning meeting, you can help Jocko pick out a few photos of himself that we'll have blown up for the anniversary party."

"What!" Leila and Gail exclaimed at once.

"And no laughing this time," Jocko growled.

Mike held up a hand for silence. "Many of our clients have been drawn to the club because of Jocko's fame as a football player. There will be possible new clients at the party in addition to members of the press. It wouldn't hurt to use several strategically placed photos of Jocko in his area." Mike rose. "Now, unless there are any objections, this meeting is over."

Leila knew that Gail would no more protest than she would. Mike had a blind spot about Jocko, and the executive director would take any argument about the idea being in poor taste as a personal criticism. This particular issue just wasn't important enough to earn Mike's ill will. The meeting broke up without further discussion.

But they were barely in the hallway when Gail mumbled, "Do you believe we're going to have to cater to that puffed-up pea brain?"

"Mike's word is law." Leila wrapped an arm around the other woman's shoulders and gave her a quick squeeze. "Can you take some good advice from a friend?"

"What?"

"Try to be nicer to Jocko."

"But he makes me crazy."

"He's probably not such a bad guy if you peel away the ego and the chauvinism."

Gail giggled. "Are you sure there would be anything left?"

"Probably an insecure human being."

"Jocko, insecure? You've got to be kidding!"

Leila shook her head. "No joke."

"Jocko, King of Insecurity," Gail said as if testing the new nickname. "Sorry, it just doesn't fit."

"Sometimes you have to look deep below the surface, Gail. Believe me. I know what I'm talking about."

"You insecure? Never!"

"For years, I was at least the Princess if not the Queen of Insecurity."

"Oh, yeah. How'd you get over it?"

"With determination."

And professional help. But if she explained that, she would have to go into other things she would rather forget.

"Let's change the subject," Gail suggested. "I would rather hear about you and Wynne. Did you see him last night?"

Leila nodded. "We had a real exciting evening, doing something I would bet you've never done on a date."

"What?" Gail demanded.

"We plastered."

"Plastered what? Each other?"

"The cracks in his living room walls."

"You're kidding, right?"

"Honest."

"Bro-ther, what do I have to do to get some excitement into your life? Plastering?" Gail shook her head sadly. "Leila, you're hopeless."

"We're seeing each other this evening, too."

"What are you going to do for kicks? Sand floors?"

"Go to Grant Park for the concert and fireworks."

"Well, that's more like it," Gail said as they came in sight of Leila's office. Wynne was waiting outside her door, portfolio tucked under one arm. Gail grinned at him. "Speaking of the plastering devil . . ."

Leila groaned inwardly. Now Wynne would know they'd been talking about him.

Eyebrows raised, he gave her a significant look. "I was wondering where you were."

"Our weekly staff meeting ran long," Leila explained. She indicated the portfolio. "Are those the pictures?"

Wynne nodded. "I think you'll be pleased."

"Let's take a look."

With Wynne and Gail following, Leila led the way into her office and cleared the few things on her desk. Wynne opened the portfolio and spread out more than a dozen glossy eight-by-tens, some color, others black-and-white.

"I had Tommy print up the best of the lot, but I'll only be able to use about half of these. So what do you think?"

"Terrific!" Gail said enthusiastically, picking up a color shot of a class in progress.

Leila could feel Wynne's questioning eyes on her. Nervously, she began examining the photos. The butterflies in her stomach soon settled, however. Most of the shots were of the clients themselves—exercising, being weighed in or measured, attending nutrition and cooking classes, participating in recreational sports. She was in the remaining shots, true, but the focus was on the clients with whom she was working...all except for one color photograph in which she was talking to a woman whose back was to the camera.

Leila picked up the exception and examined it critically. An odd feeling hit the pit of her stomach. She couldn't take her eyes off of what the camera had captured. She appeared poised, mature, confident...radiant. To Leila's amazement, all of the enthusiasm generated by her deep-seated convictions seemed to come alive in this one photograph.

"It's good, isn't it?" Wynne asked.

"Yes."

More than good. Is this how her students saw her? Leila wondered.

"No objections if I use that one?"

She wanted to object on principle, but she couldn't. There was no reason to. The photograph didn't exploit her looks. Somehow it went beyond them. She shook her head.

"You were right," she said, handing over the photograph. "You do have good taste."

"Let me see." Gail tilted her head to get a glimpse. "Leila, wow. I can't believe you quit mod—"

A knock on the open door interrupted Gail before she could finish the word *modeling*. Leila drew a relieved breath and waved Grace Vanos into the office. Maybe Leila would eventually tell Wynne that she'd been a model, but she wasn't yet ready for the questions that would go with the revelations. He would be even more dogged about getting to the truth than Gail, who knew only an expurgated version of the experience.

"You're busy," Grace said, looking around the room nervously. "I have to talk to you for a minute, but I can come back later."

Leila sensed the teenager's hesitancy in speaking to her at all. "No, now would be fine. Really."

Gail started toward the door. "I have to get going, anyway." She glanced from Wynne to Leila, then winked. "Have a good time tonight."

"I'll wait outside," Wynne offered.

He followed Gail and closed the door behind them. Grace shifted from one foot to the other, looking panicked. Leila sat and indicated the chair opposite.

"You can make yourself comfortable."

"Thanks." Grace sat gingerly on the edge of the chair as if she were ready to flee. "I—I just wanted to apologize. I'm sorry for being rude to you the other day."

Seeing how difficult this was for the teenager, Leila tried to smooth things over. "Apology accepted. I was worried I might have said something to upset you."

"No! Really, Leila. I was horrible." Grace stared down at her hands, which she twisted together in her lap. "I had some problems on my mind, and I took them out on you."

"Want to talk about it?"

"No. Everything's solved, now." Still she didn't look up. "I was thinking about what you said—about signing up for the nutrition class, I mean. If you think I should take it, then I will. I don't want to disappoint you."

Leila leaned forward and reached out to lift Grace's chin. That the girl's dark eyes seemed frightened worried her.

"Grace, I'm not the one you have to please. I know you want to make some changes in the way you look. I'm only trying to help you do it sensibly. I do think you should take the nutrition class, because I want to see you healthy and emotionally happy. That's all. Whatever you do or don't do to reach your goals should be for yourself, not for someone else."

"Well, then I *want* to join a nutrition class," Grace said quickly.

The teenager was so overeager that Leila had cause to be uneasy. Remembering her conversation with Wynne about praise addiction, she wondered if Grace could need that kind of unhealthy emotional support. No, she was probably overreacting. Everyone needed occasional approval. There was nothing unnatural in that. And Mrs. Vanos had told her that Grace had made the decision to commit herself to a new program of diet and exercise on her own. Teenagers often had problems that seemed insurmountable. Possibly Grace had conquered a few and was reviewing her goals with renewed enthusiasm.

"All right, Grace. Let's get you signed up."

WAITING PATIENTLY OUTSIDE the office, Wynne contemplated the scene Grace had interrupted a few minutes before. Leila had been nervous about looking at her photographs, as if she were afraid she might see a side of herself that she didn't like. He knew she'd felt coerced into being photographed in the first place.

Why would a woman with her looks be shy around a camera? Leila probably didn't have a bad angle and couldn't take a bad picture. Strange.

Wynne wondered what Gail had been about to say when they'd been interrupted. He'd automatically filled in the rest of the word, *modeling*. Was it possible? If so, Leila must have had good reasons to abandon what might have been a far more lucrative career than the one she'd chosen. That she might have been a model explained her attitude about appearance versus health. Models' lives revolved around their looks, a situation that had to become stale quickly.

With a typical reporter's curiosity, Wynne felt the need to confront Leila about the past. He wondered if he would be making a mistake—could be that she didn't want him to know about her past or she would have told him. Perhaps in time the revelation would be easier for her to make. He put the thought behind him with the opening of her office door.

Grace exited. "Thanks, Leila."

"No problem."

"See you."

As Grace hurried down the hall, Wynne entered the office and noticed that Leila was smiling.

"It's getting late," he said. "Want to help me eliminate a few of these photographs, or should I send them all to the editor and let him decide?"

"They're all good. I wouldn't know which to choose."

"Fair enough." He gathered the photos together. "Are you about ready to leave?"

"Anytime. I would like to stop by my apartment to change, however."

"No problem. Why don't I meet you downstairs?"

"Give me ten minutes."

About to slip the photos back into a folder, Wynne glanced at the one on top, the one focusing on Leila herself. Studying it, he could well believe she'd been a model.

The urge to ask her about her past hit him again, more strongly this time. Maybe tonight would present the perfect opportunity to do so.

AFTER CHANGING into her royal-blue clam diggers and pullover top, Leila grabbed her red sweatshirt jacket and left her apartment in the promised ten minutes. Wynne was waiting for her outside the building. A roomy canvas tote hung over one of his shoulders, and he was carrying two packages in his other arm. His car was nowhere in sight.

"Where's your car?"

"In a garage up the street."

"Don't tell me you actually parked legally for once," Leila teased him.

"I had no choice, since we'll be gone for so long. I figured we would be crazy to try to park near the lake. The place will be mobbed."

"You mean you're willing to exercise to get there?"

"Right. I'm going to exercise my arm."

He waved at a passing taxi, which screeched to a halt in front of them.

"Cheat," she murmured as he opened the door for her.

She slid across the back seat, then took the tote from Wynne before he climbed in.

"Where to, Mac?"

"I have to stop at the Federal Express office at Clark and Illinois to drop off these packages," Wynne told the driver. "Then you can take us to Michigan and Monroe." To Leila he added, "We'll walk from there."

Curious, she gazed at the two packages in his lap. "You're sending the photographs and the article separately?"

"Only one of these is going to *Glitter*. The other is something I've written...on consignment."

"Oh." Not wanting him to think she was prying, Leila changed the subject. "So what's in the canvas bag?"

"A blanket." He grinned at her. "I used to be a Boy Scout, so I always come prepared."

"Mmm," she murmured in teasing response. "I like that in a man."

Wynne raised an eyebrow but didn't comment. Leila smothered a giggle and nestled close to his side. She felt young and carefree and a little silly. Wynne always seemed to know how to loosen her up. A cautious voice told her not to get too loose, but for once Leila was tempted to throw caution to the wind.

"You're in a good mood." Wynne stretched an arm around the back of the seat and let his fingers trail her upper arm. "I hope I'm the cause."

"At least half. Definitely more than half," Leila admitted with a shiver as tingles spread along her flesh from where he touched her. "Besides which, Grace apologized for blowing up the other day. And, she's decided to take a nutrition class as I suggested."

"I'm glad things worked out."

"So I hope. I still have a strange feeling that something might be wrong."

"Like what?"

"I wish I could pinpoint the problem. Something in Grace's eyes..."

"You're psychic." Wynne leered at her. "Tell me what you see in *my* eyes."

"Tsk, tsk." Leila trailed a finger over one side of his mustache. "X-rated material."

The taxi skidded to a halt. "Here you go, Mac. Federal Express."

"I'll hurry," Wynne promised, already opening the door. "Hold that thought. We can pick up the conversation from where we left off."

With a smile, Leila leaned back and made herself comfortable. She'd only known Wynne for a little more than a week, yet she felt closer to him than she had to any man in years. Close enough to—

Not wanting to torture herself, Leila cut off that image before completing it. If things kept going as smoothly between them as they had been, intimacy was bound to come soon enough. She never would have believed it a week ago, when Wynne had manipulated her into working with him.

Wondering why he hadn't offered to show her the article as well as the photographs, Leila told herself she was worrying about nothing. Wynne Donegan wasn't the exploiting type. Even if reporters and photographers had a lot in common, Wynne was nothing like Christian.

As if to punctuate that thought, the cab door opened and Wynne slipped in beside her. He automatically wrapped his arm around her shoulders.

"All set," he told the driver.

The taxi took off at a crawl. Already the downtown streets were clogged with cars heading to the preholiday celebration. Suburbanites as well as city dwellers flooded the area every year.

"So where were we?" he asked.

"I was interpreting your X-rated thoughts."

"And?"

"I'm not sure some of those things you were thinking about are humanly possible," she teased.

They settled into a comfortable silence. Leila rubbed her cheek against Wynne's safari shirt and inhaled his after-shave, a light musky fragrance. His arm tightened around her shoulders, and his fingers tangled in her loose hair with an easy familiarity. Though part of her was content, the time it was taking to cross the bridge over the Chicago River was making her fidgety.

She turned her head so she could whisper into Wynne's ear. "We could walk faster than this cab can move."

"But we couldn't do this while we were walking," Wynne murmured in return.

"Do what?"

Finding her mouth in answer, he kissed her lightly. Even so, Leila's pulse slithered through her veins like thick syrup, and she was breathing quickly when Wynne pulled away.

"I get enough exercise anyway," she murmured agreeably, offering her mouth for another kiss.

Wynne was only too happy to oblige with a dozen more. The next thing Leila knew, the driver was interrupting them.

"Michigan and Monroe, Mac. Or maybe you folks changed your mind and want to go home," the driver suggested, staring up into his rearview mirror with unconcealed interest.

The man must have been watching the display they'd been putting on in the back seat! Leila realized, shrinking down and wishing she could disappear.

Wynne merely chuckled and pulled out his wallet. "This'll be fine, thanks."

After the driver was squared, they left the traffic jam and the high-rise buildings behind for the normally open space of the park. But a half block east of Michigan, cresting the bridge that spanned the railroad yards below, Leila realized they were in for an evening she wouldn't soon forget.

"I've never seen so many people."

"I heard predictions that the crowd will top half a million," Wynne said, pressing her close to his side as a couple of teenagers almost ran into her.

Literally hundreds of thousands of people were already spread out before them, both in the park areas and milling along the streets. Hundreds more were arriving every minute. Access streets to the area were cut off from local traffic for pedestrian use.

The food booths and entertainment stages for the Taste of Chicago had been erected in the streets directly surrounding the band shell. The event was a week-long opportunity for restaurant owners to sell the best of their cuisine in hopes of luring Chicagoans to their establishments.

Since they were both hungry, they stopped at the kiosks with the most appealing dishes on the way to the band shell. They shared Mexican, Japanese, Swedish, South American, Persian and Vietnamese specialties, which were sold in taste-size quantities. The waits were long, and dusk soon began to settle over the park.

"We'd better try to find a spot for our blanket," Wynne said. "We can get more food later."

"Are you kidding? I'm stuffed. I don't think I could eat another bite for days."

"That's too bad. I was going to ask you to come to our annual Fourth of July family gathering. But if you did, I'm afraid my mother would torture you with even more good food."

Leila thought it sounded like heaven. A real family holiday—and Wynne was offering her a chance that her own family had denied her.

"Well," she teased, "you could twist my arm."

"Then you'll come?"

Leila nodded eagerly as they reached the edge of the band shell area. Her feet stopped, not only because of her shock at the sight, but because there was no place for them to move. Ahead lay a carpet of blankets edge to edge, stretched out as far as she could see.

"We're too late," she stated.

"I was afraid of that." Wynne looked around and pointed to an area along the sidewalk under the trees and next to some hedges. "There are a few small spots left over there."

"Small" was something of an understatement. They would be wedged up against each other not to mention several strangers.

"Maybe we should forget the concert and just go down to the lake so we can have a view of the fireworks." The trees lining the park would block the view from where they now stood.

"Good idea. I brought a radio, anyway, so we can still listen to the concert."

"You really did come prepared. I'm impressed."

They set off for the lake, traversing one extralong block and crossing Lake Shore Drive in a press of hundreds of others. Police were already directing traffic, both vehicular and pedestrian. The lakeshore was a sea of humanity as far as the eye could see in either direction.

"There's a spot over there in front of that tree," Wynne murmured close to her ear as if he were afraid someone else would overhear and beat them to it.

Steering her by the elbow, he got her through the crowd only with difficulty. They had to dodge running kids, circle people stretched out on the grass and step over coolers. Finally, they claimed their stake on the hillside, spread their blanket, settled down and turned on the portable radio just as the concert was about to begin.

"Considering the inadequate new sound system, we have the better end of the deal right here," Wynne said, wedging the canvas tote between himself and the tree behind him. "You can't hear a thing unless you're directly in front of the new band shell.'

"A real shame, but right now I would like to enjoy the music, the view . . . and the company."

"Fine by me," Wynne agreed, pulling her back against his chest.

Aware of his body warmth, Leila wasn't surprised when a languorous feeling stole through her. Dreamily, she rubbed the side of her forehead against his chin and looked out over the harbor. Hundreds of people were grilling food or drinking beer on their docked boats. Other craft slowly cut through the harbor waters for better positions on the lake. Farther out, she spotted the blue lights of the fireboats and knew they were hovering around the barges from which the fireworks would be launched.

She closed her eyes and allowed the music to envelop her every bit as much as Wynne's encircling arms. She couldn't remember when she'd last been quite this happy. Wynne pressed a kiss to her temple. His mustache tickled her into smiling. She snuggled closer, content to remain quietly in his arms until the Grant Park Symphony finished the first piece.

"This is the life," Wynne murmured when a short break was announced.

"Mmm. So tell me about your Walt Disney family," Leila demanded, thinking about the next day.

"Maybe I was exaggerating just a little. You tell me after you meet them. Let's talk about something else."

"Something more interesting than your family?" Still relaxing against him, Leila was unprepared for his answer.

"Your modeling days."

She tried not to stiffen, but her attempt was unsuccessful. "My what?"

"Was it so long ago that you've forgotten already?"

"No," Leila said tightly, the magic of the evening dissipating. "I haven't forgotten a thing."

"Then tell me."

"It's unimportant."

"I don't think so, or you wouldn't be reacting in quite this manner."

Leila pulled free of his arms and faced him. Though it was now dark, mercury-vapor lamps lighted the area, allowing her to see his features. They seemed uncompromising in the harsh bluish light. Wynne was determined to get to the truth just as she knew he would be.

"Let's just say that modeling isn't the glamour job that it's cracked up to be and leave it at that. Okay?"

But he obviously wasn't ready to abandon the subject. "Meaning?" he persisted.

"Meaning it was hard work. Full of sacrifices. And disappointments."

The last referred to her ex-lover rather than the work itself. Leila's full stomach trembled violently, and she had to still the urge to panic. If she thought positively, she would be all right, she told herself.

But Wynne kept at her. "You could be more specific."

"I could, but I would rather not. Can't we just drop it?"

"Why? Why do I have to pull every detail about your personal life from you, one fact at a time? Don't you trust me yet?"

"This has nothing to do with trust. Maybe it's just too personal."

Stomach squeezing tight inside, Leila rose to her feet and looked around until she spotted the long row of orange-and-turquoise structures. Wynne clasped her ankle.

"Where do you think you're going?"

"To the rest rooms, if you don't mind." Anything to get away from the conversation. She pulled her foot free easily. "I'll be back in a few minutes."

That was a promise she couldn't keep if she wanted to. Getting through the crowd was now even rougher. People continuously streamed across Lake Shore Drive to the grassy hill and the cement strip along the lake. And when she got to the portable outhouses, the lines were at least a dozen people deep. Leila tried not to panic. She pressed a hand to her stomach and tried to will the nausea away. She couldn't react like this because someone questioned her about her past. She was all right, had been for years. She'd left all her traumas behind her in New York.

Maybe that was the problem, she thought woozily, fighting the feeling of helplessness and nausea that had a grip on her. She hadn't brought the truth into the open for ten years. Her parents hadn't been ready to hear it, and she'd gotten into the habit of skirting the truth with friends like Gail.

No one had ever forced the issue the way Wynne just had.

Her stomach lurched again. Leila swallowed hard and prayed the line would hurry. Why had she stuffed herself with so much food? She would be mortally embarrassed if she was sick in the midst of all these people, and she wasn't sure how much longer she could hold on.

WYNNE STOOD and stared through the eerie blue darkness for more than twenty minutes. No sign of Leila. She might have been swallowed up by the crowd never to be seen again. Tempted to go after her, he fought the instinct. He would never find her in this chaos. And if he left his post, she might not find her way back to him. What a hell of a way to spend an evening that had begun with such promise!

He shouldn't have pried. He'd warned himself that doing so might be a mistake, yet he hadn't had the sense to listen. But when would Leila stop being so evasive? When would she open up to him?

She'd had reason to mistrust him when he'd manipulated her into working with him. But now...*now* he thought things were different between them. Couldn't she tell he cared about her?

Damn!

Maybe Leila merely needed time. Their relationship was advancing so rapidly, the pace might be scaring her and forcing her to distance herself. He couldn't figure out why his mention of modeling should upset her so much. Unless he'd brought back bad memories of that time.

Knowing how upset she'd been, Wynne couldn't ask her directly. Of course, a reporter had other ways of finding out what he wanted to know. He thought about digging for the answers on his own. If he tried, he could find out about Leila's past. But did he want to? he wondered uneasily. If she found out about his machinations, Leila might, indeed, feel her mistrust had been well placed.

Then what would happen?

He searched the crowd again. At last he found her distinctive form as she picked her way around the people seated in her path. Wynne relaxed. She hadn't run out on him, after all. But when she came near, he noticed her features were drawn and she carried herself stiffly rather than with the fluid grace he'd grown used to.

"You all right?" he asked.

"Fine."

Her smile tight, she sat on the blanket without further comment. Wynne sat also, not quite touching her.

"Concert's over. The fireworks are about to start."

"Good."

Her back was as stiff as her voice. Daring to chance a rebuff, Wynne placed his hand on the soft flesh between her neck and shoulder and gently massaged. That she didn't move away was encouraging. That she didn't melt into him wasn't. He felt an invisible barrier between them that hadn't existed earlier.

"I'm sorry if I spoiled your evening," he told her. At least that much was the truth. He wasn't sorry that he'd pried, but that she'd react so adversely. "I really didn't mean to."

"My evening isn't ruined," she mumbled, her fingers fiddling with a tuft of grass exposed next to the blanket.

"Then why are you sitting so far away?"

"I'm not."

"You're not in my arms, either."

She couldn't deny that. Wynne could sense the tension oozing from Leila, as if she were trying to make up her mind.

The mercury-vapor lamps switched off; the blue light faded gradually. Then strains of music filled the air from large speakers set into the cement walk, and the first set of rockets burst overhead, streaking the inky darkness with twin smudges of bright light. "Oohs" and "aahs" and the shouts of excited children surrounded them.

Without warning, Leila scooted back and into his side. Wynne wrapped his arm around her and felt a flood of emotion he defined as relief. While the night sky danced with brilliant colors, she gradually began to relax, to become part of him. Relieved that he hadn't ruined the evening, Wynne tightened his grip and knew that he never wanted to feel that lonely separation from her again.

And yet, he was a man who was never satisfied with less than the truth, obviously a gift Leila was not ready to share. His mother had always told him he was too impatient, that sometimes a person had to wait to get the results he wanted. A wise mother, but her advice hadn't changed him. Maybe that need to know was what had made him a successful reporter.

But if he looked into Leila's past on his own, would he be throwing away their future?

CHAPTER EIGHT

"MEL, THIS PLACE is like fabulous," Grace said as she followed her friend into the converted loft space in Old Town. Mel had invited Grace to her mother's Fourth of July brunch.

"Yeah, I guess."

Mel could afford to be offhand since she lived there, but Grace had never seen anything like it. She and her mother had a comfortable and gracious two-bedroom apartment that would fit in the middle of this central living area with room to spare. A freestanding ribbon of pink marble streamed down the center of the open area from ceiling to floor, where it became a fireplace. The entire room was decorated in pale grays and white with delicate pink accents. The decor could have come straight out of a society magazine. "So," Mel began, "did Leila buy your apology?"

Distracted from further inspecting her surroundings, Grace frowned at her friend. "Don't put it like that. I really like Leila."

"So do I, but she would never understand if you told her the truth."

"I know, but I hated lying."

"What's the big deal? You really were sorry, and you will take the class. So why feel guilty?"

"If I don't have any intentions of using what I learn in the class, that's the same as lying."

Grace could tell Mel was about to rationalize further when a stunning blonde entered the room through the open terrace doors. She was wearing a calf-length white skirt and sky-blue blouse that accented her deep tan.

"There you are, Melanie. And this must be your friend, Grace." The blonde closed the space between them and held out her perfectly manicured hand, heavy with aquamarine-studded bracelets and rings. "I'm Sandra Bricker."

Grace stared. Her mother certainly didn't look like this. "Hi, Mrs. Bricker. Sorry if I'm late."

Grace felt the woman's piercing blue gaze sweep over her as they shook hands. She had the feeling that she came up lacking, although the older woman would be too polite to say so to her face.

"Call me Sandra, dear," Mel's mother insisted, removing her hand and smoothing hair that was already precisely in place. "Everyone does."

"Even me," Mel said, her voice odd.

Sandra Bricker circled Mel's shoulders and gave her a quick squeeze. "Melanie and I are great friends. She's a daughter any mother could be proud of, especially since she took off all that ugly weight." She squeezed again, her blue eyes traveling over Mel's delicate body. "Now she's perfect."

"A perfect daughter for a perfect mother," Mel added.

Grace thought her friend's tone sounded a bit caustic. And why shouldn't it be if Mrs. Bricker put such importance on her daughter's looks? Her own mother would never measure her or her older sister in that way.

"Why, thank you, sweetheart," Sandra was saying. "Why don't you take your little friend out onto the terrace and mingle with our guests? Vivienne is finished setting up the buffet. You can eat anytime you like."

With a sweep of her full white skirt, Mel's mother headed for the kitchen and left them to their own devices.

"C'mon, Gracie."

Mel led the way out to the flagstone terrace, with its abundance of plants, hanging flower baskets... and people, none of whom were their age. The other guests were obviously wealthy and looked at home in the surroundings.

A marble fountain in one corner of the terrace was the centerpiece for a curved buffet table. This would be no ordinary Fourth of July meal, Grace realized as her gaze swept exotic dishes in rich-looking sauces and desserts that were already making her mouth water.

"So what do you think?" Mel asked.

"This place is incredible."

"I meant the food."

Grace couldn't tear her eyes away from the display. "A million calories. At least."

"Don't worry about it." Mel picked up two china plates and handed one to her. "Enjoy yourself."

"Now, Melanie," her mother said as she brought an armload of fresh flowers to the buffet and spread them among the entrées, "don't encourage your friend to overeat. She's not as slim as you are."

Grace tried not to let the thoughtless comment get to her. She knew she was already looking better after having shed eleven pounds. Her thighs were a little flabby because of the quick weight loss, though. She would have to step up her exercise program to compensate.

"Don't mind Sandra," Mel said as soon as her mother slid back into the crowd. "Vivienne is the most extraordinary caterer. So enjoy yourself!"

That's exactly what she intended to do, Grace thought resentfully, heaping the most tempting foods onto her plate. After all, Sandra Bricker didn't know their little secret.

WYNNE'S FAMILY would have done a Walt Disney movie proud, Leila thought as she carried a bowl of potato salad out to the scarred wooden picnic table in the huge backyard. Located in Ravenswood Manor, a well-kept neighborhood on the north side of Chicago, the Donegan home was a large brick building sitting high on the west bank of the Chicago River. With its shrub-and-tree-ringed lawn and carefully planned flower beds, the place seemed as well loved as all its family members. The spacious grounds were overrun with two dozen people ranging in age from a four-month-old baby to a couple of senior citizens who were tending the grills filled with burgers and hot dogs.

Leila was pretty sure she had Wynne's siblings straight. Megan and Sean had green eyes and some shade of reddish-brown hair, as did Wynne and their father, while Doreen and the twins, Grady and Katy, took after their mother, with blue eyes and black hair. But as far as the spouses, kids, aunts and uncles were concerned, Leila knew she would need another get-together or two to keep them all straight.

The idea held a welcome ring, some bright spots for the future that her own family didn't seem willing to provide. Thinking about the widening gap she felt between herself and her parents and brother made her frown.

"How are you doing?" Wynne asked, coming up behind her and slipping his arms around her waist.

Her frown transformed into a happy smile, she relaxed against him, all vestiges of tension from the night before completely dissipated. She'd been irrational for a short while, but Wynne's unquestioning comfort had helped her through her self-induced trauma.

Wynne had been naturally curious about her background, that's all. There was no reason to suspect he had ulterior motives. He was a man she could trust.

Leila glanced up at his dimpled cheek and checked a desire to run her finger around it. Too many sets of interested eyes might be watching them openly.

"I'm doing just fine," she assured him, "other than being intimidated by trying to keep all these unfamiliar faces straight."

"*You* intimidated?"

"I have my weaknesses."

"Tell me more," Wynne teased, flaring his fingers surreptitiously under the fullness of one breast. "Maybe I can figure out how to take advantage of them."

Leila sucked in her breath at the delicious feeling spreading through her. Before she could gather her wits and think of a clever retort, Grady interrupted the private moment when he set down a massive plate of fried chicken in the middle of the table.

"Can't you keep your hands off this luscious woman for a second?" he asked his older brother. He made himself comfortable on the bench, picked a chunk from the bowl of potato salad and popped it into his mouth.

"Look who's talking," Wynne growled, slipping his fingers to a more innocent position, yet leaving his arms right where they were. "You're just jealous because, by some miracle, you don't have your own date today."

"Relieved, not jealous," Grady returned. He sighed heavily. "All those women are wearing me out."

With his more conventional good looks, Leila could believe that.

Wynne snorted. "You hate every minute, I'm sure."

She couldn't help laughing at the good-natured potshots the brothers were taking at each other. Grady grinned up at her, and in spite of the difference in coloring, she thought he and Wynne looked alike for a moment. The dimple did it, she realized, although Grady's was in his left cheek.

"Hey, you guys!" Doreen called from the kitchen window. "You know the rules around here. No shirking. I need a set of muscles."

"Your turn, big brother." Grady nodded at the chicken. "I did my share."

Letting go of Leila, Wynne warned her, "Beware of this particular Big Bad Wolf. He's a lady-killer."

He jogged toward the house. Leila's eyes followed his every movement.

"What are your intentions toward my brother, anyway?" Grady asked.

His question startled Leila, and she whipped around to face him. "I beg your pardon?"

"How do you feel about Wynne? It's obvious he's head over heels about you."

"It is?"

"My brother hasn't asked a date to a family gathering since he was nineteen, and we embarrassed him to death with our teasing. He must really have it bad for you."

That Grady might be correct both warmed and frightened her. "If so, that's the first I've heard about it," Leila stated.

"Maybe because he's shy."

"Your brother, Samuel Wynne Donegan III, shy?"

"At all the wrong times," Grady assured her.

Their conversation was cut frustratingly short by a sudden flurry of activity around them. Kids brought paper plates, cups, ice and pop from the house. Wynne's youngest brother, Sean, and two uncles dragged another heavy picnic table closer to the first while Wynne and his sisters Doreen and Megan brought folding tables and chairs outside to be set up. Swelled with pregnancy, Katy supervised, and Leila and Grady immediately offered their help. Within minutes, the dining arrangements were completed, the food was set out and the family members were standing in line.

Leila thought about the too-short exchange with Grady. If he'd been correct, why wouldn't Wynne share his feelings with her? He always seemed so bold and determined when he wanted something. Did he want her? Silly question when it came to the physical part. Things were moving so quickly that they might have shared more than a kiss the night before if he hadn't upset her with his questions about modeling.

Leila had to admit she was ready for physical intimacy with Wynne, but she wasn't sure about the emotional side of a relationship. She didn't know if she could bring herself to discuss her aborted modeling career with the honesty she knew he expected of her. And unless she could dredge up the whole ugly mess, she would feel she was cheating him in some way.

After they'd filled their plates, Wynne claimed two seats at the table with his parents, Grady and his grandfather. The boisterous good humor of the noisy family snapped her out of her more personal thoughts.

"So you're a director of a health club, Leila," Kathleen Donegan said, her musical tone hinting at an Irish brogue.

Nodding, Leila swallowed a mouthful of food. "I'm in charge of physical fitness education. I try to see that our clients—women mostly—meet their fitness goals in a sensible and enjoyable manner."

"Why mostly women?"

"How many men do you know who incessantly worry about their weight and appearance?"

Kathleen gave her husband's paunch a quick glance before saying, "I get the idea."

"Hey, wait a minute!" Samuel II protested. "I saw that sneaky look."

Kathleen adopted an innocent expression that reminded Leila of Wynne at his most charming. She tried to cover her snicker by taking a bite of chicken. Perhaps the others missed her reaction, but Wynne let her know he hadn't by squeezing her knee under the table. And then, as she was in the midst of swallowing the chicken, his hand slipped up higher....

Leila almost choked on her food but somehow managed to swallow it as Wynne's fingers did unspeakable things to her inner thigh. She tried shaking her leg to rid herself of his hand, but he wouldn't budge. At the same time, he calmly continued eating as if nothing were wrong.

Distracted, she missed Kathleen's next comment, then realized everyone at the table was watching for her reaction. Leila felt heat rise from her neck into her face. "I'm sorry. Were you talking to me?"

"I was just saying your parents must be very proud of you."

If only that were true, Leila thought, not knowing how to answer. But it seemed Kathleen didn't really expect one. Wynne's mother went on.

"Samuel and I are delighted with the way our children turned out." Her brogue more pronounced, Kathleen looked pointedly from one son to the other. "We weren't so sure about their potential for anything but mischief when they were younger. Their interests are totally different, but each one of our children is special and talented."

"Right," Wynne's father agreed dryly. "Grady is especially talented with the ladies."

"He told me he's been doing research for his brother," Sam I stated, his white mustache quivering.

"Granda, you weren't supposed to repeat that," Grady said in a stage whisper.

"Research, huh?" Leila raised a brow at Wynne's brother.

Grady shrugged. "Just trying to do my share. Wynne has to get his ideas from somewhere, you know. But I have to give my big brother credit. He had the guts to quit his job so he could chase a dream."

"Going off on his own to free-lance was risky," Leila admitted.

"Not to free-lance. I'm talking about his novel."

"Novel?" Leila was aware of Wynne tensing as she stared at him. "What kind of novel?"

"It's a wonderful story," Kathleen assured her. "About a young woman who—"

"It's not all that wonderful," Wynne interrupted. "I mean, it's popular fiction, on the glitzy side. I think it has merit because I'm trying to pass on some of my own values, but my mother would have everyone believe it's literature. She's never even read a page."

"Can you believe it? My own son and he won't let me see what he's writing."

"Probably afraid you'd critique it to death," her husband muttered.

Kathleen swatted him playfully, and Samuel lifted an eyebrow, promising some unnamed form of revenge. Leila was so intrigued by their easygoing manner—how different they were from her own more reserved parents—that she almost forgot the direction the conversation had taken.

Almost.

She turned her attention back to Wynne. "So, how long have you been working on this novel?"

"Six months."

"Strange that you never mentioned it."

Now Wynne was looking rather uncomfortable.

Grady spoke up in his stead. "I told you he was shy at all the wrong times."

Wynne gave his brother a threatening glare, which Grady seemed to enjoy immensely. Ducking his dark head, he chortled into his food. Leila wanted to know more, but she decided discretion was called for at the moment. She would wait until later, when she and Wynne were alone, to continue her questioning.

Let Wynne have a taste of his own medicine when she pried into his personal business!

A short while later, Leila had sampled most of the food but stopped before she felt full; she was not about to repeat her mistake of the night before. She took her plate to the garbage bag and dumped it. Other family members had likewise finished their meals, and the children began clamoring for a boat ride. Wynne volunteered to take them.

"We've always had some kind of motorboat to take advantage of the river. Da's version of a Sunday drive," Wynne explained. "He goes upriver instead of driving out to the country. You'll come along, won't you?"

"Of course. Think I'm afraid of a little water?"

"You wouldn't want to swim in *this* river," he assured her, leading the way to the opening in the bushes that would take them down to the boat. "All right, three maximum," he told the pack of kids who followed.

That meant they'd have to break up into several groups. They began squabbling as to who would go first until Uncle Wynne threatened to cancel due to stormy tempers. That calmed the loud voices immediately, and Wynne chose the first three. They clambered down the steep incline to the dock using wooden steps set into the bank.

As they settled into the boat, Wynne kept everyone entertained with stories. Leila could see he was a natural favorite with his nieces and nephews. He would make a terrific father.

They spent the better part of the hot muggy afternoon ferrying kids, then adults, up and down the river, but Leila didn't mind. She was having the time of her life.

She wanted this sense of belonging, this closeness, with her own family. She'd had it once upon a time before she'd moved to New York. This day with Wynne convinced her to try again. Somehow, someday, she would recapture that special relationship she'd lost.

They were entertaining the kids with a softball game when the skies darkened. A storm quickly brewed, and dark clouds released a downpour. Everyone scrambled for the house, but within fifteen minutes the rain had ended, and kids and adults alike trouped back outside. The game resumed on the slippery grass, and it wasn't long before Leila found herself bottom down, mud splattering her long legs and white shorts. She didn't mind until Wynne began laughing. She promised to get even with him for that.

Evening and the end of the gathering came too soon. Leila was tired, filthy... and sorry to leave. Impulsively, she hugged Wynne's mother and received a warm embrace and an invitation to come back. Feeling let down, she followed Wynne to the car.

"Anxious to get home?" he asked as they pulled away from the curb.

Leila glanced back at Samuel and Kathleen, who stood on the porch, arms wrapped around each other. She waved and received two of the same in return.

"Actually, I'm not."

She wouldn't mind hanging on to this feeling of contentment forever.

With his free hand, Wynne found her knee and stroked it coaxingly. "We could stop at my place and listen to the crickets in the backyard."

Leila felt a thrill shoot through her, as if she were turning inside out. Wynne wasn't thinking about crickets any more than she was. Somehow, she managed to keep her voice even when she said, "Sounds nice."

"If it doesn't rain some more."

Leila thought about her mud-splattered legs. "An impromptu shower might improve my appearance."

"Nothing could make you look any better in my eyes," Wynne assured her.

Andersonville was barely more than five minutes from Ravenswood Manor. Another thing to envy, Leila thought, wishing she didn't feel as if she lived a continent away from her parents. But her mother and father weren't uppermost in her mind when Wynne helped her from the car, his bold fingers wrapping themselves around her side and stroking the fullness of her breast. Shivers crawled along her delicate skin, making her nipples tighten in response.

She swallowed hard as Wynne led her up the path, because she knew what was going to happen in his house. She might be nervous, but she was ready, Leila told herself. More than ready. She'd been waiting half a lifetime for someone like Wynne to come along. He was everything she wanted in a man—warm, charming, devilish, compassionate... and best of all, worthy of her trust.

"Hey, loosen up," he whispered as they stopped in front of his door. He ran his hand up along her spine and massaged the back of her neck. "My crickets aren't going to eat you."

"How can you be sure?" she asked lightly.

"I've trained them to be vegetarians. Exotic women are more to my taste, anyway."

"Exotic?"

"Mmm." He kissed her lightly. "Spicy...." He kissed her a second time. "Sexy...." And yet again, deeper this time. "Scintillating...."

"Don't you think we should be doing this in the house?" she murmured.

"Why? Afraid the crickets will spread rumors?"

"Well, they do a lot of chirping."

Wynne let go of her to unlock the door, but after he swung it open, he guided her inside without bothering to dispel the darkness by turning on a light. He quickly secured the bolt, then found her by using the Braille method, his fingers reading her growing excitement when they came into contact with her breasts. His hands moved over her body with bold familiarity. Leila's heart began to pound. Unsure of what to expect from this man who usually teased and coaxed, she was surprised when he pressed her back against the wall and kissed her in a breathtakingly aggressive manner.

Tongue entwined with his, Leila flowed against him, her softness to his hard. Desire coursed through her, hot and damp. And Wynne was as ready as she. The proof lay trapped against her upper thigh, taunting her. Her body responded naturally, her hips shifting and pressing against him in a sinuous movement, forcing his expulsion of air and the removal of his mouth from her own.

"Try that again and you'll have to hold me up," he growled.

Embarrassed by her sensual reaction, Leila tried to move away, but Wynne held her fast. Her pulse beat rapidly, and her voice sounded odd to her own ears when she whispered, "Any better suggestions?"

"Let's go upstairs."

He didn't press the issue, but coaxed her lovingly, nuzzling the side of her neck, placing small kisses along her jaw and on her nose. Even though she'd thought she was ready for this, even though she'd known what would happen before she entered the house, Leila was torn. Part of her wanted to protect herself; part of her wanted to give Wynne her trust, something she'd held back from all men for the past ten years.

Trust . . . a gift so difficult to part with, yet so precious when offered. She'd given a man that gift once before only to have it tarnished.

But this time would be different, Leila argued with herself. Wynne was different. He would never use her.

As if to confirm that, he stroked her hair and whispered, "You're not irrevocably committed, you know. I still could take you home."

Chasing away her remaining doubts, Leila placed her hand in his, giving him her trust, which was so fragile.

"You're sure this is what you want?"

"I'm . . . sure." Her answer included much more than the physical, but the words wouldn't come.

Wynne kissed her sweetly, as though giving her a moment to change her mind. "You're so edgy." He used his free hand to rub the back of her neck, making some of the tension drain from her. "Don't be, not with me."

Leila tried to think of something humorous to say so she could hear him laugh, but it was getting more and more difficult to concentrate on anything but the sensations Wynne created where he touched her. Finally, he drew her through the living area, dark ex-

cept for the yellow light being cast by the street lamp
and shafting through the bay window.

He stopped in front of the fireplace, lit a candle on
the mantel, picked up the holder and led her on. He
raised the hand he held and kissed each finger, making Leila shiver. Lilting shadows flirted with the stairs
as they climbed. With each step, her nerves asserted
themselves. Her muscles had tightened once more by
the time they entered the bedroom. But he kept on,
moving past the hulking dark shadow of his bed.

Leila swallowed a nervous laugh. "Where are you
taking me?"

"To paradise and back if I can manage it."

Leila couldn't stop the laugh from escaping her as
they entered the bathroom. He placed the candle on a
shelf and turned on the shower. He kissed her, chasing away her desire to laugh and rousing her deeply
buried sensuality. Then he was undressing her and she
him, both flinging shoes and clothing to the floor.
Desire of another kind began to consume her.

Wynne swept her into the spacious stall, where
stinging needles of pleasantly warm water danced
along her sensitive flesh. He slid the door shut, and
they were enveloped in a steamy darkness except for
the glow of candlelight, which continuously changed
shape against the glass.

"This is all happening so fast, but I feel as if I've
been waiting forever for you," he murmured, as if to
reassure her.

The words were perfect. Leila couldn't have phrased
the sentiment any better herself. But then Wynne always seemed to know the right thing to say. Fascinated, she watched through lowered lids as he took her
mouth and held it captive in a lingering kiss.

He found the bar of soap and laved her skin, working his way from her shoulders down her arms to her fingertips. Then he began again at her neck and traced a soapy path through the valley between her heavy breasts down to her navel and lower, not stopping until he dipped the bar boldly between her thighs. Gasping with pleasure, Leila steadied herself by leaning backward onto the ceramic tiles while the shower beat a sensual tattoo against walls, glass, bodies. Wynne soaped his hands, and setting the bar on its shelf, made a twin foray from collarbone to breasts.

Leila watched as he lifted their fullness and soaped her hardened nipples with the rough pads of his thumbs. Her breath came quick and shallow. A surge of desire wiped away any remaining shyness and made her bold. She pushed herself forward and slid against Wynne in an erotic series of movements meant to wash him . . . and excite him, as well.

"I can't wait," he murmured, pressing himself against her thighs.

"Then don't."

Wrapping her arms around his neck, Leila lifted herself and opened to him. Wynne slid in easily, his entry aided by the traces of soap clinging to them both. Mouths melded as did bodies. They moved to the water's familiar cadence.

Another shower in another time threatened to intrude. Leila shoved back the memories to their proper place: the past. What was done was done. Wynne was her present, maybe her future.

She lost herself to sensation and urged him on with fevered hands and lips until, a moment later, she reached fulfillment.

They sagged together against the ceramic tile. "Was that the kind of impromptu shower you had in mind?" he asked, reminding her of her comment in the car.

"Even better," she murmured, now comfortable enough to call on her humor. Amazing the way Wynne was able to bring both the passionate and the light side of her nature to the fore. "But I still owe you one for laughing at me when I landed on my behind in the mud."

"You can collect anytime. *Any*time."

"Braggart."

"Try me."

"And give you a swelled head?"

"That's the idea."

Leila slapped at him playfully, making him back away from her. "I think it's time to dry off."

A wicked thought struck her as she slid open the door. She distracted Wynne by kissing him. Then she backed out of the opening while flipping the shower handle to Cold.

"Aaah! I'll get you for that!" he yelped as he did a frantic dance while trying to shut off the shower.

"I certainly hope so."

Leila grabbed a towel and dried herself as she headed for the relative safety of the bed. Wynne took his time stalking her. Candlelight silhouetted his lanky form, so she could see his deft movements as he ran a towel over his body.

"What are you planning to do to me?" she questioned warily, wondering if he would continue the silly game she'd started.

He set one knee on the bed next to her hip. "Did I get you to paradise?"

Leila smiled up in the dark and ran her fingers over his damp hairy thigh. "You bet."

"Then I guess it's time I brought you back."

With that he straddled her fully. Leila allowed her hand to continue its lazy exploration through crisp hair until she found him ready as promised. She circled him and slipped her hand along his velvety length. Sucking in his breath, Wynne sprawled forward, enveloping her with his damp heat.

This time their lovemaking was leisurely, a drawn-out agony sweeter than any Leila had ever experienced. Only once did her thoughts stray past the physical to the emotional bonds that beckoned seductively. But those bonds could be deceptive, crippling, destructive. She wasn't ready, she thought, trying to contain a sudden panic that threatened to engulf her. She still couldn't let go fully, couldn't share her secrets.

Surely Wynne would understand and would accept what she could give for now.

And give she did, with every fiber of her body, until satiated at last, she drifted with him deeper into the night, content in her lover's arms.

WYNNE WOKE WITH A START, alone and naked in the middle of his bed. Daylight poured through the windows. He shook away the cobwebs of sleep. Had Leila left him in the middle of the night? Disappointment washed through him until he noticed two sets of athletic shoes neatly placed next to the open bathroom door. And their discarded clothes were hanging over the shower stall as naturally as if they belonged together. He liked that idea.

A glance at the clock told him it was a few minutes after six. That gave them plenty of time to breakfast together before he drove her home. Pity that Leila had to be at work in a couple of hours. Rising to see what she was up to, Wynne grabbed the towel that had been discarded at the foot of the bed and wrapped it around his hips.

"Leila?" he called, expecting to hear her answer float up from the kitchen.

"I'm in here." Her voice came from a nearby room.

She was in his office! He hurried down the hall to his haven in the turret, anxious that she might have found the copy of his manuscript.

Relief stopped him in the doorway. Leila stood next to his desk at the windows overlooking the garden. He was mesmerized by the very sight of her. Early-morning sunlight slanted over her form and cast a golden halo around her dark hair, which spilled in waves across her shoulders and down her back. She'd wrapped his top sheet around her voluptuous curves in Roman fashion, but the material dipped low in back, revealing the perfect curve of her spine. Wynne grew hard just looking at the exposed flesh and re-membering the feel of it under his hands.

Leila turned. A happy smile gave her a special glow. She'd never looked so achingly beautiful.

"The view here is lovely," she said. "I don't un-derstand how you can get any work done."

"Sometimes the view is what inspires me."

She was inspiring him now, but definitely not to write. Wynne moved into the room, his eyes roaming over every inch of her before settling on Leila's face. Her winged eyebrows convinced him she knew what he was up to. He advanced; she retreated and slipped away from his grasp.

"I like what you've done in here."

Following the natural curve of the room, Leila wandered from the wooden desk and shelves on one side to the seating area on the other. He'd been lucky to find a secondhand sofa and chair that he'd liked. The dark rattan was softened by cushions with a muted geometric pattern. The casual furniture fit the sunny area perfectly, as did the striped area rug.

"I'm glad you approve," Wynne said, continuing to pursue her.

Leila stopped and faced him. "So, you get a lot of work done here."

"Sometimes."

"Free-lance articles. Novels you don't talk about...."

A scarce yard between them, Wynne stopped short. Had she seen his work? Considering he'd just sent his revised proposal to his agent, he should feel more comfortable with the idea. But he didn't. Only two things in his life made him unsure of himself. The novel... and this woman who was challenging him.

"You found my manuscript?"

"I didn't look." Her sniff seemed intended to give him the impression that she was offended, even if her warm open expression said otherwise. "I was hoping you would offer to show it to me."

"What if I offered to show you something more personal, instead?"

Her eyes dropped to the towel, which accentuated rather than hid his erection. "I've already seen it." Her tone lowered to a pitch that was sexy even while it expressed her amusement. "Very nice."

"Maybe you'd like another look ... in this room ... by sunlight."

"Perhaps I would."

Her hands moved to her shoulders. With a deft movement, Leila loosened the sheet, which slithered over her breasts and caught on her full hips. She flicked her bottom and the sheet puddled around her ankles. Wynne could hardly breathe as his fingers fumbled to release the towel. Her long leisurely look in itself made the demands of his body more urgent.

"Very, very nice."

Leila pressed herself against him and wrapped her arms around his neck. She became the aggressor— touching, stroking, nipping him in all the right places until Wynne felt as if he might explode. She led him to the couch, pushed him to the cushions, slid up over him. Dazed by the intensity of the desire rocketing through him, Wynne allowed her to do what she would.

And what she did to tease and seduce was enough to make any man her love slave, he thought hazily as Leila continued to work her magic on him. When she rubbed her inner thigh against him intimately, he couldn't hold back any longer. Finding her hips, he anchored her over him, then thrust up and into her with a sigh of satisfaction.

She set the pace. He let her. All the while, he watched her changing expressions. Leila's lush sensuality, usually well hidden, was revealed in all its intensity on her incredible face. He'd never seen anything like it. The sultry fire in her eyes, the blush of arousal tinting her complexion, the natural seductiveness of her parted lips were guaranteed to turn on any healthy man.

Turn him on and bring him home, Wynne thought as the tension built to an unbearable high. He caught her breasts with both hands and raised his head to capture a tempting nipple. He surrounded her with the wet warmth of his mouth. She cried out. The sound came from deep within her, urging him past the breaking point. The tension flared, fragmented, then flowed out of them in a simultaneous culmination of passion.

Laughing breathlessly, Leila leaned forward, her soft breasts pressing against his chest. Her head found the hollow made by his collarbone and fit there perfectly. She was perfect.

"You're so perfect. How could any man resist you?"

The words flew past his lips even as he thought them. Leila tensed and her pliant body tightened against his. Wynne tried not to let her silent response bother him. He stroked her hair in a calming motion, letting the thick strands slip through his fingers, and all the while he could feel her accelerated heartbeat refusing to slow.

She was upset; he sensed the unspoken. She was holding herself back from him, not physically, but in every other way that mattered. He had no right to expect more, not in this short time that they'd known each other. But he did.

He tried to make a joke of it.

"Hey, you could hurt a guy's feelings. This is a moment we're supposed to share. You know. Saying nice things. Sexy things. Teasing each other."

But Leila wasn't smiling when she moved up and off of the couch. He could swear he saw a glimpse of fear in her eyes before she turned away to retrieve her sheet. She wrapped the material around her.

"I'm not perfect, Wynne." She stared down at her hands as they fumbled with a knot. "And I don't want to turn on just any guy."

"I'm glad. I was just trying to tell you how sexy I find you." Wynne stood and lifted Leila's chin so she had to look at him. "I want to be the guy you turn on. It's a compliment, Leila. Why are you upset with me?"

"I'm not upset with you. Just a bad memory."

One she obviously wasn't going to talk about.

"You're sorry you stayed."

"No!" She cupped his cheek. Her widened eyes gave her a pleading look. "Please don't think that. I'm glad we got to know each other... better."

But Wynne could sense all was not well. Though she was trying to hide it, she was still upset. Not wanting them to part with any doubts between them, he tried to salvage the situation.

"Why don't we get dressed and have breakfast together. I could use a strong cup of coffee and a couple of eggs. I make a pretty good omelet. What do you think?"

"Breakfast together—sounds like a great way to start the day."

The words were right, the tone wasn't. and Leila's smile seemed a bit forced.

What in the world was wrong?

Wynne was beginning to think he didn't at all know the woman with whom he'd shared such intimacy. Leila took such care of herself outwardly. But what about the inner person Leila herself was so concerned with? How could he get to know her inside when she'd raised an invisible barrier that kept him out?

CHAPTER NINE

"WHERE'S THAT REPORTER fella?" Elizabeth asked Leila as the Saturday afternoon aerobics class was gathering. "I haven't seen him around today."

"He's done with his research and with the article. He mailed it to his editor the other day."

"How disappointing." Jane spoke up, her usual pucker and frown nowhere in sight. "I wanted to add some things I didn't think of when he interviewed me."

Other voices echoed her sentiment. Leila was touched by the obvious affection the women had for Wynne, even though he'd only begun working on his story a little more than a week ago. Then again, why should she be surprised? She hadn't known him any longer.

Jane went on. "You know, Leila, you're even more foolish than I thought if you let that nice man get away. You're not getting any younger."

The unexpected advice left Leila too stunned to reply. She hadn't realized the attraction between her and Wynne had been so apparent to others. And she couldn't imagine Jane Radcliff caring *what* she did.

"Isn't it time to start class?" Fran asked.

The other woman's conspiratorial expression told her that Fran was trying to get her off the hook. A grateful Leila asked the women to take their places.

She turned on the cassette player. As she led the warm-up exercises, she wondered what the women would think if they knew how far she and Wynne had taken their mutual attraction.

She herself didn't know what to make of the relationship. It seemed to be progressing at tornado pace. Always wary around men who appealed to her too much, Leila wished she could just let down her guard. Wanting a normal healthy partnership that was both physically and emotionally satisfying wasn't too much to ask. She was certain not only that she deserved that kind of a relationship, but that she was capable of dealing with one. She merely needed some time to adjust.

Wynne had been paying her a compliment when he'd told her she was perfect and irresistible. She knew that. If only his words hadn't sounded so familiar, so like the ones Christian had invariably used to seduce her. With unerring clarity she had remembered an incident that had occurred shortly before she'd ended her modeling career.

Christian had spread photographs of her across the coffee table. He'd been choosing which to include in his new portfolio, one that would feature her shots exclusively. In them, she wore everything from evening gowns to lingerie to bathing suits. Though she knew she had posed for each and every photograph, Leila had been mesmerized by the stranger who stared back at her from the eight-by-ten glossies. Surely she couldn't be looking at herself—this woman sizzled with open sensuality.

She hadn't been able to define what disturbed her the most—the way the clothes seemed ready to melt off her, that Christian had backlit the lingerie, giving the viewer teasing glimpses of her flesh, or that the expressions her lover had coaxed from her were so intimate. But Leila had been uncomfortable looking at this stranger who indeed was herself, especially when Christian had handled the photos as if he were touching a flesh-and-blood woman.

She remembered what he'd said exactly. "How could any man looking at these resist you?"

And then he'd kissed her to make her forget about her doubts. But the doubts had lingered, had grown stronger, and in the end, had been justified.

Wynne was different, Leila reminded herself as the shift in the music's tempo brought her back to the present and to the aerobics portion of the class. She had to stop being so sensitive, so negative. She would work on loosening up with Wynne, starting on their date that night.

James lay next to Brenna and listened to her steady breathing. Perhaps she was relaxed enough to sleep, but he was wide awake. He was falling for the woman. He'd told himself not to let it happen, that he was making a mistake. He'd been correct, as usual.

She was holding back....

Wynne stared at the computer monitor in frustration, not knowing quite how to develop the delicate psychological balance between James and Brenna any more than he did in his own affair with Leila. He hadn't planned to transfer his very real experience to his story, yet his doing so subconsciously didn't surprise him. He was finding it more and more impossible to keep his fiction separate from his life. That was only natural, he assured himself. A writer drew on experience, altered and used it to create a new reality.

So why was working with his own feelings on paper getting him down?

Wynne was mentally replaying the morning's scene with Leila in his office when the telephone rang. He answered, hoping it might be her. Instead, Harry Benton's voice boomed over the line.

"How's it going, Donegan?"

"You tell me."

"The article is great, especially the slant. I only have a few revisions. Can you work on these tonight and Fax them to me in the morning?"

That would mean breaking his date with Leila that evening, but sometimes cancellations and disappointment were inevitable. He was sure she would understand that they were right down to the line with this story. The magazine was scheduled to be on the stands in less than a week.

"Sure, Harry. No problem." Wynne reached for a pencil and pad of paper. "Now give me the bad news."

Actually, the changes weren't all that extensive. Harry was looking for more quotes, more focus on a few of the clients. The editor's comments took only minutes.

Wynne recognized his own ulterior motive when he asked, "What did you think of the pictures?"

"Great selection. The one of the Forester woman is dynamite. If I didn't already have the cover set, I would think about using that one."

"That good?"

"Better."

Wondering if he was crazy to chance messing up what might be the best thing he'd ever had happen to him, Wynne only hesitated a second. "Leila used to be a model."

"No kidding. Maybe that's why she seemed familiar. I figured my imagination was playing tricks on me. That happens when you hit the golden years, you know."

"You've got a few good ones left in you, Harry." The voice of reason objected to what he was about to say, but Wynne ignored it. "How would you like to do me a favor?"

"Name it, Donegan."

"You've got more contacts in New York than I do. Find out what you can about Leila's modeling career. How long it lasted. What she was worth. Why it ended."

"How long ago?"

"I'm not sure. She's thirty now. She's got a few years of work behind her. And before that, school. Try between eight and twelve years back."

"You're not asking much."

"I'll owe you one, Harry."

"A big one."

"Agreed."

Harry was silent for a second before asking, "Hey, Donegan, what's it to you, anyway?"

"It's personal. Use a little discretion, huh?"

"So that's how it is. You're sure you—"

"I'm sure."

"I'll see what I can do. Maybe my art director or one of the staff photographers can come up with something."

"Thanks."

But as Wynne hung up and dialed Leila's work number to cancel their date, he knew she wouldn't thank him for prying into her past. Then again, if Harry didn't find anything, she would never have to know.

EARLY SUNDAY MORNING, Grace took the jogging path through Lincoln Park toward the hill overlooking the baseball diamond. That's where Mel had suggested they meet when Grace had called earlier. Grace knew Mel had been upset, but her friend had refused to explain why over the telephone.

Hearing the thump-thump of a faster jogger behind her, Grace moved to the right. A nice-looking eighteen- or nineteen-year-old guy gave her a thorough once-over as he drew alongside her. He winked before speeding on his way. Her pulse accelerated even while she stopped in her tracks. Was it possible the guy actually thought she was attractive?

Grace stood there in confusion for a moment before realizing she was only a hundred yards from her destination—she recognized Mel's slim figure even at this distance. Her friend was sitting on the grassy hillside, hunched over, arms around her legs, head resting on her knees. Grace closed the gap.

"Hey, Mel!"

The blond head slowly rose and turned toward her. As Grace drew closer, she could see Mel's face was tear streaked and bloated from crying. Something really was wrong.

"Hi, Gracie."

"Mel, what's going on?"

"It's Luke. He dumped me last night."

"You're kidding." Grace plopped down in the grass. How could any guy in his right mind dump someone who looked like Mel?

"Do I sound like I'm kidding?" Mel asked with a sob.

"What happened?"

Tears rolled down Mel's thin cheeks. She bit her lip as if she were trying to get control of herself, and for a moment Grace didn't think her friend was going to explain.

"He said I needed help."

"What kind of help?"

"A-about my obsession with food."

"You told him!"

"Of course not. He just sees how much I eat sometimes and thinks I'm fat."

"He said that?"

"He didn't have to. All I had to do was look in the mirror."

"Take a better look, then," Grace said, wondering why was Mel doing this to herself. "You're thin. Beautiful. Any guy would think so."

"Luke doesn't. My thighs and butt are still too big."

"*Mine* are still too big," Grace said, slapping the side of her leg. "Yours aren't."

"Well, they won't be for long. I'm going to do something about it so I can get Luke back."

"Do what?"

Mel set her jaw and turned her head forward to stare out toward the lake. Worried, Grace swallowed hard and put a hand on her friend's shoulder.

"Do what?" she repeated. "Mel, tell me."

"I...I've got to stop eating until I'm thin enough."

"You mean binging. You're going to stop binging, right?"

"No, Grace. I mean eating. I'm going to stop eating until I've lost at least ten more pounds."

"You can't do that." Mel didn't have ten pounds to spare. "You'll make yourself sick."

"If I do, it'll be worth it."

"No guy is worth that!"

"Luke is."

"Mel, what's wrong with you?"

"I'm fat. That's what's wrong."

"Luke didn't say that!"

"Fat and disgusting," Mel continued. "No wonder Luke doesn't want me. No guy would want me looking like this."

Grace was getting nervous. Mel was talking crazy. She didn't have an ounce of extra flesh on her. Actually, Grace personally thought Mel was a little too thin, but then everyone said you couldn't be too thin or too rich, and so she'd never made a big deal about it. These past few weeks she'd thought Mel had merely been trying to maintain her weight loss without giving up everything she liked to eat. But this was different. This was serious. She had to talk Mel out of doing something she might regret.

Remembering how understanding and sensible Leila Forester had been, Grace said, "Mel, maybe you should talk to Lei—"

"Don't even finish!" Mel's blue eyes blazed with anger. "My mind is made up."

"I'm not going to let you do this."

"You can't stop me."

"Your mom can."

"You would tell her?" Mel jumped to her feet and backed away. "I thought you were my friend!"

"I am your friend."

"No you're not. You just don't want me to lose more weight because you've got such a long way to go. If you tell my mother or anyone else, I'll never speak to you again."

"Mel!"

But Mel's back was already to her. Without saying another word, the blonde stalked away. Hurt by her friend's insult, Grace swallowed hard and watched her go. Mel had been striking out because she felt threatened—Grace knew that—but she didn't really mean her unkind words. Mel would come to her senses and apologize.

Meanwhile, what was she supposed to do? Grace attempted to think about Mel's threat logically. She herself had tried fasting lots of times, but she'd never actually been able to continue doing so for more than a day or two. She'd felt weak, light-headed and nauseated. Mel would get tired of that feeling fast and wisen up.

A little voice inside her told Grace that what they'd both been doing to be able to eat things they liked wasn't much wiser, but she ignored it. She had to ignore the voice or she wouldn't lose any more weight. The very thought made her stomach clutch. If she broke Mel's trust, the blonde might turn around and tell on *her* and she couldn't let that happen.

There was really nothing Grace could do.

SUNDAY WAS LEILA'S LAST DAY off before the anniversary party the following Saturday. The workweek promised to be hectic, so she made an extra effort to get herself organized. She spent the morning cleaning, shopping for groceries and doing her laundry. Then she tempered her disappointment about her canceled date with an afternoon spent holding Wynne's hand while touring the Shedd Aquarium.

They started in Leila's favorite gallery—Tropical Salt Water. After admiring the brightly colored specimens occupying the large tanks—parrot fish, wrasse, butterfly and lizard fish, among others—they moved on. The short walk gave her time to think about the car she'd rented so she could pay a surprise visit to her parents that evening. And that reminded her of Wynne's family.

"Have you talked to your parents lately?" she asked.

"They stopped by yesterday afternoon."

"While you were working on the house?"

"Yep. Mom gave me loads of advice on decorating, as usual, and Da gave her a hard time. What a couple of characters!"

"But nice characters."

Wynne squeezed her hand. "Glad you approve."

"I do. They're so different from my parents. Yours seem to have the ideal relationship."

Wynne grinned. "Think you could love one man for a lifetime?"

Leila couldn't take her eyes away from his. Normally sparkling with humor, they were intent on her. "I would like to think it's possible."

Suddenly nervous by the serious turn of conversation, she looked away and noticed the crowd gathering around the Coral Reef Exhibit, the aquarium's largest.

"Let's go watch," she said, leading him to the circular exhibit.

A diver equipped with a mike in her mask relayed information about coral formation and the fish that lived around reefs as she fed the tank's occupants.

"Wouldn't it be fun to do that?" Leila asked.

"Get in the tank with those nurse sharks and eels?"

"Not in the tank. In the Caribbean. I've been to the Bahamas and to Grand Cayman. I'd love to go to the Virgin Islands next."

"That would be a pretty expensive trip."

"But worth every penny." Leila would love to share the experience with Wynne. "I'm sure you'd like a water vacation, too. Snorkeling is like entering another world . . . and I'd love to learn to scuba dive."

Wynne agreed, "It would be an interesting experience."

His terse reply made Leila wonder if she'd made him feel uncomfortable. He probably couldn't afford such a luxury on the money he made as a free-lance writer. Leila sighed wistfully. "Well, it's nice to dream about, anyway."

They watched the diver in the tank feed an eel. Leila noticed Wynne had grown quiet, an unusual state for him, but by the time they moved on to another section of the aquarium, he was his old self.

The next hour seemed to speed by as the time to part approached. Leila felt less and less like being away from Wynne. Their date ended in the parking lot with a tender kiss.

"I know you're going to be busy this week, but I'll call you," Wynne promised as he opened the door of her rental car for her.

"I'll be looking forward to it." Suppressing a sense of loss, Leila waved cheerfully as Wynne headed for his own car.

Certain that her parents would have returned from Peoria sometime that afternoon, she set off for Crestview in positive spirits. Her mood shifted when she arrived only to find her old home locked, the car gone. Since she hadn't thought to bring her keys to the house with her, she couldn't get in. She would wait anyway. Leila made herself comfortable on the front steps, but she grew tired and disappointed as the skies darkened. Perhaps her mom and dad had decided to stay in Peoria an extra day.

Not wanting to leave without letting them know she'd been there, Leila found a flyer in her glove compartment, scrawled a message on the blank back side and tucked the folded paper into the screen door, where her parents would be sure to find it. Dispirited, she set off for the downtown area. By the time she returned the rental car and arrived at her apartment, the hour was late. She showered, set up the coffee maker for the morning, then fell into bed exhausted.

The following week was equally hectic and frustrating due to all the extra work she'd taken on as chairperson of the anniversary party committee. A new problem seemed to creep up each day. Final arrangements had to be settled with the printers, entertainers, decorators, caterers and outside janitorial service. While Gail and Jocko were handling their share of the work, they still needed to discuss every little hang-up with Leila.

And although her parents called to tell her how sorry they were to miss her, Wynne didn't. . . .

Leila tried not to think about what his silence might mean, but she was only human, with all the normal insecurities that went with starting a new relationship. He'd seemed so serious at the aquarium. Had he scared himself off? she wondered, finding it difficult to think of Wynne as having cold feet about anything. Maybe her talk about an expensive vacation was giving him second thoughts.

Or perhaps his avoiding her was due to a totally different reason. The article? While she'd seen the photos, he hadn't offered to show her the copy.

Images of Wynne and memories of being with him kept creeping into her thoughts, making Leila wonder if she wasn't more attached than made her comfortable. She was able to block him out of her consciousness only occasionally, as she did early Thursday afternoon, during the final organizational meeting for the party.

"The cleanup service will make their people available at 2:00 a.m. so we can be in business as usual by late Sunday morning," Gail reported.

"Good." Leila scribbled a note. "That'll make Mike happy."

"He's happy with my pictures, too." Jocko rose and opened the large package he'd left near the door. He spread the mounted 3-by-4½-foot photos along the wall. Leila hadn't visualized their impact from the small snapshots they'd chosen. Jocko strutted, posed and preened in near life-size. She felt as if she were looking at six more of the real thing.

"Great job, huh?"

Leila could tell Gail was restraining herself when she said, "They do convey a vivid sense of your personality."

"Hey, thanks. I knew this was a great idea and that you'd have to admit you were wrong. Want to help me figure out where to hang these?"

"I appreciate your asking, but I think that privilege should be all yours."

"We have one more item on the agenda." Leila broke in before Gail could add anything that might upset their co-worker. "I want to make sure you have firm commitments from all your staff members to be here."

"No problem. When the Jock speaks, his staff listens."

Gail swallowed a snicker. "My people will be here."

"Remind them to be on time and that they'll be expected to give tours to guests. Mike wants this to be a one-on-one experience so potential clients will get the idea that we specialize in individualization."

"If that's it, I've got work to do," Jocko said, indicating the photos that he was already restacking.

"Meeting's adjourned."

Seemingly busy making notes to herself, Gail sat right where she was until Jocko left. He'd no sooner vacated the room than she flipped her notebook closed. "Well, have you heard from Wynne or not?"

Leila sighed and slumped back into her office chair. So much for putting the man out of her mind. "Not since Sunday."

"I thought he promised to call you."

"He did."

"But this is Thursday. That's four days."

"Really?" Leila fiddled with her pencil and finally threw it down on the desk. "I guess I have too much work to keep count."

Gail stated the obvious. "You *are* upset. So what are you going to do about it?"

"Do? I have tons to do before Saturday."

"That's not what I meant, as if you didn't know it. And what about Saturday night?" Gail demanded. "Is Wynne going to be your escort?"

"Good question since I haven't asked him yet. And I don't intend to call him, either," Leila added quickly, so Gail wouldn't get any ideas. Her forehead pulled into a frown. "Not that I wouldn't under different circumstances."

"You want me to handle this for you?" Gail rose to her full, if unimpressive, height. "I can be tough when the occasion calls for it."

That made the wrinkles smooth from Leila's forehead. "You're—"

"Impossible." Gail grinned.

"Knock, knock."

The familiar voice made Leila's gaze fly to the door. "Wynne!" Pulse accelerating as if she were in the midst of an aerobics class, Leila cringed inwardly as she realized he might have overheard their conversation. "How long have you been standing there?"

"Why? Been talking about me, I hope? No wonder my ears were burning."

How could he act so cocky considering the circumstances? Leila wondered, both resentful and grateful that he'd shown up unannounced. She couldn't help but stare at the welcome sight and note every detail of his appearance. Instead of his usual shorts and T-shirt, Wynne wore a pair of neatly pleated tan trousers and a summer cotton pullover, its long sleeves pushed up to his elbows, its green a shade that intensified the color of his eyes. For once, his lock of unruly hair was brushed neatly back from his forehead.

"I guess this is my cue to leave," Gail muttered, giving Leila one of her famous expressions, this one conveying the idea that Leila should "go get 'im."

"Gail, don't leave yet." Wynne pulled a handful of magazines from the leather case he was carrying and waved them in front of her. "At least not until you take a look at the current issue of *Glitter*."

"The article!" Gail grabbed two copies from Wynne and passed one to Leila, who still sought refuge behind the desk.

"Page 86," Wynne informed them as he sat in the chair opposite Leila. His loud sigh indicated his relief.

Already reading, Gail took the chair next to him.

Leila flipped the magazine open to the article. The first thing that caught her eye was the one photograph that focused on her. It filled the right-hand page. Shifting uncomfortably, she began reading Wynne's text, then spent the next ten minutes absorbing copy while trying to get covert glimpses of him as he watched her. She saw past his neat exterior and realized Wynne wasn't his usual exuberant self. Slumped in the chair, he looked tired and a little strung out. He smothered a yawn and then caught her staring.

When he winked mischievously, she turned her attention back to the magazine. Her pulse was thrumming, and the pounding of her heart seemed to echo throughout her body. Even distracted as she was, Leila realized the article was true to the concept they had formulated together. She continued to read with a growing sense of pleasure and accomplishment. Though Wynne had done the writing, he had captured the spirit of her personal philosophy on these pages. She was thrilled—and ashamed that she'd ever doubted him.

"It's wonderful, Wynne."

Rising, Gail echoed her sentiment. "I can't wait to show this to my staff. I can take this issue, can't I?"

"Sure." He stood and handed her another. "Take this to pass around, but tell everyone the issue is on the magazine racks now and that you expect them to buy their own copies."

"Will do." Gail took the second copy and headed out the door. She was looking directly at Leila when she said, "See you Saturday night, Wynne," then quickly closed the door.

Leila felt like strangling her meddlesome friend. What if Wynne's only reason to be here was professional—to drop off copies of the magazine?

"What's Saturday night?" he asked Leila.

"The anniversary party."

"Open house?"

"Invitation only."

"Oh."

Leaning over her desk, Wynne looked down at her expectantly, and before she could help herself, Leila blurted, "I was going to ask you—"

"I accept."

"—but you didn't give me the opportunity since you didn't call."

There. It was out in the open. He would know she was not pleased with him.

"Does that mean you changed your mind?" he asked, his quirky smile challenging her.

"I should!" Leila rose and circled her desk. Arms crossed over her chest, she stopped in front of Wynne.

"I've got plenty of men's phone numbers in my little red book."

Sitting back on the edge of her desk, Wynne softly urged, "Throw it away." He took hold of her single braid and tugged gently until she moved toward him. "Mine is the only number you'll need from now on."

"Sure of yourself, aren't you?"

"If you had wanted to ask another man, you would have. But you want me." He pulled her closer until she was snug between legs that curled around her thighs and trapped her like a vise. "The same way I want you."

Leila couldn't stop her body's reaction to his closeness, yet she levered one palm against his chest while she lifted his right hand and singled out the index finger. "Not so quick. You'd better have a damn good excuse for not using this dialing finger. It certainly doesn't *look* broken."

"It was otherwise occupied . . . burning up my computer keyboard." He freed the finger and used it to stroke her cheek and trail the length of her neck. "I swear I meant to call you Monday night, but my agent messed up my plans."

"You have an agent?"

Wynne nodded. "Robert Martin. Remember the mysterious second package I sent to New York last week on the way to the lake? That was the revised proposal of my book—the first hundred pages and a chapter-by-chapter outline. Rob brought it home and read it over the weekend and was excited enough to bring it to his Monday lunch date with an editor named Sylvie Feldman. He'd already told her about my book, and she'd expressed interest in seeing it, so he turned the package over to her."

He paused for a long shaky breath that made Leila aware of his deep-seated excitement. "And?"

"And Sylvie took it back to the office, where she decided to read a few pages. She didn't stop until she finished the entire proposal. She called Robert before leaving for home and told him she wanted the book."

"You sold it?"

"Not exactly. I don't have a track record writing fiction. But Sylvie wants to see the completed manuscript as soon as possible."

"Congratulations. You must be thrilled."

"That's putting it mildly. Thrilled and scared. The rest of the book was still in rough draft. I started rewriting like a demon on Monday afternoon and didn't stop until dawn. Since then, my hours have been topsy-turvy—absolutely crazy. *I've* been crazy. Writing. Getting too little sleep. Not getting to see you. I'm a mess. Am I forgiven?"

Though she shared Wynne's happiness and could see the truth of what he'd been going through in his tired face, Leila wasn't about to make her capitulation that easy for him. She raised her eyebrows.

"I'm not sure. The least you could have done was given me a quick call so I didn't think you left town in a hurry or something."

He gave her one of his most charming smiles, guaranteed to melt the resistance out of her.

"I promise I won't let it happen again. And I'll make it up to you."

"How?"

"I can start with this."

Before she could blink, Wynne had pulled her to his chest and kissed her until she pressed against him.

"A good beginning," she said breathlessly, wanting more.

He kissed her again, long and lingering, until every nerve in her body demanded attention. His hands splayed across her spine, massaging, comforting, seducing. She visualized the last quite clearly.

"And we can do something together tonight as long as it doesn't expend too much energy," Wynne promised.

She couldn't help but tease him. "Well, that eliminates some very thought-provoking suggestions...."

He groaned and tilted his head so their foreheads touched. "I hate to admit this, but I was thinking of an early movie, maybe dinner."

"I guess I can save the suggestions for later."

"Maybe you should write them down so you won't forget them."

"Don't worry." She ran a fingertip along the length of his mustache straight to his dimple. "I have a memory like a steel trap."

"That's good to know." He kissed her finger, then the tip of her nose. "I wouldn't want to miss anything."

"You won't if I can help it."

"So when can we get out of here?"

"After my class—" she checked her watch "—which I have to run to make right now!"

"Let's go." At her questioning look, he asked, "Why do you think I brought so many magazines?"

Releasing her, he grabbed the stack. They headed down the hall to the aerobics room. Most of the regulars were already waiting for her.

"I've lost thirteen pounds!" Grace was announcing to the others as Leila and Wynne entered.

Amidst congratulations, the women became aware of Wynne's presence.

"Wynne Donegan, what are you doing here?" Jane Radcliff demanded, but her face was wreathed in a smile that simply amazed Leila.

"Just stopped by," he said, his tone nonchalant. "I don't imagine anyone here would be interested in seeing the newest issue of *Glitter.*"

He was surrounded immediately. When he passed out the magazines, the women huddled in small groups to read the article and exclaim over the pictures.

Only Mel stayed back from the group and did warm-up exercises by herself. Leila had noticed that she and Grace hadn't been speaking all week. While Grace threw herself into the exercise routines with renewed enthusiasm on one side of the room, Mel had stayed as far away from the other girl as possible and had attacked the exercises with a quiet intensity.

Leila took a good look at the blonde. She appeared a little haggard...almost fragile. Perhaps Grace wasn't the only one who should be taking the nutrition class. Now wasn't the time to make a fuss, however. She didn't want to bring up the subject before the group. But she would have plenty of opportunity during the following week, after the madness of the anniversary celebration was over.

"Look at this picture of our class!" Jane exclaimed. "My picture in a national magazine. I'm famous! I'm going to the nearest newsstand to buy a bunch of copies."

"Me, too," Elizabeth said, her agreement echoed by a half-dozen voices.

"What about today's class?" Leila asked.

"Missing one day won't hurt a thing," another client insisted.

The consensus was that it indeed wouldn't, and the women were so excited Leila didn't have the heart to disagree. "See you all Saturday."

The room emptied quickly. Mel hung back until Grace was out the door. Leila again wondered what had come between the friends.

"You're frowning," Wynne whispered.

"Not at you."

Wynne followed her gaze to the blonde, who'd finally made up her mind to leave. "What's wrong?"

"I wish I knew." Leila spoke in a low tone so no one but Wynne would hear. "I guess she and Grace must have had a major falling-out or something."

"Teenagers. Never a dull moment. They probably fought over something silly, and things will work out by next week."

"Probably." All Leila wanted to think about now was Wynne. "Since my crew has mutinied, I don't see why I couldn't leave a little early today."

"Great." He was already guiding her toward the door. "I'll get a newspaper and go over the movie listings while I wait for you in the lounge."

"I won't be long," Leila promised.

She was as good as her word. Relief and excitement combined, making her shower and dress in a hurry so she could rejoin Wynne. When she found him, he was relaxed in an easy chair, his head back, eyes closed. The paper lay spread in his lap, open to the movie section.

She poked his foot with a toe. "Hi, there. I'm not disturbing you, am I?"

He jerked upright and smothered a yawn. "No. I just closed my eyes for a second."

His exhaustion was apparent to Leila. "Sure you want to go out? I can take a rain check."

"I'm positive. I don't know how much longer I could go without getting my Leila fix. I've been having withdrawal symptoms for days."

Warmed and flattered, she smiled as she always seemed to be doing around Wynne. "Did you pick a movie?"

"I'm not fussy. Any of the features at Chestnut Station would be fine with me," he said, mentioning a nearby movie theater complex.

Since he left the decision to her, Leila chose a thriller, but even the plot twists and turns and action sequences weren't enough to keep Wynne from yawning. He stretched an arm around her shoulders so she felt his jerk every time he almost nodded off. Leila was content just to be near him until the movie's steamy love scene made her squirm and wish she and Wynne could duplicate the action on the screen. She had a feeling it wasn't to be, at least not that night.

When the movie ended, Wynne's head was nestled against hers.

"Hey, sleepyhead. Time to go home."

"I'm relaxed...not asleep," he argued between more yawns. As if to prove it, he rose, pulling her up out of her seat with him. They crossed the theater toward the exit. "And we haven't had dinner."

"Forget dinner. You're going to bed."

That woke him up. "Sounds promising. Coming with me?"

"No. You need some well-deserved rest." She circumvented Wynne's attempt to slip his hand from her shoulder to her breasts. Though the theater was dark enough that no one would see, she firmly placed the hand on her waist. "I want a lively date Saturday night, not one who's sleepwalking."

"If I weren't so half-witted at the moment, I would be insulted."

"Don't be. I understand how important your book is to you, and I want you to do a good job on it ... as well as on me," she added, bumping his hip with her own. "What's the title, anyway?"

"*Hot Bodies*."

Leila laughed. "You're perverted."

"I rather thought I was inspired."

After ascertaining he was actually awake enough to drive, Leila let Wynne drop her off in front of her building, then sent him on his way with a warning to be careful. She didn't want anything to happen to him...or to the relationship that was beginning to look so promising.

CHAPTER TEN

A LITTLE AFTER EIGHT on Saturday evening, Wynne checked in with the bouncer at the entrance to The Total You. A young woman at a terminal scrolled through computerized data until his name finally was highlighted on her monitor. If this affair was invitation only, Wynne decided, half the city must have been on the list. The bouncer gave him the go-ahead.

Wynne entered the main lounge area, which had been set up with cozy seating arrangements so that guests could break into small groups and talk while consuming champagne and hors d'oeuvres. Gold and silver metallic streamers and balloons had been strung from the ceiling, while bouquets of fresh flowers in pedestal containers had been placed in strategic niches. Live music filtered through the open double doorway leading to a seminar room that had been converted to a dance floor for the evening.

Because the hour was still early, the crowd was thin enough that he easily spotted Leila circulating among the guests. She was a vision in black, her outfit surely designer. A strapless Lycra unitard clung to and accentuated her every curve, over which a see-through smocklike garment trimmed with bugle beads hung to midthigh. She'd pulled her hair to the crown of her head. Thick waves spilled over one shoulder from a silver-and-black cone-shaped clasp that matched her dangling earrings and high-heeled sandals.

Dressed as she was, Leila looked like she belonged....

Wynne remembered their conversation at the aquarium about vacationing in the Virgin Islands and how it had put him off kilter. He had to remind himself that Leila had never complained about their casual dates. And she had invited him to be her escort for the evening when he was sure she could have had one of the wealthier men in the room, if that had been what she wanted.

She wanted *him*. The thought bolstering his suddenly fragile ego, Wynne stepped forward. He caught her near the bar between greetings and casually circled her waist. What he really wanted to do was to pull her into his arms and kiss her thoroughly. "Hi, spectacular looking."

"It's about time you showed." After checking out the clothes that Wynne had bought especially for the occasion, Leila ran her fingers down a tan lapel. "You're pretty spectacular looking yourself tonight. You look incredibly handsome. Must be the suit."

"This old rag?"

"Rag, huh?" Her dark eyes sparkled with disbelief.

"You can tear it off me later."

Color suffused her cheeks, but before she could respond, a young woman at the other end of the bar called to her. "Leila, everything is super."

Leila turned to wave at the client. "Thanks, Karen. Have a great time." She recentered her attention on Wynne. "Now, where were we?"

"Tearing my clothes off."

She leaned closer to whisper, "Unfortunately, we have a long evening ahead of us before we can indulge in our flights of fancy."

"Nothing like a working date," he said in mock complaint.

"Well, it doesn't have to be *all* work. I think I can slip away from my duties long enough for a dance or two."

"You mean I get to hold you in my arms?"

"Maybe you'll get to do a lot more than that tonight."

"Are you sure you're not just leading me on? I was game the other night, but you sent me home."

"I like my playmates wide-awake, thank you."

"At the moment," he assured her, "my senses are all fine-tuned."

"At the moment, Leila needs to check on the caterers." Mike Kramer ended their private exchange. He gave Wynne an intense look before explaining. "Jocko said something about a crisis in the kitchen."

Leila groaned. "I knew I should have handled the caterers myself." She touched Wynne's arm with a possessiveness that got him right down to his toes. "I'll be back shortly. Have a glass of champagne."

Wynne's eyes were glued to Leila as she walked through the crowd. Her body swayed with an unconscious grace and sensuality that had to be natural to her. Tonight more than ever before, she looked every bit the successful model that he now knew she had been—thanks to the information he'd gleaned from Harry.

"I haven't had a chance to tell you what a great article you wrote," Kramer said, interrupting his thoughts. "Your verbal portrait of The Total You will get us more new clients than paid advertising would."

Wynne had noticed issues of *Glitter* magazine carefully placed on every available horizontal surface. "I'm glad we could be of mutual assistance to each other."

"So am I, but I'm beginning to wonder what you were after, Donegan." Kramer's expression was speculative. "A story, or my director of physical fitness education?"

"How about both."

Chuckling, Kramer slapped him on the back. "Can't say as I blame you. Ah, I see someone I have to greet personally. Catch you later."

Kramer smoothly cut through the crowd to a middle-aged man and woman who were obviously wealthy, if Wynne could judge by the woman's jewels. He stepped over to the bar and took a glass of champagne. A sip told him it was a quality product. But then there was no question that this whole operation was quality.

Just like Leila.

Tuning out the music and noisy voices, Wynne thought about the conversation he'd had concerning her early that morning.

Harry had relayed the information Wynne had been seeking. A decade before, Leila had spent a year in New York as a photographic model, working exclusively with Christian Manley.

Now one of the top Manhattan-based, globe-trotting photographers, Manley had still been struggling then. Wynne was familiar with the name and reputation if not with the man himself. Supposedly

Manley had quickly risen above the unknowns because Leila had been in hot demand.

Harry suggested Wynne dig up the 1978 Christmas
issue of *Sophisticate* magazine in which Leila had been
featured in a lingerie spread. That afternoon, Wynne
headed for the main branch of the Chicago Public Li-
brary where he found bound copies of the magazine
going back to its inception.

He must have stared at the Christmas cover photo
for a full quarter of an hour. Dressed only in a lace-
trimmed, red silk teddy and lacy stockings, Leila vir-
tually sizzled off the cover despite her youth and the
then fashionable thinness that bordered on fragility.
Her full breasts pressed against the silk fabric in an
enticing display while her exotic features conveyed
both innocence and a natural sensuality. Above all,
her eyes seemed focused and alight with desire, an effect that made Wynne physically uncomfortable, perhaps because he remembered being captivated by
Leila's similar expression the morning they'd made
love in his office.

After studying the inside spread in *Sophisticate*,
Wynne believed that Leila had been an overnight sensation. Harry had told him that she'd been Christian's discovery—as well as the photographer's live-in
lover. Her quitting modeling had been totally unexpected, and it had stirred speculation when Leila simply dropped out of sight.

High-pitched laughter brought him back to the
party. Aware that he'd been in his own world and
people around him were beginning to give him curious looks, Wynne picked up a copy of *Glitter* just so
he'd have something to do. He opened the magazine
to his article and the stunning picture of Leila. Ten

years and perhaps twice as many pounds had added to her appearance rather than detracted from it. He was still studying the photograph when a familiar pair of arms circled his waist from behind.

"If there had been time," Leila said, peering over his shoulder, "Mike would have had every page blown up. He would have lined the entry halls with your story just as Jocko did the recreation area with his own photographs. Who knows? Our esteemed executive director may choose to do that yet."

"Then we'll both be famous," Wynne said. He set down the copy. "Crisis over?"

"Everything's in control."

"Then how about one of those dances you promised me?"

"I think that can be arranged." Leila tilted her head. "Mmm, a slow number."

Wynne allowed her to lead him to the next room. He pulled her into an acceptable public embrace and enjoyed her scent, a perfume as exotic as the woman herself. He was amazed once again at the turn fate had taken by bringing him to The Total You and into the arms of a special woman named Leila Forester.

But what was a relationship without complete trust and honesty?

Surmising that whatever had happened to Leila ten years before had helped make her the woman she was today, Wynne wanted to know more about that part of her life. But how would he ever find out? The last time he'd brought up her modeling career, she'd literally panicked. Would she ever be able to talk to him about what had gone wrong?

Perhaps more importantly, would she ever tell him about her relationship with Christian Manley?

LEILA REVELED IN THE FEEL of Wynne's arms around her as they moved to the music. She wouldn't mind staying right where she was for the rest of the evening if she didn't have other duties waiting on the sidelines. A pang of guilt niggled at her for shirking them, but she decided to think of these few relaxing moments as a well-deserved break. She'd been working as hard as Wynne all week.

Suddenly realizing that he seemed to be off in his own world, Leila assumed he must be thinking about his novel. She put just enough distance between them to converse. "How's the writing coming?"

"Good, now that I've gotten over my initial panic. I had a long rejuvenating sleep when you sent me home the other night, after which I revised the chapters I'd been working on like such a maniac."

"Sounds like you weren't able to stop by the hot-line center this morning."

"Are you kidding? I would have made time, no matter what. I stick to my commitments."

She should have known, Leila thought. "So have you heard anything about that kid, Vincent?"

"As a matter of fact, I spoke to him today. He said he called his mother a couple of times. Unfortunately, they haven't settled anything yet."

"But establishing communications is a start. You should be proud of yourself. A week ago Vincent was threatening suicide, but you talked him out of it. Maybe next week you'll talk him into going home."

"I hope so. I feel like I have a personal investment in this case. Policy doesn't seem to matter when you're working with someone who needs help."

"You're an admirable man, Wynne Donegan. You really care. That's nice." Leila nuzzled the edge of his mustache with her nose, then kissed the spot on his cheek where his dimple would pop if he smiled. "It's one of the things I appreciate most about you."

"Most?" He pulled her tighter against him. "Tell me about the other things."

"Later."

"Promises, promises. We're going to have a lot of catching up to do at this rate."

"I'm a woman of my word. We'll have all night."

When the music ended, Leila opted to stay in Wynne's arms for one more number. It might be their last opportunity to be alone in the midst of the crowd. The dance floor was overflowing, as was the lounge area. People must have been herding into the club in droves.

Obviously on the same wavelength, Wynne commented, "Quite a crowd here tonight."

"In addition to clients and their guests, everyone who is anyone in this city was invited. It looks as if they all showed up."

"I haven't seen so many designer gowns and jewels in one area since I covered a charity ball that was held to fund a shelter for battered women," Wynne told her.

"I'm surprised you didn't get involved in that cause, too."

"I did. I wrote their publicity brochures."

"Sometimes I think you're too good to be true, Wynne Donegan."

Leila nestled her forehead against his cheek and thought about the truth of that statement. Of all the people she had met in her life, Wynne was one of the best. How lucky could a lady be? Other than his manner of getting what he wanted—which could be annoying—the man didn't seem to have any faults. And Leila didn't want to look for problems where there were none.

As if to illustrate her good fortune, an altercation at the doorway made her take notice. Jocko and Gail were arguing about something. As quickly as Leila could blink, the man was pulling an obviously reluctant partner into his arms and dancing her out to the floor. The small woman seemed to be steeling herself for the ordeal, while the big lug seemed rather smitten . . . as if he were attracted to Gail.

Leila tried to swallow a giggle, then laughed outright at the strange sound that erupted from her.

Wynne squeezed her waist. "What's up?"

"Over there," she said, pointing to Jocko and Gail, who looked more as if they were struggling with each other than dancing. "How's that for an unusual couple?"

"Better not let Gail hear you say 'couple,'" Wynne warned her.

"You're right. She would probably try to strangle me, even if she had to stand on a chair to do it."

They both laughed at that. Wynne tried some fancy footwork, then settled into a more leisurely pattern. "Talking about couples . . . did you see Grace?"

"Where?"

Wynne turned her as he said, "Dancing."

And with a dark-haired teenager who was pretty cute, Leila noticed. Why not? The girl was attractive in spite of the weight she was still determined to lose. Her iridescent green taffeta dress set off her coloring, her makeup played up her large eyes, and her hair had been spiked into a more fashionable version of the curly mop she usually wore. Bold features animated,

Grace was talking to the boy as if her shyness had evaporated with the pounds she'd lost. He smiled down at her, and she appeared absolutely entranced.

Leila looked around to see if she could spot Mel, but if the blonde had come to the party, she didn't seem to be on the dance floor. Leila wondered how serious a wedge had been driven between Grace and Mel. A permanent break would be a shame, since there were so few teens at the club. Before she had time to speculate further, the music ended.

Reluctantly, she stepped back, out of Wynne's arms. "I think I'd better start circulating again."

He frowned and picked up a thick strand of hair from her shoulder, then ran the prickly edges along her neck. "Couldn't we just disappear, instead?"

The sensation made Leila shiver all the way down to her toes. "You're trying to corrupt me."

"Am I succeeding?"

"Umm . . . let's say I have to fight the temptation you're putting in my path with everything I have."

"All right. I give up." He dropped the lock of hair and raised both hands in a gesture of surrender. "I'll behave . . . for now."

Leila gave Wynne's tie a sharp tug. "And you accuse me of making promises."

He slid an arm around her waist and led her off the dance floor. "Why don't we get a couple of glasses of champagne and mingle together? There's no reason I can't work alongside you, is there?"

"I'd like to see someone try to stop you."

But they'd barely made it to the bar when Jane Radcliff joined them and took possession of Wynne's free arm as if that's exactly what she had in mind.

"My friends are dying to meet the man who wrote that fabulous article. You don't mind if I borrow Wynne for a few minutes, do you, Leila?"

Leila was faced with a familiar pucker and frown until she said, "No, of course not. Wynne deserves to have celebrity status tonight."

Her pinched features transformed by a wide smile, Jane hurriedly dragged her prey toward the other end of the room. Wynne looked over his shoulder at Leila for a second. His expression was good-humored, if resigned.

Trying to discern any club members she knew but hadn't yet greeted, Leila took a swift glance around the room. Her gaze skipped over several vaguely familiar-looking people until it settled on Fran, Elizabeth and Grace with her dark-haired dancing partner, all filling plates at the hors d'oeuvres table. About to join them, she stopped cold in her tracks and snapped her eyes back toward the elevators, where Mike Kramer was talking to a tall man with a chiseled profile and hair that shone golden even in the dimly lighted area.

It couldn't be.

But she knew it was.

Feet frozen to the floor, Leila wondered what the hell Christian Manley was doing there!

More important, she wondered how she could escape before he spotted her. Too late. Smiling, Mike was pointing in her direction. In a gesture that bespoke male bonding, Christian slapped Mike on the shoulder and set off straight toward her. The crowd parted, letting him through. There was no doubt in Leila's mind that he was stalking her. She fought the urge to panic and held her ground. This was *her* territory, not Christian's.

So why was her heart beating like mad?

Leila told herself that she couldn't be afraid to face him after all these years. But a secret part of her knew she was terrified.

Christian stopped directly in front of her and stretched out an arm to the bar as if blocking any escape attempt she might be contemplating. Leila felt the blood sizzle hot through her veins. How dare he!

"Leila. Wonderful to see you. You've grown even more beautiful, if that's possible."

The sights and sounds of the party faded until Leila felt alone and trapped with the man who had brought her to the lowest point in her life. But she was no longer young and trusting, she reminded herself. Nor was she in love—not with him. She was a different person now—mature and hopefully strong enough to hold her own. She raised her chin.

"Christian." No welcoming greeting passed her lips, which she set in a tight smile meant to convey her disdain. "What are you doing here?"

He picked up a glass of champagne from the bar and raised it in a toast. "Celebrating."

"What? Another lucrative contract? Another boost to your professional ego?" She looked around, purposely changing her expression to one of trusting innocence, that commodity he'd taken from her under false pretenses and from who knew how many other women. "Oh, my, you don't seem to have a date. No gorgeous unsuspecting young woman on your arm who can help further your career? I'm disappointed in you."

"So you still care," he said with a knowing smile.

His arrogance infuriated her. "Bastard." She'd mentally described him using the word a million times, but she'd never had the opportunity to label him in person. Somehow, the syllables rolling off her tongue didn't give her the satisfaction she'd thought they would.

His smile widened. "Such passion. I remember your passion well. What about you? What do you remember, Leila?"

His eyes were all over her, making her feel as if he were touching her. Making her feel used and incredibly naive again. A vivid memory from their past flashed through her mind: a contract lay on the coffee table, awaiting her signature, one she refused to give; he cajoled, seduced, then threatened; still she wouldn't sign.

"I remember everything about you, Christian."

"Good."

Could he possibly think that was a plus? Leila wondered, staring at his self-assured expression. Then why shouldn't he be confident? He was a stunning example of the male species, more attractive than he had been ten years before. And he was a professional and financial success. That he was a rotten human being had never seemed to bother him before. She doubted that he'd changed for the better.

"In answer to your earlier question," he went on, "I'm in Chicago on a shoot. To be specific, I came to this party because I knew you would be here. The article in *Glitter* was quite informative," he explained. "And Mike Kramer was most cooperative in extending an invitation when I called him about it yesterday. Your boss is quite the celebrity seeker."

Leila shook her head. He hadn't changed. "And you eat that up, don't you?"

"Don't you?"

"No."

"Then why was your picture in *Glitter*?"

"Because I chose to put it there," Wynne said, seeming to have come from nowhere.

He smoothly slid between them and placed a possessive hand square in the middle of Leila's back. Already rapid, her pulse accelerated even more at the idea of a confrontation. She knew Wynne was waiting for an introduction, but she wasn't about to oblige. Instead, she used his return as an excuse to get away from the golden-haired photographer, who smiled in smug amusement at them both.

"I was just on my way over to the hors d'oeuvres table to say hello to some of the women from my afternoon aerobics class."

Without another word, she brushed by the man who had almost ruined her life. Wynne followed close behind. He didn't say a word until they had crossed the room. Fran and Elizabeth were nowhere in sight, although Grace was filling another plate with appetizers. Leila was thinking that the teenager was going to be sorry in the morning, when Wynne took her arm and made her face him.

"All right, what was that all about?"

"I saw Fran and Eliz—"

"The man," he clarified.

Leila looked him straight in the eye when she said, "That was nothing." As far as she was concerned, Christian meant nothing to her other than a bad memory and the reminder of her former gullibility.

"It didn't look like nothing. He had you cornered."

"No big deal." She didn't want to lie, but she wasn't willing to reveal her entire history to Wynne. Not here. Not now. Maybe never. "He was just some wise guy with an unoriginal come-on." Leila kissed Wynne lightly. "Forget about him, okay?"

Wynne neither agreed nor disagreed, and she could sense he didn't believe her explanation, but at least he didn't continue to press her.

Leila looked around until she saw a couple of people she recognized. Hooking her arm through Wynne's, she led him to the group and made introductions. They talked for a while, then moved on. Even as she concentrated on the guests, Leila became aware of Christian's continued presence. The photographer always managed to stay somewhere within her line of sight while charming female guests.

On edge, her stomach knotting with the tension, Leila tried to soothe her nerves by moving into Wynne's comforting warmth. But while he wrapped an arm around her shoulders and conversed as though nothing were wrong, she could feel his aloofness. He had to be as aware of Christian's presence as she.

Then the photographer moved closer and dropped his pretense of being interested in anyone other than Leila.

A few moments of Christian openly staring at her was all that she could take. She felt ready to explode. And Wynne stood tensed at her side, waiting for an explanation. She sensed his dissatisfaction with her.

She had to get away from both men for a few moments until she could regain her composure. But where to go?

The ladies' room—a haven where neither man could get to her!

"Excuse me, but I have to powder my nose," she told the guests she was speaking to, then assured Wynne, "I'll be back in a couple of minutes." She tried not to take his silence and piercing stare as an accusation.

Deciding to avoid the nearest rest rooms, which were sure to be filled to capacity, Leila cut through the crowd in the opposite direction. The women's locker room had been left open for tours. She would seek asylum there. Perhaps she could even lie down on one of the wooden benches and breathe deeply until her stomach settled.

But as soon as she entered the outer area, she knew she wasn't alone. The gut-wrenching sounds coming from the next room told her someone was in one of the toilet stalls in the process of being sick. The woman coughed and gagged, the rough sounds scraping up Leila's spine and threatening to trigger her own like response.

Her instinct was to leave so she wouldn't be sick herself, but if someone needed help...

She took a steadying breath and moved toward the inner room as the other person flushed the toilet, unlocked the door and left the stall. Leila hesitated in the doorway. A familiar figure in green taffeta lurched toward the sink and turned on a faucet, then stooped over, filled her cupped hand and rinsed out her mouth.

"Are you all right?"

Grace jumped and banged her head on the still-running faucet. She whipped around quickly, her face white, her expression horrified. She wouldn't meet Leila's eyes.

"I-I'm f-fine."

Without looking up, the teenager rushed past Leila. Water dripped from her face and hands onto her beautiful dress.

"Grace, wait."

The girl ran through the locker room and pitched open the door so hard the wood smashed into the ceramic wall. Leila told herself to go after Grace, but she couldn't make her legs move. The past hour had been too much of an ordeal.

First Christian, now this.

Her past had finally caught up to her, and she felt more devastated than she would have believed possible.

Leila leaned against the doorjamb for support. She closed her eyes, pressed her hands to her stomach and willed herself to breathe deeply. She was healthy, she reminded herself, both physically and mentally. She had been for years.

But Grace wasn't, or wouldn't be for long if she wasn't stopped. And Mel. Dear God, Mel! She was so thin, so fragile....

How could she have not realized? Leila asked herself. How could she have let this happen? Of anyone who knew them, she should have suspected what those girls were doing to lose weight. Everything was so clear now. Rapid loss. Shortened tempers. Obsession with food. Need for approval.

Who was better qualified to recognize the symptoms of bulimia than another bulimic?

Although she had gotten her own eating disorder under control through therapy before she left New York, Leila knew she was in the same league as a recovered alcoholic. The substance she had abused had been food. She no longer binged and purged, but she would forever be on guard against returning to the destructive pattern that had once been part of her daily life.

The beginning of her illness would always be burned in her memory. It had been at a party like this one, filled with New York hotshots. Too much rich food and drink, too many calories. Christian prodding her to be sociable to further her career as a model. Christian warning her against gaining so much as another ounce. How many times had he urged her to lose ten pounds so she would be camera thin? She'd been at the end of her wits, feeling stuffed and guilty. She'd been in the ladies' room, crying.

A successful model had given her the solution. "It's easy," the rail-thin young woman had assured her. "Eat and drink everything you want, then go in the bathroom and stick a finger down your throat. I do it all the time."

Never, Leila had thought. She could never do something so gross, so disgusting.

But it had been easy. Not the first time, maybe, but later. It had gotten so easy after a while that she'd been able to stop using her fingers. She'd developed her stomach muscles to act independently, to better control her frequent purging. She hadn't seen bulimia as a sickness, then. She hadn't even been able to give a name to what she was doing to herself. She only knew that losing weight and keeping it down was something she had to do, not for herself, but for her lover.

And Christian had loved her even more with each pound she'd lost. He'd told her so. He'd told her how absolutely perfect she'd become....

Leila often wondered if he realized how she was able to eat and still take off unwanted pounds. Pounds unwanted by Christian, the ambitious photographer who saw in her an easy meal ticket, who used her as a stepping stone for his own career, who badgered her to sign a contract that would make them both famous.

But she hadn't signed the damned contract and hadn't become famous and had lost Christian.

She'd hit bottom at the age of twenty—disillusioned by love, her life controlled by an eating disorder—and had wondered if there was anything left worth living for.

At a friend's urging, she'd sought professional help. She'd turned her life around. She'd been determined to help others look at body image in a different way than she had. So what was she doing alone in a bathroom reliving the horror she'd put behind her? Why couldn't she tell Wynne everything? And what was she going to do about Grace and Mel?

Leila had thought she had her life neatly in hand, everything in comfortable order. Suddenly, her life seemed like such a mess.

AFTER SPENDING another uncomfortable hour at the party, Wynne brought Leila back to her apartment. For once in his life, he didn't know what to say. She'd wanted to leave early and had told Kramer she wasn't feeling well. Her boss hadn't been pleased, but he hadn't objected, either, perhaps because Leila truly didn't look well.

She turned in the doorway, effectively blocking him from entering. "I'm exhausted. And I have this horrendous headache. Would you mind very much if I didn't ask you in?"

"I mind." The situation was even worse than he thought if she wasn't willing to be alone with him or to talk to him. He tried to hide his deep-seated anger with coaxing. "What about all those promises you made earlier?"

Then Leila did something he didn't expect. She wrapped her arms around his neck and rested her head on his shoulder. "I'm sorry." Her voice quivered when she spoke, and her body trembled. "So sorry."

Wynne felt awkward and didn't know how to respond. She'd taken the wind out of his sails, that was for sure. How could he be angry with a woman who suddenly seemed so defenseless? He held her close, wishing he didn't have to let her go, wishing she would let him in, even if to do nothing more than hold him through the night.

Leila lifted her head, kissed him softly, then stepped back.

"Will I see you tomorrow?" he asked.

"I need some time..."

"Monday, then?"

"Yes, Monday. Come by about six."

Wynne sure as hell didn't like having to wait that long, but he was afraid to push. Trying to coerce her might be a mistake, and he was in too deep. He would wait.

"Monday," he echoed, backing away from the door.

By Monday he would have some answers—and since she wouldn't give them, he would use his own methods. The first thing he wanted to know was the identity of the blond stud who'd been his nemesis, who'd caused Leila to shut him out. Wynne had seen the guy talking to Kramer. The executive director would be able to provide the guy's name.

Somehow, though, Wynne didn't think that particular answer would come as much of a surprise.

CHAPTER ELEVEN

GRACE AND MEL were her priority. Leila made that decision without any qualms. Her own problems could be put on hold for a while longer. She was an adult who could take care of herself, but they weren't much more than kids. Someone had to look out for their welfare. Leila was certain their parents had no idea what they were doing to lose weight. Bulimics learned early on to be clever about hiding their secret, as she well knew.

The girls were so young—much younger and more naive than she had been when she'd developed her eating disorder. And they had obviously formed a support system to keep each other going, to tell each other they were okay when they weren't. Their recent falling-out might have temporarily interrupted that support, and maybe she could use that to her advantage. No matter what she had to do, Leila was determined to make the teenagers face up to their problems and seek help.

Acting as if nothing were wrong, Grace showed up in Leila's aerobics class Monday afternoon. Mel didn't. Leila couldn't help but worry even more about the older girl. How far had Mel taken her eating disorder? Leila suspected the blonde's health was already in serious jeopardy.

After class, she stopped Grace in the hall. "We need to talk about a few things. Why don't you come to my office where we can have some privacy?"

"I, uh, can't. My mother's expecting me for dinner."

Grace turned away, but Leila caught her arm before the girl could take more than a step toward the locker room. "I'm serious. *Now.*"

She could see the wheels turning behind the transparent young face. Grace was trying to decide what action would be in her best interest. Leila knew she had no tangible power over the teenager—she was neither her mother nor one of her high school teachers—but she had the leverage of what she'd witnessed.

Thank God it was enough.

"All right. I guess I can spare a couple of minutes."

Though she agreed outwardly, Grace's inner resistance was visible in her stiffly held back and her mutinous expression. Her attitude didn't daunt Leila. She had been there. She understood. She knew all the tricks of denial and was confident that, given the opportunity, she could make Grace admit to her problem.

When they got to the office, she let the girl enter first, then closed the door behind them. She took her time settling herself in behind her desk. The more uncomfortable Grace became, the more effect Leila hoped to have on her.

Her back straight and removed from the chair, Grace pasted a tense smile on her lips. "So what's up?"

"I've noticed you and Mel haven't been speaking lately. I was wondering why."

"We had a difference of opinion, that's all."

"Opinion on what?"

"Nothing that would concern you."

"You're wrong. I am concerned. I care about both of you, and I've really been worried about Mel lately."

As if those words relieved her anxiety, Grace visibly deflated. Good. Leila wanted her to think the other girl was the topic under discussion...for the moment.

"So why are you talking to me instead of her?" Grace asked, settling back against the chair.

"How can I when she's not here? Besides, you're her friend, aren't you? I thought you could tell me what was wrong. Mel hasn't been looking too healthy the past month. Last week she was acting odd. And then she didn't show up to the party Saturday. I was sure she planned to go."

Grace looked down at her fingers, which she twisted together. "I guess she changed her mind."

"Then she isn't sick?"

"I don't know. Like you said, we haven't been speaking."

"I thought maybe she had the flu...just like you did Saturday night." Leila decided to plunge ahead and put the girl on the spot. "Or was there another reason you were in the bathroom throwing up?"

Grace's head snapped up. She couldn't hide her frightened expression. "No, you're right. I had the flu. One of those twenty-four-hour bugs. I was really sick. Maybe that's what Mel has, too."

"If it's a twenty-four-hour bug, she should be over it by now. But she isn't, is she?"

"W-what do you mean?"

"She's been binging and purging—throwing up—for a long time. And now you're doing it, too, aren't you?"

"I'm not doing anything! I was sick Saturday, that's all. Now I'm fine."

"You're not fine if you're bulimic, Grace," Leila said, finally bringing into the open what she was sure was the truth. "Eating everything you want and then getting rid of it may seem like an easy solution to your weight problem, but trust me, it isn't."

Dark eyes wide, Grace protested, "I don't know what you're talking about."

"I think you do."

"No!" The teenager rose quickly, almost knocking over the chair in the process. "I don't know anything about this bulimia thing and neither does Mel. There's nothing wrong with us, so just leave us alone!"

She stomped toward the door.

"Before you leave this office, Grace, listen to me, please," Leila pleaded.

The girl's back was to Leila, her hand already on the knob. Without letting go, she turned and waited.

"I want to help you," Leila continued. "Both of you. I know all about bulimia and what it can do to your body and your mind. I know how it can make you feel. You eat and then you get depressed and angry with yourself and feel guilty, so you get rid of the food and feel even more guilty because you know what you're doing isn't right. You get to the point where you think you can't stop. But you can. I can help you stop before you make yourself really ill." Leila didn't express her fears for Mel, that the other girl might already need more than counseling. "I promise you I'm on your side. I want to talk to you and Mel together. You tell her that.''

''This is ridiculous. We're not—''

''Tell her.'' As sympathetic as she was, Leila knew she had to be tough. ''I expect to see you both tomorrow afternoon. If the three of us can't discuss this like adults, I'll contact your parents. I'll tell them exactly what you've been doing to lose weight.''

Someone had to tell their parents eventually, but Leila was hoping she could convince the girls themselves to do it.

Grace blanched. ''If you tell my mother,'' she said, her voice low and firm, ''I'll run away from home.''

With that unexpected threat added to the implied admission, Grace slammed out of the office and left Leila shaken.

LEILA WAS STILL WORRYING about the alarming threat a few hours later while changing and applying some makeup before Wynne showed up at her apartment. Sick at heart that Grace might have been serious about running away, Leila knew that she couldn't go to the girls' parents until she'd exhausted every other means of persuasion at her disposal.

Honest with herself, she knew of only one thing that might work—forming a bond with Grace and Mel by telling them about herself. Some gritty facts might convince them that the disorder could literally destroy their lives. Perhaps if they knew what she and others had gone through as bulimics, the girls might be willing to listen to reason.

Staring out her living-room window at the soothing view of the lake, Leila fought the agitation that rose at the prospect of disclosing personal information she hadn't shared with anyone since leaving New York. Just thinking about doing so brought back some of the pain and heartache. She might be healed physically and psychologically, but not emotionally. Why? What would it take?

Her telephone rang, interrupting her thoughts. Lifting the receiver, she checked her watch and noted that Wynne was early. Only a quarter to six.

"A gentleman here to see you," the guard at the front desk told her.

"Send him right up."

Leila glanced at her reflection in the plate glass. She straightened the collar of her fuchsia silk jump suit and ran her fingers through her loose hair. She couldn't believe how uptight she was. She regretted sending Wynne away the other night, but she'd had no choice. She'd been too distraught, too much in a state of shock to make explanations. Even now, though she intended to apologize, she wasn't about to make some kind of confession. She didn't know if she ever could.

The knock at her door set her nerves on edge. How would Wynne act? What would he say? Would he pretend Saturday night had never happened? She would never know if she didn't answer, Leila chided herself, crossing the room. When she opened the door, however, she was in for a surprise.

"You!"

"Leila." Christian's golden brows arched in response to the arm she automatically raised to bar his entrance. "Aren't you going to ask me in?"

As arrogant as ever, her former lover smiled down at her. Once upon a time, Leila would have melted under that smile, but no longer. Once upon a time, her heart would have raced at the sight of Christian's golden good looks and hot body accentuated by an elegant designer shirt and fashionable linen pants. Now he merely appeared silly. A male peacock. Her taste in men's clothing must have changed, Leila thought, deciding she preferred Wynne's neon-orange shorts and the armless bright green sweatshirt.

"Leila?"

"Why should I let you in?"

"Why did you have the security guard send me up if you didn't want to see me?" His expression changed to a knowing one. "Oh, you're expecting someone else—the stooge from Saturday night."

"Wynne is not a stooge. He's a better person than you ever were." Not knowing why she didn't slam the door in Christian's handsome face, Leila stepped back and let him pass. She had a few things to settle with this man, things she hadn't had the guts to tell him when their relationship ended. "Let's get this over with."

"Such enthusiasm."

Christian took his time and looked around carefully as if appraising every item in her apartment. Then he made himself comfortable on a couch and studied her critically, as well. Leila felt her skin crawl when he seemed to evaluate her as thoroughly as he had her furniture. She couldn't care less if she measured up to his exacting standards—not that he viewed her any more personally than he would a piece of meat.

"If you're trying to psych me out so you can have the advantage, it's not working," Leila told him.

He ignored the accusation, merely asking, "Aren't you going to offer me a drink?"

"No. You might get the mistaken idea that you're welcome in my home."

Not in the least fazed by her hostile attitude, Christian threw an arm over the back of the couch and crossed his leg in a show of easy confidence. "I thought you would be happy to get together now that you're over your initial shock at seeing me so unexpectedly."

"Happy? Whatever gave you that idea?"

"We do have quite a history together."

"Not one that I would recommend," Leila told him, perching on the arm of the couch opposite. She looked straight into his eyes and challenged him. "Our mutual past is nothing to brag about. You saw to that."

"Come, now. Don't keep lying to yourself, Leila. You weren't mature enough to handle a sophisticated relationship. Admit it. And while you're at it, admit we had some incredible times together, as well."

His voice dripped with sensuality as it had in the past when Christian had wanted to seduce her...or to photograph her. What was he up to? Leila had no doubt that Christian had some underlying motive for being there.

"Put in the perspective of why the relationship ended," Leila corrected him, "the good times kind of lost their luster. You were using me all along, plain and simple."

"No more than you used me."

Incensed by the unfair accusation, Leila balled her hands into fists. "That's a load, and you know it!"

"Do I? You came to New York a starry-eyed nineteen-year-old looking for excitement."

"I was looking for a fun vacation from the tedium of studying, yes, but I had no dreams of grandeur, no intentions of staying in New York." Merely thinking about what had followed shot adrenaline through her system, making Leila fidgety. She stood and stepped closer. "You were a sophisticated older man who swept a naive young girl from the South Side of Chicago off her feet. You introduced me to a whole new world that I didn't even know existed."

"And you took to it like a duck takes to water."

"You seduced me and then you kept me off balance so I would do just about anything to keep you. No, I wasn't the one doing the using."

"A matter of perspective, isn't it?" Christian's brow was marred by a frown. "You were eager for the glamour that came with being a model."

"I was eager to please you. You made me want you. You were part of this very elaborate package, Christian, and you made it clear that I had no choice but to take all or nothing. I didn't really understand what that would mean in the long run, and so I bought into your special brand of manipulation. I loved you so much that I would have done anything for you," she said, thinking of what she'd done to herself to lose weight for him.

"But you didn't, did you?"

If he knew about her eating disorder, that sacrifice obviously meant nothing to him. The only thing he'd cared about had been the damn contract!

"I had to draw the line somewhere. Thank God I wised up before I did something I would regret for the rest of my life. If you had had any real feelings for me, you wouldn't have suggested I pose for smut. Suggested..." Becoming more agitated and sick feeling by the moment, Leila drew closer until she was practically standing over him. "That's a laugh. You demanded. You tried to force me into it."

"My photographs of you would have been art, not smut."

"Don't flatter yourself. Call a spade a spade. You were a pander, not an artist."

Christian's tan paled as he stood and took the advantage of height. Leila wouldn't be intimidated. Confronting Christian was giving her a deep sense of satisfaction—as if she were filling in some part of her life that had been frozen in time incomplete. She was glad he'd finally given her the opportunity she hadn't had the courage to make for herself when their relationship ended.

"I was offering you a contract with the leading men's magazine in the world!" Christian bellowed.

"Posing for pornography! You wanted to use me to turn on every man in the country the way I did you. And why?" Heart pumping painfully at the memory, Leila had to restrain herself so she wouldn't hit him as he deserved. "Because you thought my body would make your name as a top photographer. You thought using me was a quick way to get where you wanted."

Christian bared his teeth in a victorious grin. "I made it without you, didn't I?" He looked around her apartment as if he found it lacking. "But you couldn't make it without me."

"Is that what this is all about?" she cried. All the misery he'd caused her came back to haunt Leila. Anger made her insides tremble. "Is that why you're here—to rub my nose in your success? Oh, God, you're still a poor excuse for a human being."

The telephone rang just then, interrupting their argument. But Leila wasn't finished. She picked up the receiver, issued a sharp "Send him up" before the guard could say a thing, then slammed down the phone.

"You don't know the first thing about relationships," she went on. "Actually, I pity you."

"I know I wasn't perfect, Leila, but then no one is. I did care for you in my own way—more than I've ever cared for another woman. Whether or not you accept that is up to you. I know I never should have given you the ultimatum to do the shoot or leave. I realized my mistake the moment you walked out the door."

Christian's carefully modulated voice had slid into a low pitch that was supposed to win her over. She wondered why he was bothering. What did Christian want from her?

"Am I supposed to take this speech as your way of making an apology?" She didn't bother to hide her suspicion or hostility.

"I'm not apologizing for anything," he said smoothly. "Getting you to sign that contract and pose for the layout wasn't anything personal. It was business, pure and simple."

"There was nothing pure about that deal. And that was the trouble with you, Christian. You were all business and no heart. My problem was that I was too stupid to realize it."

"I can change."

His words and his accompanying provocative expression surprised the breath out of her. Leila was speechless even as Christian reached out and fingered a lock of her hair. His touch revolted her, but she didn't seem able to do anything about it.

"I remember how good it was between us, Leila. Don't you? I'm going to be in town for the next week.

Why don't we get together? The sparks are still there. I can feel them.''

"That's antagonism—or are you so egotistical that you can't tell the difference?"

Christian's blue eyes were all over her, stripping her bare. "You're just as beautiful as ever. Even more so. That picture of you in *Glitter* knocked me for a loop."

He slid his hand around her neck and inched closer. Leila shuddered at his touch but held her ground. Rage grew in her and multiplied, the emotion making it difficult for her to breathe properly. Christian must have misinterpreted her feelings, for he went on with a confident smile.

"We could work together again. No nudity," he added quickly. "You could still be the top photographic model, not only in this country, but in Europe, as well. I'm famous there, too, you know. Of course you'd have to lose a few pounds—"

The reference to her weight made her see red. Without holding back her considerable strength, Leila pushed Christian away from her, then slapped him across the face so hard that his head snapped back.

"That's what I think of your proposal. Now get out!" she ordered him. "And don't come back."

Features glowering and color staining his cheek, Christian stepped away from her. "You'll be sorry you did that."

Her heart was beating so hard she could hear it pulsing in her ears, but Leila liked the sweet taste of victory that spilled from her lips. "No, I won't. I only regret I didn't do it years ago."

She strode toward the door and opened it with a jerk just as Wynne arrived. He stopped short and quickly glanced from her to Christian.

"Hi, you're right on time," Leila said, knowing her voice didn't sound natural.

Wynne's absolute silence frightened her. Willing her heart to calm down, she slid into his side and kissed his cheek as Christian shoved past them, and hopefully out of her life for good this time.

WYNNE HELD HIMSELF STIFFLY, even after the golden-haired man had stormed down the hall and Leila had moved into the living area. He was waiting for an explanation and could hardly believe that none was forthcoming.

"Aren't you going to come in?" she asked.

He stepped into the apartment and closed the door behind him. "Now what?"

She seemed uncomfortable, as well she should. "Now we can do whatever you want. Have a drink... go out for a walk... take in another movie. One that won't put you to sleep this time."

He ignored her effort to lighten the thick atmosphere with teasing. "How about talking honestly? Or is that too much for you to handle?"

Leila's tense smile faded only to be replaced by an openly worried expression. "If you're referring to the man who just left, don't worry about him. He won't be back."

"Why was he here in the first place?" Wynne asked, pressing the issue. He moved closer to her, yet kept a purposeful distance between them. "To go after you with another unoriginal come-on like he did the other night when he cornered you at the party?"

"Something like that. Sit down, would you? You're making me nervous."

"Why? Do you have reason to be?"

Wynne had had that talk with Mike Kramer. His suspicions about the stranger's identity had been confirmed, but he wanted Leila to volunteer the information.

"What is this?" Leila demanded, her apprehension turning to impatience. "You don't own me, Wynne Donegan, and I don't owe you any explanations."

"Excuse me. I thought we had something special going for us, but I guess I was mistaken." Hurt by her sharp tone and uncaring attitude, he turned to go. "Maybe I should leave."

"No, wait. Please. I'm sorry. I didn't mean that the way it sounded. I'm just a little upset, and I shouldn't be taking it out on you."

Wynne wasn't about to be sympathetic, at least not until Leila decided to be honest. He faced her and silently urged her to tell him everything she'd been holding back. "Upset about what?"

"The guy is . . . *was* an old friend. We parted badly. That was years ago," she hurriedly added. "He saw the picture of me in *Glitter* and decided he wanted to renew our acquaintance."

"All the way from New York?"

"No, he was in town on a shoot . . ." Her sentence trailed off, and she stared at him. "New York?" she echoed.

"That's where Manley lives, isn't it?"

Her voice odd, she asked, "You know him?"

"Of him. We've never been *introduced*." He emphasized the last word so she would know he was ticked.

"Believe me, Christian Manley is someone you wouldn't want to know, Wynne. I wish I had never met him."

The way Leila threw herself onto the couch disclosed the anger that was still simmering below her surface. Wynne followed and sat next to her. He took her hand, kissed the palm and tucked it between his.

"Why, Leila? What's the big mystery?"

"Let it be. It's in the past."

"No, it's not. Whatever happened is still affecting you. Something's coming between us, Leila. *He's* coming between us as surely as if someone inserted a wedge."

Wynne could see the truth of his words in Leila's vulnerable expression, and still she tried to deny it.

"Look, he hurt me when I was too young to deal with the situation properly. But I just got a whole bunch of grievances off my chest. Maybe now I can finally forget about Christian completely and concentrate on us."

"Sounds good. At least it's a start. So why don't you tell me what went wrong between the two of you."

"I've been through that once tonight."

"But not with me."

"You don't need to hear the gritty details."

She pulled her hand free. He could tell she was withdrawing, but he wasn't about to let her off so easily. "I do need to hear them, and you need to talk about them with someone who cares about you."

"Wynne, please, can't we just drop it?"

He knew he was taking a chance when he asked, "Like you dropped modeling at the beginning of a promising career?"

Wynne felt as if he could cut the silence with a knife. Leila backed herself into a corner of the couch and stared at him as if she were trying to discern how much he'd guessed and how much he knew for sure. He waited, certain she wouldn't try to change the subject at this point.

"Would you like to explain that statement?" she finally asked.

"You're the only one who has all the answers."

"If you want honesty from me, then I deserve the same from you."

She was right, of course, but this was the moment he'd been fearing. If he admitted going behind her back to get the information, he might lose her. The question was, did he have her to begin with?

Perhaps it was time he found out.

"I know that Manley discovered you," Wynne began after taking a deep breath. "That you were under an exclusive contract with him. And that you lived with him. I also know that you dropped out of sight without explanation when you were in hot demand."

"How, Wynne? How do you know all this?" Her forehead pulled into a frown of distress, and the pitch of her voice rose. "Who did you have to interview to get your answers?"

"Does it matter?"

"Yes! Damn it!" Leila hit the back of the couch with the flat of her hand. "This is my life you've been prying into!"

"I wouldn't have had to pry if you hadn't been so secretive."

"Who do you think you are to be privy to my every thought, anyway?" Leila asked indignantly.

"Only the man who's falling in love with you."

Wynne hadn't known he was going to make the declaration. Hell, he hadn't even defined his feelings for Leila until that moment. But once said, the words weren't to be retracted, because they were true. He was falling hard, and it was already too late to stop the momentum.

With that realization, Wynne knew that Leila had the power to hurt him as badly as Christian had her. She was staring at him oddly, as if she were trying to decide how she should respond to his statement. When she began, she spoke carefully, as though she didn't want to hurt him. But she avoided the issue altogether.

"You make it sound as if I've committed some kind of a crime because I quit modeling. I was twenty years old when I decided to start over and do something worthwhile with the rest of my life. It's only natural that I prefer to forget an unpleasant period."

"But you haven't forgotten, and you've never gotten over it. That's my point." Wynne was growing exasperated. "You've continued to use whatever happened to you in New York to push people away when they get too close. Christian Manley may be out of your life physically, but how long are you going to let your memories come between us?"

"Wynne, I don't love the man, if that's what you think. I despise him."

"I kind of figured that out for myself. What I don't know is why."

Her dark eyes went glassy, and he could tell she was holding back her tears with effort. She gulped hard, and he could see her throat muscles knot. She was trying to make up her mind. Wynne wanted to take her in his arms and beg her to tell him, or perhaps to force the information from her.

No, neither was true. He wanted Leila to give him her trust freely.

That had been the problem all along, the thing that continued to frustrate him. Even when he'd had Leila in the most intimate of ways, he'd known what he'd been missing.

"I-I'm sorry," she finally said. "It's just so complicated. I need time to think."

Wynne rose. "Fair enough."

"Where are you going?" She caught his hand and pulled herself up. "You're not leaving?"

"I'm giving you the time you need, Leila," Wynne said gently. He stroked her cheek. A large tear freed itself from her lashes and wet his fingers. "When you come to a decision, let me know. I hope you'll make the right one and soon. I love you."

Wynne walked away from her before he could change his mind. He hoped she would call him back, tell him about the past, heal the separation before it could widen. As he opened the door, he could have sworn she whispered that she loved him, too.

That was a start, something to give him hope.

But did she love him enough to give him the honesty and trust he needed, as well?

GRACE MADE HER WAY to Mel's bedroom, wishing the other girl had answered the door herself. Making small talk with Mrs. Bricker had made her anxiety surge. Dread of the necessary confrontation mounted until her stomach began to ache.

She stopped in front of Mel's door and hesitantly knocked.

"I'm trying to take a nap, Sandra," Mel called out. "I'll get something to eat later."

"It's not your mom."

Mel didn't answer, but Grace heard movement. A few seconds later, the door opened. Circles darkened the delicate skin under Mel's eyes, which narrowed suspiciously.

"Here to blab?" she asked.

Grace shook her head. "To warn you." Mel was her friend, after all, even if they hadn't been speaking.

The blonde stood back and let Grace pass, then slammed the door. "Warn me about what?"

"Leila is onto us."

"You told her?"

"Of course not." Grace fidgeted with her purse. "She caught me. At the club's party."

"The party? You threw up there?" Mel was looking at her as if she were an idiot. "What a dumb thing to do."

Grace's eyes filled with tears. She hadn't expected Mel to strike out at her when she was trying to do the other girl a favor. She turned to leave.

"Wait a minute!" Mel caught Grace's arm. "I shouldn't have said that. I'm sorry."

"I'm sorry, too." Grace blinked away her tears and took a closer look at her friend, who had obviously lost more weight. "Haven't you been eating anything?"

"Oh, a few bites of salad here, a small piece of fish there to keep my parents from suspecting. But I get rid of it as soon as I get away from the table."

Sure that Mel would have to give in and eat soon, Grace chose not to comment. "I just wanted you to know Leila demanded we both see her at the club to-morrow.''

''And if we don't . . .''

''She said she'd tell our parents.''

''I suppose I can figure out a way to handle my mother.'' Mel flopped back on her bed. ''Maybe I'll tell her Leila's been giving me a hard time lately.''

''Mel, no. You can't get Leila into trouble. That wouldn't be fair.''

Mel wore a stubborn expression that frightened Grace. A lot of things were frightening her lately. ''My mom would believe Leila,'' she said in a small voice.

''Great! What are you going to do, then?''

A bleak feeling washed through Grace, and her eyes filled with tears once more. Trapped in a maze of a nightmare, she couldn't seem to find her way down the right corridor.

What *was* she going to do?

CHAPTER TWELVE

LEILA SPENT A SLEEPLESS night thinking about Wynne's unexpected declaration of love and its consequences. She couldn't put off making a commitment to a new relationship forever. And indeed, Wynne was the first man who had ever made her believe that her life could have a happy ending. All she had to do was reach out and take what her slightly rumpled Prince Charming was offering.

That's exactly what she intended to do, Leila decided as she yawned her way through the next workday. Her senses didn't fully awaken until early that afternoon when she spotted Melanie Bricker among the clients using the indoor track. The teenager saw Leila, as well, but she looked away furtively.

Leila jogged to catch up to Mel. Her long legs made it a cinch to pull up to the girl, despite her lack of sleep. "Have you heard from Grace lately?"

"I saw her...last night," Mel said, heaving a breath between words.

"Did she tell you I wanted to talk to you both together?"

"She told me...but she's not...here."

And if Leila waited for Grace to show, Mel might sneak off. "Then I'll settle for you."

"Forget it." Mel puffed as she struggled to pull ahead. "You can't intimidate me."

Leila stayed with her easily. "I don't want to intimidate anyone, Mel."

"So talk."

"Not here."

Leila knew they would need privacy and figured the chances of getting the stubborn girl into her office were slim. As they took the turn, she spotted an empty racquetball court. While others would see them in the room through the floor-to-ceiling glass wall, they wouldn't be able to eavesdrop on the personal conversation.

Pointing to the empty court, Leila said, "Let's go in there."

Mel seemed as if she were going to resist even that suggestion. Then she shrugged and stepped off the track, taking the lead. Leila followed closely, and once they were alone, decided not to mince words.

"Bulimia is a very dangerous method of losing weight."

"So?"

"So you have to stop before you ruin your health."

Leila examined the girl carefully. Mel's blond hair hung thin and lifeless. Her skin seemed dry, and both it and her eyes had a yellowish tinge that even the mercury-vapor lamps couldn't disguise. Could Mel possibly have looked like this for long without Leila noticing?

Mel was still breathing heavily when she asked, "Who said I started?"

At least she wasn't pretending she didn't know what Leila was talking about, although she wasn't exactly being honest, either.

"Mel, don't lie to me, or to yourself. You have to set realistic goals. You've already gone past the ones you should have set for yourself.'' Leila turned to their reflections in the glass wall. "Take a long look at yourself. Your hips and ribs and collarbone are all showing. You must be ten pounds underweight now.''

Mel crossed her arms in front of her thin body. "That's your opinion.''

"How much do you weigh?''

"And *that's* none of your business.''

Leila decided to try a different tack. "You're exhausted. You were puffing out there like you didn't have an ounce of oxygen to spare. I know you weren't on the jogging track for very long, since I didn't see you when I went by a few minutes earlier. If you were eating sensibly, your energy level would be a lot higher. You wouldn't be straining. I've noticed you've been having the same problem in the aerobics class the past week or so.''

Still Mel wouldn't admit to anything. "Why don't you bug someone else?''

"Because you need my help.''

"I don't need your criticism. I want to be like you. Perfect.''

"Mel, no one is perfect. You're already far thinner than I am. And you shouldn't try to be like someone else, anyway. You're an individual, your own person.''

"Then why don't you leave me alone and let me be what I want?''

"Because I'm worried about what you're doing to yourself.''

"You don't know anything about it.''

That was the closest the teenager had come to admitting she had a problem. Leila knew it was now or never. She took a deep breath. "I do, Mel. I'm a bulimic just like you are."

"You throw up to lose weight?"

"Not anymore. I recovered ten years ago, but I can't ever forget what happened to me. I lived in a nightmare for the better part of a year. I was a model, and my photographer kept telling me I needed to lose a few pounds because the camera made me look heavier," Leila explained carefully. Mel didn't have to know about her relationship with Christian to get the idea. "And then I went to all these parties—there were incredible spreads of food and drink at every one of them. I tried to watch what I ate, but I couldn't lose weight that way. Another model told me her secret of eating and losing at the same time, so I did what she did—binged and purged."

"Did it work?"

"Too well," Leila admitted. "Some days I ate as many as twenty or thirty thousand calories—more than ten times the amount a normal person eats—and I still lost weight."

"So?"

"So it wasn't healthy, Mel. Not physically. Not mentally. I was robbing my body of important nutrients while all I could think about was food until it became an obsession. I was hungry all the time. I never felt satisfied, because within minutes after stuffing myself I would have to empty my stomach. And then a while later I would be starving again. But you know how that is, don't you? You know how horrible that makes you feel . . . how guilty?"

But Mel didn't admit any such thing. "Even if it was true," the teenager said airily, "I know what's best for me. No matter what you say, I'm going to be perfect just like you. Then Luke will do anything to get me back." She started to leave but paused long enough to add, "Oh...and don't bother threatening to call my parents. They don't care how I lose weight as long as I don't embarrass them in front of their snobby friends."

With that, Mel walked out on her and back onto the track.

Even though Leila was deflated at her failure to talk sense into either teenager, she didn't believe that Mel's parents could be so uncaring. And she knew that calling them was exactly what she had to do. Mel left her with no alternative.

Leila followed up on that decision immediately after teaching her aerobics class. She hurried to her office to make the calls. Mrs. Bricker's reaction to Leila's warning that Mel had developed a serious problem wasn't exactly what she had expected, however.

"My daughter isn't some psychotic!" Mel's mother exclaimed.

"I didn't say that she was. What I meant by 'psychological' is that bulimia is an eating disorder supported by a person's distorted self-image. Melanie refuses to admit she's too thin now, and—"

"Melanie is her father's and my business, not yours, Ms Forester. We signed her up at the club because she was obese. Now she's not. She's acceptably thin. You've succeeded at your job. You should be satisfied. We are."

Leila began to wonder if Mel had been correct in her assessment of her parents. "Mrs. Bricker, I have good reason to be worried about Mel."

"Enough, Ms Forester." Sandra Bricker's tone was frosty enough to send a chill over the telephone line. "You keep your nose out of my family's life or I'll speak to Mike Kramer about you. If you go on persecuting Melanie, I'll see that you're fired."

With that, Mrs. Bricker hung up. Leila must have stared at the phone in shock for a full five minutes before she tried again, this time calling Grace's mother at her place of employment.

"Mrs. Vanos, it's about Grace."

"Oh no, she hasn't hurt herself, has she?"

"Not in the way you might imagine. She's not injured," Leila began cautiously. "But she's been doing something to lose weight that certainly isn't healthy."

"Don't tell me she found a way to get diet pills." Mrs. Vanos sounded exasperated. "I've told her time and again that pills aren't the solution."

Leila took a deep breath. "Neither is throwing up."

"Pardon me?"

"Your daughter is bulimic, Mrs. Vanos. That means she eats whatever she wants, then throws up to rid herself of the unwanted calories."

"Are you sure?"

"I caught her at it."

"Oh, Lord, I never even suspected." Real concern strained Mrs. Vanos's voice. "Thank you for calling me, Ms Forester. I promise to speak to Grace about this as soon as I get home from work."

"If there's anything I can do to help, let me know."

Having dealt with that problem as best she could under the circumstances, Leila turned her thoughts to straightening out her own life. Wynne would appreciate a little honesty from her, she was sure. She only wondered how much she could make herself tell him without falling apart.

"Brenna, I love you," James said, not liking the desperation in his voice. When had he become so vulnerable? "At least the part of you I know."

"What you see is what you get."

"Nice package...but I don't believe it. There's so much more to you than meets the eye. You're a complex woman, Brenna, and that not only excites me but frustrates me, as well."

"I wouldn't want you to be frustrated."

Brenna moved closer and loosened the tie that held her kimono together. James got a quick flash of full breasts and a slender waist before she pressed her lush body against his. He'd sworn he wouldn't let her distract him from their personal confrontation this time, but he was only human. There was no way he could prevent himself from responding. With a groan, James held Brenna to him and kissed her as she had undoubtedly expected he would.

Making love again wouldn't solve anything, but it sure as hell would make him feel better for the moment. It was afterward he was worried about....

Wynne sat back in his office chair and threw down the hard copy he'd been reading over.

The relationship between the protagonists in *Hot Bodies* was getting too close to home for comfort. Somehow he'd managed to transfer his problems with Leila to the printed page. He hadn't been doing so consciously—the words just seemed to write themselves, maybe because his problematic relationship with Leila seemed to pervade his every waking thought, his every dream. Now it was taking over his writing. He didn't know how to stop this growing obsession. He wasn't sure that he wanted to. The only thing he was sure of was his love for a woman who might never return the feeling.

Wynne pushed himself away from his desk, rose and stretched. He couldn't remember when he'd eaten last. No doubt something substantial in his stomach would help him think straight. On his way downstairs to scare up some dinner, he was surprised when the doorbell rang. He wasn't expecting anyone. One of his siblings must have ignored his warning to call first to make sure he wasn't immersed in his writing. Probably Grady.

The last person in the world he expected to see when he opened the door was Leila. But there she stood, smiling uncertainly and holding out a large brown paper bag.

"I hope you like Chinese."

"I love Chinese." Wondering what to make of her unannounced appearance, Wynne blocked her way and waited for further explanation.

Leila lowered the bag. "Are you going to make me eat dinner alone on your porch steps?"

"I don't know. Do I have a reason to let you in?"

"You're going to turn down free food and semi-interesting after-dinner conversation?"

He gathered this was her concession to his demand that she be open with him. Adrenaline rushed through him, but he tried to keep a rein on his elation. "Conversation first. Dinner later. Agreed?"

"If that's the only way you'll let me in."

"My house, my rules."

Leila forced the bag on him. Accepting that as her way of agreeing, Wynne took the food and moved out of her way. She was putting on a good face for him, but he could sense her underlying nervousness, making him wonder at what cost she had capitulated. That she had come around so quickly filled him with a buoyancy that lifted his spirits. Perhaps she cared as much about him as he did about her.

"Make yourself at home."

Wynne set the bag on the fireplace mantel and ignored the incredible smells of food only by sheer willpower—even when his stomach rumbled and protested being denied. Leila sat forward on the edge of the couch, as though she wanted the option of making a quick escape in case she changed her mind. She really was nervous.

"Aren't you going to sit down?" she asked.

"Sitting is what I've been doing for the past eight hours or so. I don't get much exercise in my line of work these days. Stretching my legs feels good." He leaned back against the mantel, keeping his manner casual when he really wanted to take her in his arms and tell her how glad he was to see her. "So, what shall we talk about?"

"You're not going to make this easy on me, are you?"

"This isn't any easier for me, Leila." Whether or not she believed him, that was the truth. His empty stomach was knotting from tension.

"I don't quite know where to start."

"New York would be fine."

"New York." She took a deep breath. "That was my sophomore year of college. One of my best friends was going to NYU to get a degree in film. Jeanne was working on an ongoing project for a class, so she really couldn't come home for Christmas. She invited me to visit her. Manhattan was every bit as exciting as I had dreamed it would be. Jeanne introduced me to fascinating people—''

"One of whom was Christian Manley."

Leila nodded. "He swept me off my feet. Love at first sight. I was so impressed by him . . . and amazed that a man with his talent and sophistication wanted me. I didn't take time to question his motives."

"Why would a woman with your looks be amazed that a man was attracted to her?"

"My looks."

The two words were filled with such rancor. Leaning forward, elbows on her knees, Leila clasped her hands together tightly. She remained silent for a moment, and Wynne could sense the pain it cost her to continue.

"That's what Christian was after, all right, but I was too green to read him correctly. I thrived on his compliments, would do anything for more. I didn't have much in the way of self-confidence," she explained. "I mean, I knew I was attractive, but I was . . . insecure, I guess. At first, I thought Christian was joking when he said he wanted to take test shots of me. Then I decided that was his way of giving me the come-on. I didn't even mind. I wanted him more than I'd ever wanted anything in my life."

Wynne fought back an unexpected wave of jealousy. "So you posed for him."

"And the next thing I knew, he had a real assignment for me. I agreed because I wanted to be with Christian—and for the fun of it. I have to admit I was attracted to the glamorous life, as well. I figured I'd go back to school with some terrific memories.''

"But you never returned."

"No, not then. While I was thinking this was a one-shot deal, Christian was making big plans for me, and I fell right for them—hook, line and sinker. He was a fast worker. The day I was supposed to fly back to Illinois, I moved into his loft with him, instead. From then on, there was no turning back.''

Bitterness was a tangible thing coloring Leila's words. Wynne could sense her anxiety increase as she got closer to the heart of the matter. He grew apprehensive for her. She was staring down at her clenched hands now, as if she didn't know how to continue.

"Some young women try to break into modeling for years and never succeed," Wynne prodded.

That was enough to get her going again.

"Luck of the draw, I guess. I was a novice without any formal training, and yet Christian landed me an amazing number of jobs. I'm not talking about conventions or catalogue work, but ads and fashion layouts in top women's magazines—high-class assignments.''

"I saw the Christmas issue of *Sophisticate*."

Shifting uneasily, she asked, "What did you think?''

"I was fascinated."

Meeting his eyes directly, Leila licked her lips and took a deep breath. "Christian insisted on shooting that right after we made love.''

Wynne forced his face to remain expressionless. "That made you uncomfortable.''

"Very. But it didn't stop him from insisting. And it didn't stop me from doing what he wanted.''

She dropped her gaze then, and Wynne sensed a deep-seated shame she'd never overcome.

"After that," Leila continued, "Christian became even more demanding. The shooting sessions became more openly erotic. When I objected, he insisted I knew nothing about marketing, that he was selling a concept." She laughed. "He was selling me, all right."

Wynne was beginning to get the picture, one he didn't like. And Leila looked as if she were about to cry, as if she needed a shoulder to lean on. He couldn't deny that need, couldn't stand to be the cause of her pain without doing something to help her through it. Joining her on the couch, he put his arms around her and pulled her back against his chest. She held herself stiffly. Wynne stroked her hair and kissed her temple.

"Go on," Wynne urged. "You're doing just fine. I'm not judging you, if that's what you're afraid of."

Leila relaxed a bit, and Wynne drew her even closer. She rested her cheek against his chest and tucked her head under his chin. He felt a strong wave of compassion and protectiveness roll over him—and a growing anger toward the man who had taken advantage of a trusting young woman.

"You were right when you told me I wouldn't want to know the bastard," Wynne told her.

"It took me a long time to come to grips with the truth," Leila said, "but I finally realized Christian wanted me not because he loved me, but because of what he thought I could do for him."

He continued to stroke her hair comfortingly. "What opened your eyes?"

"Christian put together a special portfolio, including only the hottest shots of me. I never posed nude," she added, as though trying to reassure him. "I might as well have, though, considering how steamy some of those photographs turned out. Anyway, he used the portfolio to sell me to the executives at a top men's magazine. They agreed I was centerfold material. The contract was all drawn up and waiting for my signature before I knew anything about it. I refused to sign.''

''And Christian kissed you off?''

''Not immediately. He thought he could get me to change my mind, because he'd convinced me to do everything else he wanted up to that point. He couldn't understand my objections. I thought I'd seen Christian in all his moods. Loving, demanding, cajoling. But I'd never seen him in such a rage. He accused me of trying to ruin him when taking this job could set us both up with big money, lucrative future contracts and fame. We went around and around for days, until finally he told me that if I didn't agree, I could pack my things and get out. That's exactly what I did...after I literally tore up the contract and threw it in his face. It's the closest I came to telling Christian what I thought of him until yesterday.''

Wynne gave her a reassuring squeeze. ''Be glad you had the opportunity. Not everyone gets that chance. What a bastard! You must have been heartsick when you made the break.''

''That's putting it mildly. I was twenty years old and felt as if my life were over. I'd been seduced by Christian and his glamorous life-style, and I was left with nothing, not even self-respect. I stayed with Jeanne for a few months and got some professional counseling. That helped me resolve my...problems. Then I came back to Illinois and finished school. You know the rest.''

Wynne didn't think so. He couldn't put his finger on it, but he sensed she was still holding back. Maybe it was because she'd mentioned "problems" instead of talking about resolving her feelings for Christian. At least they'd made a start.

"You turned your life around," he said. "That's the thing that matters. It's all that matters to me."

Leila pulled out of the close embrace and kissed him on the cheek. "You're very dear for saying that."

"I'm not fishing for compliments, just the truth. I only wish you had told me about Christian before he showed up."

"Why?" She gave him a piercing look. "Would you have punched him out?"

"That's a distinct possibility. And no disparaging remarks about my physical condition, either."

Leila's laughter made Wynne's heart skip a beat. It was the first positive reaction she'd had since entering the house. A good sign. He placed a kiss on the tip of her nose, but before he could aim for her mouth, she sobered.

"I've never been able to tell anyone, Wynne, not about the real reason I left Christian. The story was too sordid and humiliating. I vowed I would never let anyone have that kind of control over me again."

Wynne thought about the statement. No wonder he'd felt Leila had been trying to distance herself. She'd been afraid of being used again.

"I can understand why you didn't trust me—or any other man whom you didn't know really well—but why didn't you talk to your mother and father about what happened? Your parents could have helped you."

"No. Especially not them. They would only have made things worse. I never could do anything right in their eyes."

"Surely you're exaggerating."

Leila's expression darkened and Wynne knew he'd reawakened other disagreeable memories.

"You think so? If I was crazy about a boy in high school, my father was sure I would get pregnant and disgrace the family. If I talked about going to college, my mother would worry that I would never find a man who would want to marry me and give her grandchildren. When I moved in with Christian, my father practically disowned me. He thought any woman who lived with a man or who wanted to be a model was immoral. And when I moved back to Illinois, my mother told me I'd better make up my mind about what I wanted to do with my life. One person could only handle so many failures. How could I tell them anything?"

Wynne could understand her reluctance, but he tried to reassure her. "All parents give their kids a rough time."

"Yours don't."

"Ha! You weren't there when I was growing up. My parents might be supportive of my career choice, but they had plenty to say about other areas of my life. I didn't always like their interference, but I knew they were coming from a different generation with different ideas, different values. I knew they only wanted the best for me because they loved me. And I'd bet your parents love you, too. Sometimes people don't know how to express their emotions in the way we would like. You never even gave them a chance to help you after you left Christian."

"They wouldn't have understood."

"Maybe not, but they would have loved you anyway. I think you needed that reassurance. Instead, refusing to talk about what happened caught you up in a self-defeating cycle. You never recovered emotionally the way you should have after all those years."

But she would have that opportunity now, Wynne vowed. He would make sure the channels of communication stayed open. He fought the niggling feeling of guilt about his own lack of complete honesty. He'd never told Leila why he'd wanted to get to know her, had never mentioned that some of the problems in their relationship seemed to be feeding his imagination when he wrote. But, of course, the two situations weren't exactly comparable.

"I talked to a therapist and to my counseling group in New York," she told him.

"That was a good start. But those were strangers, not the people who really counted in your life. You've been pushing us all away."

Leila's brow furrowed. "I never really thought about that before. Maybe it's true. I don't know." Her forehead smoothed and her lips turned up when she added, "I don't want to push *you* away, Wynne."

"I'm glad."

"You're good for me."

That was what he wanted to hear. Placing his elbow on the back of the couch, he leaned his head against a closed fist. "Why?"

She traced his bottom lip with a fingertip. "Because you make me laugh."

"A clown could do that."

"I don't like clowns."

"What else?"

"You're even more stubborn than I am."

"Is that supposed to be a compliment?" he asked.

"You bet. You got to me in spite of all the invisible barriers I built between us."

"Tell me more."

Leila trailed the finger down his chin and onto his chest. "You have a great heart."

"How do you know?" She could probably feel it pumping like mad. Wynne could hardly believe this woman cared about him enough to share a past that she'd kept hidden even from her parents. "You can't see it."

"Well, it has to be at least as great as the rest of you."

"Now I know you're putting me on."

"Where's the famous Donegan confidence?"

"Sometimes it goes into hiding around you."

She was trailing the finger even lower. Wynne had no doubts that Leila was done talking for the evening, whether or not she'd told him everything. He sensed pushing her further would not only be futile, but might be damaging to the fragile bond they'd begun to form. "Are you trying to seduce me?"

"No. I'm trying to give you an anatomy lesson," she said, laughing softly.

"As long as I know what's happening."

He knew that in reality Leila was trying to distract him from any serious conversation. She obviously didn't want to return to an uncomfortable subject. She was managing to convince him so nicely that he decided to let her off the hook.

For now.

Dusk was settling over the room as Wynne stripped off his T-shirt and kicked off his sneakers. Leila bared her own feet and began to unbutton her blouse. Clad only in a pair of shorts without any briefs underneath, he decided to let Leila make that discovery for herself. He stood so his legs bumped her knees. She reached out and caught the elastic waistband of his shorts, then tugged ever so slowly, her eyes pinned to her labor. Her face was fascinating to watch as desire made its unmistakable imprint on her features.

"Remember to tell me when you find a good part," he teased.

She gave the garment a sharp tug, and warm laughter spilled from her lips. "There's one coming up right now."

Wynne stepped out of the shorts and left them in a puddle on the floor. His heart was hammering so loudly that he could barely hear himself when he softly urged, "Feel free to explore."

"Like this?" she asked, running her hand up between his naked thighs.

Wynne sucked in his breath. "You've got the right idea. Improvise as much as you like."

Leila investigated first with her hands, then with her mouth.

"Would you like to go upstairs, to bed?" he asked with a groan as she gave him unspeakable pleasure.

"I'm not sleepy." She stripped off her blouse and unsnapped her bra, freeing her full breasts. "Besides, we've made love there before."

"Is that what we're doing?" Her breasts were already in tune to his arousal. He took her hardened nipples between forefingers and thumbs and made her moan with pleasure. "Are we making *love*?" he asked, with emphasis on the last word.

In silent answer, she pulled herself away from him to strip off her shorts and bikini briefs. Then she lay back on the couch and stretched out her arms. Wynne straddled her waist and slowly trailed his erection down her belly before enveloping her more fully with his whole body. She was touching his arms and his chest, watching his every movement, her fascinating deep-set eyes telegraphing her desire. He found her mouth for a deep lingering kiss. If this wasn't love it was the most all-consuming emotion he'd ever experienced.

He explored her heavy breasts and narrow waist with eager hands. But another part of him was even more anxious to penetrate her innermost mysteries. When his questing fingers slipped below her waist to find her hidden warmth, Leila sighed in ecstacy and opened her thighs.

Wynne murmured, "Don't you think it's time our good parts got together for an anatomy lesson of their own?"

As he entered her, he thought Leila was the most desirable, sensual, passionate woman he'd ever been with. More important, she was the only woman he'd ever truly loved. He just hoped she was feeling the same sweet agony as he—one that went beyond physical desire.

"THIS IS ABSOLUTELY DECADENT," Leila was saying a satisfying half hour later.

She was sitting on the couch in bikini briefs and open blouse, her long bare legs curled to the side. She couldn't keep her eyes off Wynne, who sat close to her. He was naked as a jaybird, even though they'd turned on a lamp to shatter the descending darkness. But if he wasn't worried about the neighbors seeing him through his bay window, she certainly wasn't going to object. Her eyes were being nicely entertained.

"Decadent and delicious," Wynne agreed, taking another sample of the princess prawns, a spicy Szechuan dish. He indicated the coffee table covered with open cartons. "Too bad we let all this get cold."

Leila arched a brow. "Do you really mind?"

"Not a bit. I wouldn't have changed the order of things for all the tea in China."

"Tea! That's what's missing."

"Nothing is missing as far as I'm concerned. I have everything I want right here."

Leila flushed happily. He wasn't looking at the food, but at her.

"Have another pot sticker."

She picked one of the pan-fried dumplings from its box and held it out to him. He took a bite only after kissing the fingers that held it. She ate the remainder of the appetizer herself. She'd never felt so happy and lighthearted in her life.

Maybe it was because she'd finally shared some of her secret memories with someone she cared about. Wynne undoubtedly had been correct about her pushing people away so she wouldn't have to talk about her past. Could her estrangement with her parents be more her fault than theirs? A pang of guilt niggled at her as she ate a mouthful of black mushroom pork. The food reminded her that she hadn't told him everything. But she would, she promised herself, when the time was right.

"I had some good news this morning," Wynne told her.

"About your book?"

"About Vincent."

"He's going home?"

"To a halfway house that's supervised by a psychologist," Wynne told her. "It's actually a place that houses eight older teenagers who refuse to go home. They can stay for a limited time during which they're prepared for the outside world—finding work, getting an apartment, that kind of thing."

"Then his mother wouldn't take him back. How sad."

"Actually, she said she was willing to let him come home if he could prove he was willing to change. Vincent has promised to find a job and enroll in night school. His situation may work out yet."

"Thanks to you." She took a bite of garlic chicken and decided to make it her last before she got too full.

"Thanks to Vincent."

"He wouldn't have come around if you hadn't talked him into seeing the light," she argued.

"But I couldn't have talked him into anything he didn't really want to do in the first place."

Leila frowned at him and set down the cartons. "Will you stop trying to dodge the credit? Please take my compliment in the spirit in which it was intended."

Wynne's cheek dimpled as he grinned at her. "Okay. You win. I'm one terrific guy."

"You really are." Leila leaned toward him and smacked him on the cheek. "My terrific guy."

"Yours?"

"All mine. At least you'd better be," she threatened playfully.

"By what right do you stake this claim?"

"Love."

"Whose?"

"Mutual."

Wynne's grin widened. "That's the kind of talk I like."

Leila tilted her head coyly. "I thought you preferred a different kind, one infintely more personal."

Wynne's brows shot up in a display of interest. "That, too."

"Why don't we go upstairs and have a discussion, then?" Leila rose, purposely allowing the blouse to gape open. Wynne had made her sensuality blossom, and she was enjoying exploring it as she never had before.

Wynne lunged for her and drew her into his arms. Laughing, Leila pressed against the arousal her teasing had coaxed to life.

"I do love you, Leila."

Heart pounding, she knew it was time to admit what she'd been afraid to say to another man since her experience with Christian. "And I love you, Wynne."

Leila could deny it no longer—she was wild about the man. And this time, nothing could come between them to ruin her happiness.

CHAPTER THIRTEEN

LEILA AWOKE from a sensual dream only to realize she was experiencing the real thing. Wynne was tracing lazy patterns on her stomach while placing soft kisses at the edges of her mouth.

"Morning, Sleeping Beauty."

"Mmm." Leila yawned and stretched, her movement pushing the flesh of her hip into Wynne's hand. "I thought I was Little Red Riding Hood."

"That was when I was the Big Bad Wolf."

"You're doing a pretty good job of living up to your reputation."

"You think I'm bad, do you?"

"Marvelously so." Wondering why he was fully dressed, Leila wrapped her arms around his neck and initiated a kiss that heated her blood. But Wynne untangled himself and pulled back. "Leave this bed and I'll send the woodsman after you," she warned.

"Your threats pierce my heart," he said theatrically, placing his hand over the area in question, "but if I get back in that bed, you'll be late for work."

"Work?" Leila groaned. "I hardly slept all night."

"And whose fault was that?"

"Yours?"

"I think we get to share the blame on this one." He tugged at a strand of her hair and winked mischievously. "At any rate, I brought the rest of your clothes up here," he said, indicating the small pile at the end of the bed. "I already started the coffee, and I was just about to run out to a nearby bakery for fresh rolls. I should be back by the time you're out of the shower."

"I'd rather have *you* for breakfast."

"Compliments will get you everywhere." Wynne smacked her on the lips, then headed for the door. He gave her a lazy grin. "If you're not dressed by the time I return, you *will* be late for work."

"If you consider that a threat..."

Wynne laughed. "Get up, you insatiable woman."

He blew her a kiss and left the room. Leila could hear him singing jovially—if off-key—all the way out the front door. Yawning again, she forced herself out of bed and into the bathroom, where she made quick work of her shower. She combed out her hair and dressed in record time, even for her. Unable to find a blow-dryer, she French-braided her hair into a single plait. The only problem was that she didn't have anything to hold it together except her fingers. She looked around both the bathroom and the bedroom to no avail.

The office! Thinking Wynne would have rubber bands there, Leila entered the turreted room that reminded her of a castle. Smiling, she hummed an old song about fairy tales coming true if you're young at heart. At the moment, Leila felt as if she were a teenager—young, carefree and very much in love. If that wasn't a fairy tale...

How lucky could she be?

About to open the middle desk drawer, she spotted several printed pages lying next to the computer. She caught the two words on the top line: *Hot Bodies*. When he'd revealed the title of his book, she'd accused Wynne of being a pervert. Now she wondered just how hot his story was. The temptation to take a peek at a sample of his writing was irresistible. Letting go of her hair in trade for the pages, she made herself comfortable in his chair and began reading.

By the time she'd finished the scene, she was glad she was sitting down. She had to be imagining things, Leila told herself, willing her pulse to slow. This couldn't be what it seemed. Surely this wasn't *their* relationship she was reading about. Perhaps if she could locate another part of the manuscript...

Leila frantically searched the desk until she found a stack of pages held together with a large metal clip. It was an early chapter of the book. Removing the fastener with fingers that trembled, she read the first page. The heroine, Brenna, was working as a show girl in Las Vegas. She was arguing with her manager about going topless. If she would agree, the manager told her, she could make more money.

Leila couldn't read another word. Holding the pages in lifeless hands, she stared out of the window at a large maple tree in back. No wonder Wynne hadn't wanted to show her his manuscript. No wonder he'd never even told her about the gist of the story. She thought about their conversation of the night before—all the things she'd so painfully revealed. She could only be glad she hadn't told him everything, that she'd kept the information about her eating disorder to herself.

Wynne had known about Christian, so what was to say that he hadn't known more of the story than he'd let on? She hadn't been able to open up and give herself completely to Wynne; Brenna had been as evasive with James. She'd been a model who hadn't wanted to pose nude for a men's magazine; his heroine was a show girl who didn't like the idea of baring her breasts to audiences. The coincidences came too close for comfort. Perhaps Wynne had been trying to get a few extra sordid details out of her, Leila realized bitterly.

The thought made her sick to her stomach. She felt like throwing up. If she had had any food that morning, she just might be tempted...

"Leila?"

Startled by the unexpected sound of Wynne's voice, she swiveled the chair around to face him. He stood frozen in the doorway, the muscles of his bare legs tense, his hands planted firmly on the woodwork. He was staring at the sheaf of papers clenched in her hand. When he looked back up, his green eyes were wary.

"How could you?" she asked.

"How could I what?"

He was trying to sound convincingly candid, but there was an edge to his voice that Leila didn't trust. He knew, damn him! She'd made no mistake!

"Do this to me," she whispered.

She clutched the copy in one hand and flung it across the room toward the doorway. Wrinkled papers fell short of him and fluttered around Wynne's feet, but he didn't look down, didn't stop staring at her.

"You didn't even bother to disguise me," Leila went on, forcing her voice to remain steady. She didn't know how she could be so calm. She wanted to cry, to mourn her own stupidity, but she would not lose control—not in front of him. "The least you could have done was make Brenna a slender blonde with blue eyes."

"She's not you. Leila, I told you about Brenna when I first met you. Don't you remember? I said you reminded me of someone else."

He was sounding very reasonable, but Leila wouldn't allow herself to be fooled. She clutched at the arms of the chair, as if anchoring herself to something solid could stabilize her rapidly beating heart. "You didn't tell me she was a character in a book."

"Only because I was—and still am—feeling self-conscious about writing fiction."

"And you didn't tell me you were using me for research purposes."

"I've never used you," he said, not too convincingly. "When I saw you, I had to meet you. I felt as if a cardboard character had come to life before my eyes. You were flesh and blood, a multifaceted woman a man could love. I admit that's why I wanted to get to know you better and why I asked you to come to the zoo."

"You're admitting it—you did use me!"

"It wasn't like that!"

Even while he denied it, Wynne shifted uneasily in the doorway. She could sense his tension even at this distance. That might be an indication of how well she knew him, but Leila was afraid she didn't know the real Wynne Donegan at all.

"Tell me how it was, Wynne," she pleaded in a low voice. "Convince me you're any different than Christian."

"Damn it, Leila!"

"No! Damn you!" Leila stood so quickly the chair flew backward and bounced off the desk. "I can't believe I was stupid enough to let this happen to me twice."

"I'm not Christian. I love you."

"At the moment, you couldn't prove it by me."

Wynne stood fast in the doorway, blocking her exit. "Give me a chance to explain, would you?"

"Do I have a choice?" Leila crossed her arms over her chest. Maybe that way she could keep her body from trembling. "I don't think there's a thing you can say to change my mind, but give it your best shot."

"All fiction writers reshape their own realities to some extent. I didn't even realize how true that was until I really got into my revisions and began to flesh out my characters," Wynne insisted. "I already had a first draft of the manuscript, so the story itself was pat. What it lacked was heart and gut-level passion. Somehow my own uncertainties about our relationship got mixed up in James's emotional makeup. I didn't even know I was doing it until I read the revised pages. And as far as Brenna goes, I may have modeled her more loveable qualities after yours, but—"

"No 'buts.'" He had only confirmed her suspicions, and Leila wanted nothing more than to end the discussion and get out of his house. "You betrayed me and abused my trust, Wynne, plain and simple."

"It *isn't* that simple."

"It is to me." The back of her eyelids stung as she futilely tried to stare him down without bursting into tears. "All right. If you really love me and want to prove you weren't using me," Leila said, "then you'll agree to destroy the manuscript and computer disks of *Hot Bodies*."

"You can't be serious." Wynne's widened eyes and appalled tone conveyed his shook. "Do you know how much of my life—of *me*—is tied up in that book?''

''Don't you mean your ego? You can always write another book, Wynne.'' *But you won't always have me,* she added silently. Not if he intended to continue with this particular story.

''Leila, please...can you hold off passing judgment on me for a while longer? At least until I finish *Hot Bodies*? I'll be done with the revisions in a few weeks, and I'll be happy to let you read the whole manuscript. Then you'll be able to see I haven't abused your trust.''

He hadn't agreed, just as she'd feared he wouldn't. ''I've read enough, thank you. And I've heard enough, too. I won't be your guinea pig for one more minute.'' She stepped closer. ''Please let me pass.''

Leila faced him almost nose to nose. She didn't think he would move. His features were pulled into a mask of frustration, and she feared he would rage at her the way Christian had. Just when she was about to repeat her demand, Wynne stepped out of her way.

Sure that she'd picked the wrong man once more, Leila brushed past him, walked out of Wynne's house and out of his life.

She practically ran to Broadway, where she flagged a taxi. How could she have been so stupid? At least with Christian, she'd had youth as her excuse. But this time, she had age, experience and a far more developed intellect on her side. So how could she have let herself be taken in again?

That question rolled over and over in her mind on the way home. She allowed herself the luxury of a short cry, but her increasing anger seemed to burn the tears out of her, and she was dry-eyed and calm on the outside by the time the taxi pulled up in front of her building. Twice! She'd let herself be used by a man twice. She was still pondering the irony of the situation long after she'd entered her apartment.

While she was changing clothes, the telephone rang. The insistent shrill rattled her.

Wynne, no doubt.

She waited until the ringing stopped, then pulled the line from the phone.

Her nerves were jumping, her stomach doing a tumbling act. She was in no shape to go to work. First she had to calm down. Usually early, Leila decided that for once she would take the luxury of being late and to hell with anyone who dared object. She made herself a cup of herbal tea and a slice of plain toast. She had to force herself to get both down, but by the time she finished, she felt a bit better.

Who was to say that she would ever feel whole again?

Leila contemplated calling in sick, yet she abandoned that idea. Her mind needed to be occupied with work...with anything other than Wynne. She was more than an hour late, a first for her. She'd expected a few raised eyebrows from fellow employees or even a friendly warning from her boss. What Leila hadn't counted on was a wild-eyed Gail attacking her before she set one foot in her office.

"Thank goodness you finally showed up," Gail said breathlessly, stopping Leila from going farther by grabbing her arm.

"I don't believe it. The first time I'm more than a few minutes late and we have a crisis. Okay, Gail, what happened? Did Jocko booby-trap your office again?"

Even as she teased Gail, Leila realized something far more serious was going on.

"No, it's not Jocko. I have an important message for you." Her brows pulled together. "Did you know there's something wrong with your telephone?"

Leila immediately stiffened and shook her arm free. "I'm not the least bit interested in anything Wynne Donegan has to say to me."

Gail gave her an odd look. "Wynne didn't call. It was Mrs. Vanos, Grace's mother. Oh, Leila, I don't know how to tell you this...."

Something in Gail's manner got to Leila. Her pulse was already accelerating as she asked, "Has something happened to Grace?"

"I'm afraid so. Mrs. Vanos said to tell you she had that serious talk with her daughter last night." Gail appeared stricken as she blurted, "This morning Grace was gone. Both she and Mel have run away from home."

WYNNE SAT AT HIS DESK and stared at his monitor screen and the winking cursor that kept reminding him he was supposed to be writing. It was already half past noon and he hadn't revised more than a paragraph or two. Not only was he unable to work, he was unable to think about anything but Leila. If only he could make his mind a blank, or, as he could so easily do with a file on a computer disk, delete the scene that had taken place that morning.

But Leila's allegations haunted him. The truth was too complex for him to sort out easily, let alone explain to another person.

He hadn't used Leila, not in the way she'd accused him of doing. He wasn't anything like Christian. He loved her more than anyone or anything.

More than Hot Bodies? a voice in his head asked.

The two weren't comparable, Wynne silently argued, and Leila had been grossly unfair to demand he prove his love for her by destroying what was literally a part of him. Why couldn't she have waited to read the entire manuscript as he'd suggested, instead? Foolish question. Deep in his gut, he knew why. He'd thought they were making headway the night before when she'd finally opened up to him, yet even then, he'd known she was holding back.

She still didn't trust him—that was the crux of the matter. Nothing he could have said to her would have changed her mind about him.

And without trust, how could love survive?

LEILA CALLED MRS. VANOS and learned that Grace had left a terse note saying that she was leaving. The teenager had taken a shoulder bag of clothing and the money she'd been saving for a new stereo—maybe a hundred dollars or so. Her mother had contacted the Brickers hoping to convince Mel to tell her where Grace might be. Sandra Bricker had gone to her daughter's room to find that Mel, too, had left. Mrs. Bricker had insisted the girls were merely playing a prank to get attention and would be home by bedtime.

While Mel's mother seemed merely to be irritated, Mrs. Vanos was in near hysterics and blaming herself for being a poor mother, for not having seen what Grace was doing to lose weight and for not stopping it sooner. Leila tried to assure her that she might never have found out, but she wasn't certain she succeeded in comforting the poor woman. The attitude of the police didn't help. Policy dictated the girls hadn't been gone long enough to begin an official investigation. And Leila herself didn't have a clue where to search.

She spent the day jumping every time she heard a telephone or someone approached her in class or the hallway. But there was no word about the girls' whereabouts. When her office phone rang late that afternoon, she answered, hoping against hope that it would be good news.

"Leila, this is your father."

"Dad?" Her father never called her at work and rarely called her at home. Gripping the receiver hard, she sat up straighter. Her chest squeezed tightly. This couldn't be more bad news. Please, God. Enough was enough. "Is everything all right at home? Mom...?"

"Your mother's fine."

She collapsed back into her chair and let out a relieved, "Oh."

"I guess that says something about what a jackass an old man can be."

"What do you mean?"

"I call and you panic. I guess I don't call enough."

Leila knew he wasn't the only guilty one. "Maybe none of us does anymore." A lump settled square in the middle of her throat as she thought about the warm close relationship Wynne's family shared. Someone had to make the first move. "I love you, Dad."

Her father cleared his throat. Leila thought he was embarrassed by her admission, until he said, "Me, too, honey." Then he quickly changed the subject. "I saw the article about the club in *Glitter*. I wouldn't normally buy the magazine myself, but one of the neighbors gave it to your mother yesterday," he explained. "Why didn't you tell us you were going to be featured in it?"

"I didn't think you'd be interested."

"Of course I'd be interested. You're my daughter, aren't you?" he asked gruffly. "I like what I read about the club and your work. About you. You're a real caring and dedicated person, if I can believe this Donegan fellow. He showed me a whole different side of you that I've never seen."

"Maybe because I haven't put my best foot forward around you and Mom in a long time . . . but I'm going to change that," Leila promised.

The stress of the day was really getting to her. The backs of her eyelids stung like crazy, and she didn't think it would take much more to make her crack.

"And maybe you can teach an old dog new tricks," her father added. "Well, listen, I better not keep you from work, or you might get yourself fired. I wouldn't want that."

"Thanks for calling, Dad. It really meant a lot to me." She could hardly keep her voice from breaking. "And I promise you, we'll be seeing more of each other."

"Good. You know—your mother tells me she likes those Sunday brunches. And it wouldn't kill me to put on a suit for once—if you still want to go to that place you told me about, that is."

"I'd love to." Tears were already streaming down Leila's face. "We'll make plans soon, okay? I'll call you in a couple of days."

"Good. I'll tell your mother."

As she replaced the receiver in its cradle, Leila began to cry in earnest. She couldn't remember having a day that had been so emotionally draining. If only her father's call could make up for Grace and Mel's disappearance and Wynne's betrayal....

But had he betrayed her—or had she jumped to conclusions?

Wynne had asked her to read the entire manuscript before making up her mind about him. She'd basically done the same thing to Wynne that her father had done to her when she'd decided to stay in New York. She hadn't given Wynne the benefit of the doubt, because she hadn't been able to give him her complete trust.

But now, Leila wondered if she hadn't been wrong. It was difficult to think of someone who volunteered on a hot line for runaway kids as a user.

The more she went over the past couple of weeks with Wynne, the more afraid Leila was that she'd made the biggest mistake of her life.

CLUTCHING A LARGE BAG of burgers and fries to her breast, Grace scurried down Broadway, giving the people around her furtive looks. The low-income midnorth neighborhood called Uptown was creepy. The hotel she and Mel were staying in was even creepier. But their money wouldn't last long. They had to stay someplace cheap until they could find jobs. Then they could get a real apartment and live decently on their own.

Even as she assured herself that she and Mel could manage, Grace questioned her boldness. Who would give a fifteen-year-old a job that paid enough so she could support herself? Someone, she assured herself.

Someone had to! She couldn't go home. Her mother must have been disgusted at what Leila told her. Ashamed at the thought of disappointing the only person who'd ever really loved her, Grace knew her leaving had been for the best.

About to reenter the hotel, she found her way blocked by a sleazy older guy with greasy dark hair. He smiled, showing a gold front tooth.

"Hey, baby, where you goin' so fast?"

"To my room," she mumbled. Pulse picking up, she tucked her chin into her chest and tried to get past him.

He shifted his stance so she couldn't get by. "Why not take me with you? I ain't busy tonight."

Grace tried not to breathe. The guy smelled as if he hadn't had a bath in weeks. "No, thanks."

"Twenty bucks."

"What?" Her head flew up, and she realized he was taking inventory of her. Her skin crawled and she hated the feeling. Even more, she hated the way her chest was squeezed tight, the way her spine crawled with fear.

"Come on, baby, don't try to come on big-time. Not when you're staying at a flophouse like this one. Okay. Tell you what. I'll make it thirty. But I get something special for the extra ten."

"Keep your money! I'm not a hooker!"

The sleazeball laughed. "Well if you ain't now, baby, it's just a matter of time, ain't it? You change your mind, ask the desk clerk to put you in touch with Silva. I can get you all the work you can take."

Frightened, humiliated and close to tears, Grace pushed by him, but his laughter followed her into the filthy lobby and up the rickety stairs to the third-floor room. Her hand was trembling so, she could hardly get the key in the lock. She was ready to scream by the time she got the door open.

The room was almost dark. Mel lay on the lumpy double bed, her thin arms raised to her head. Her legs twitched and she whimpered softly.

"Mel, you okay?"

Grace locked the door behind her and set the bag on the single broken-down dresser. The thin girl's body gave a tremendous jerk. Mel sat up and hugged her knees. She began rocking back and forth.

"What's wrong?" Grace asked, suddenly more frightened than she'd been with the sleazeball.

"I—I don't know. I feel so weird. My muscles are jumping or something." Mel shifted to a new position on her hands and knees. "I was trying to take a nap, but I can't sleep. I can't even get comfortable."

Grace turned to the dresser. "Maybe you'll feel better if you..." Spying the biggest roach she'd ever seen scuttle over the food bag, she faintly said, "Eat."

"No! I told you I'm not eating until I'm so thin Luke will want me again." While Mel argued, she crawled around the bed on all fours like an animal. She moaned again, louder this time. "God, I wish this would stop."

Nervous, Grace gulped. "Mel, you're scaring me. We should do something."

"Like what?" Her expression stricken, the blonde stopped moving for a minute. "Go home? You've got to be kidding. I can't go back there. My parents don't want to deal with anything but their social lives."

"I meant get you to a doctor."

"A doctor would call my parents."

"Not if we give him fake names."

Mel shook her head stubbornly. "No way. He'd make me eat."

Grace knew better than to argue at the moment. "What, then?"

"I don't know, Gracie." Mel began to cry. Harsh sobs wracked her slender frame. "Help me, Gracie. Make this go away."

Grace rushed to the bed and put her arms around her friend. Mel was all skin and bones. No flesh. What there was to her seemed to be going into spasms.

"I'm here, Mel."

"You won't leave me alone, Gracie, will you?"

"No, Mel." She forced the words out past the lump in her throat. "I won't leave you."

As she hugged Mel, Grace was crying, too. Silently. This was her fault. It had been her idea to run away and, in spite of the fight they'd had the week before, Mel had stood by her, had refused to let her go alone. Now she had to be equally loyal. She couldn't let her friend down by going against Mel's wishes and calling her parents.

But there was a small scared voice inside her asking what she was going to do if something happened to Mel that she couldn't handle.

CHAPTER FOURTEEN

WITH TREPIDATION making her heart beat double-time, Leila approached the now familiar house in Andersonville. The doubts, argument and subsequent rift of the day before came back to haunt her, making her slow down as she climbed the stairs. She hugged her shoulder bag to her chest. She wasn't here to make up with Wynne, she reminded herself, no matter how attractive that prospect might be. She'd swallowed her pride for the girls' sake, not for her own.

Reaching the porch landing, Leila stood and stared at the doorbell for a moment. The damn thing wouldn't bite her, for heaven's sake...but Wynne might. Even as she thought it, Leila's rational side took over and denied the idea. She rang the bell.

A minute later, Wynne answered the door. His feet were bare, as was his chest. An old pair of ratty-looking shorts hung low on his hips making her think he'd just jumped out of bed and pulled them on. That impression was furthered when she raised her gaze to the unruly hair covering his forehead. He masked his surprise with a wary expression.

"Leila. What are you doing here? Shouldn't you be at work?"

She tried not to feel anything about his neutral tone, but it hurt nonetheless. "Sorry if I've disturbed you, but I have to talk to you."

He stepped back. "Come in. I didn't mean to be rude."

Wynne might have been talking to a delivery person or a meter reader, Leila thought ruefully. Then again, what had she expected? She entered but didn't move out of the entryway while he latched the door. His close proximity flustered her, almost made her forget her reason for being there. When he turned, Wynne's expression was expectant, hopeful.

"I don't know how to say this," Leila began, "except . . . I need your help."

Something akin to disappointment washed over his features, but he quickly hid the reaction with an expression as neutral as his voice. "How?"

"Grace and Mel have run away, and I thought with your contacts—"

"When?"

"The night before last. Grace's mother is frantic." Leila clung to the strap of her shoulder bag as if it were a lifeline. But Wynne was the anchor, the one who could help. "Mel's parents are finally admitting this might be something more than a prank or a statement the girls are trying to make."

"Come into the kitchen. You can tell me the whole story over a cup of coffee."

Leila followed him through the house, feeling both part of the old place she had helped patch up, and yet a stranger. She had done that to herself—alienating Wynne just as she'd managed to separate herself from her parents.

At least she was learning.

Once in the kitchen, she sat at the table and worried the smooth old wood with nervous fingers. His back to her, Wynne moved around the room, preparing the fresh pot of coffee, gathering mugs, filling them, pulling the milk carton from the refrigerator and taking the sugar bowl from a shelf. His actions seemed to be played in slow motion, torturing her, making her agonize about what might have been.

How she wished yesterday had never happened.

And how did he feel? Was Wynne thinking the same things? Was he ruminating on how unfair she'd been to him? He didn't say anything until he sat across from her, mug in hand, his words far from personal.

"So, what's the story with the girls?"

Leila told herself to be grateful he was speaking to her at all. "You remember how disturbed I was by the way Grace was acting, don't you?" When Wynne nodded, she explained, "I finally figured out the problem. She's bulimic."

"You mean she eats and throws up?"

"That's putting it simply, but yes, she does that." Leila took a sip of coffee and set down the mug, wrapping both hands around the warm ceramic. "And so does Mel, who probably taught Grace. The night of the party, I caught Grace throwing up in the ladies' room."

Wynne gave her a searching look. "One of the reasons you were acting so out of character that night— other than Manley's presence, that is."

"The two reasons were pretty much inseparable."

Leila spoke more to herself than to Wynne. After all, she'd become bulimic to please Christian the ambitious photographer. But she wasn't prepared to discuss that with a man who was acting so reserved with her, albeit for a justifiable reason. She should have given Wynne the benefit of the doubt. Hindsight didn't help.

"I tried reasoning with both girls," she went on, trying to keep her mind on the right track. "They wouldn't listen to me, so I had to warn their parents. Mrs. Vanos had a talk with Grace the other night. It was enough to make Grace run, just as she threatened to do. Mel left probably out of misguided loyalty to her friend, because Mrs. Bricker said she never even mentioned our conversation to her daughter."

"I'm sorry."

"So am I. I feel as if it's my fault—"

Wynne placed his hands around hers. "You can't blame yourself."

"I can and I do." His comforting gesture brought a lump to her throat. "I wasn't paying attention. It was my job, but I let it happen."

"Your job is to help people get fit and healthy, not to play watchdog."

"I'm not talking about a job description, Wynne, but a moral obligation. I should have seen the signs."

She pulled her hands from his and put them to her forehead. She tangled her fingers tightly in her hair. It was all she could do to keep from crying again. She felt as if a water tap had been connected to her eyes. A mere word or thought could turn it on.

"Oh, Lord, where could they be?" she whispered.

"Do they have any money?"

Leila took a deep breath for control and lowered her hands. "A couple of hundred dollars between them."

"Then they're not in the streets..."

She took a deep breath of relief.

"Yet," he finished.

Leila slammed her fist against the table, making the mugs jump and slosh coffee over its surface. "I'll never forgive myself if anything happens to those girls."

Wynne reached for a napkin and mopped up the spilled liquid. He kept eye contact with her, and his was the voice of reason when he said, "Hopefully, we'll find them before anything bad does happen."

"Then you'll help?"

"You wouldn't be here if you didn't believe I would."

Leila nodded. She'd known he would help her, just as she should have known he would never use her intentionally. He'd said it wasn't that simple. Love was never simple. She believed him now, when it seemed to be too late. She wanted to apologize, to give him the gift of these words, but they stuck in her throat. It wasn't merely that she didn't know how, but that her confession would be wasting time. Precious time to two lost girls who needed to know someone cared about them.

"I can get on the telephone right away," he said. "Alert the hot line and some local shelters."

"Thanks. I'll help in any way I can. Do you need me?"

Wynne stared at her long and hard. Leila's pulse began to race.

"Not for this," he finally said. "I can take care of it. Why don't you go on to work. I'll call you there if I hear anything encouraging."

Heart dropping to her toes, Leila rose and gathered her shoulder bag. For a moment, she thought he might admit he did need her. Incredibly sad that no such confession was forthcoming, she was about to leave for The Total You when she changed her mind.

"Look, at a time like this, we have to put aside personal differences and work together."

Wynne gave her a searching look before agreeing. "All right, but I only have one telephone here anyway. You'll still have to go back to the club or to your apartment to make some calls. Maybe you can reach their parents and their schools, find out the names and phone numbers of friends. It is possible that they could have gone to stay with someone or that they told someone where they would be."

Leila nodded. "I'll call if I get anything that could remotely help."

Then she left for the club, where she was frustrated by dozens of useless telephone calls and a day-long wait that turned out to be fruitless all around.

THE TELEPHONE SHRILLED, waking Leila from a restless sleep. She blinked into the darkness. The illuminated numbers of her digital clock glowed 2:45 a.m. Maybe Wynne had found out something positive. Lifting the receiver in midring, she expected to hear his familiar voice rather than one so young and frightened.

"L-Leila?"

She shot straight up in bed. "Grace?"

The sobbing teenager wasn't exactly coherent. "I d-didn't know wh-who...to call."

"You did the right thing, Grace. I've been so worried about you and Mel." Switching on the bedside lamp, Leila blinked against the sudden brightness. "Are you all right?"

"N-no!" The teenager sobbed harder. "I-I'm fine . . . but M-Mel . . ."

"What about Mel? What happened to her?"

"I couldn't m-make her wake up!"

Leila was already climbing out of bed. "Where are you, Grace?" she asked, taking the phone with her toward the dresser, where she began pulling out clothes.

"C-Cook County Hospital emergency room." Grace sucked in a jagged breath. "They won't let me see her. No one will t-tell me anything."

"I'll be there as soon as I can."

"P-please, hurry!"

"I will, Grace. Hold on. I'll help you."

But first she would alert Mrs. Vanos and the Brickers. And Wynne, Leila amended. Having put out the word to his sources, he deserved to know, as well.

Leila dressed as she made the calls. Mrs. Vanos wept with relief and thanked Leila profusely. His tone irritable, Mr. Bricker warned her that the press had better not get hold of the information. That his priority was not his daughter's condition angered her; she held on to her temper with difficulty. Wynne offered to drive her to the hospital, but she decided not to wait. A taxi would be quicker. He promised to meet her in the emergency waiting room as soon as possible.

The night was hot, the kind that made tempers flare. In addition to normal emergencies, there were sure to be victims of muggings and gang-war violence at Cook County, the hospital where the indigent of the city turned for free medical care. A sheltered girl like Grace had to be terrified in such a setting.

A taxi took Leila to the hospital in a matter of minutes, and she ran into the emergency waiting room. It seemed ready to burst at the seams. Her gaze skipped over the poverty-stricken patients, relatives and friends. A man sat in a wheelchair, his left leg straight and bound in place. An old man was trying to comfort his female companion, whose withered face looked as if it had been used as a punching bag. A youth held a pressure pack to a bleeding wound.

Huddled in a corner, her tear-streaked face pinched and white against the dark curls that lay plastered around it, Grace sat alone. She appeared so lost, so forlorn, until she saw Leila. Her expression immediately transformed to one of relief and hope, Grace bounded out of her chair and pushed past a rough-looking youth who yelled a string of curses after her. Grace ignored him and flew into Leila's arms.

"I'm so glad you came."

Leila hugged the girl and stroked the head pressed to her shoulder. "I'm glad you called me. Your mother will be here soon. And Mel's parents."

Grace tried to push away from her, but Leila wouldn't let go completely. She wasn't taking the chance that the teenager might run out into the street.

"How could you call them?" Grace cried, her expression stricken.

"I had to. You know I had to call them, Grace."

The girl dropped her gaze. "My mother must be so disgusted with me."

"No, she's not. She's worried." Leila lifted Grace's chin so the girl would have to look at her directly. "Your mother has been miserable and feeling guilty since you left. She was terrified that something would happen to you. You and your sister are all she has, you know."

Grace relaxed and Leila could tell she wanted to believe that. Obviously, the frightened teenager was anxious to go home. Certain that Grace wouldn't bolt out the door, Leila let go of her.

"Really? Mom doesn't hate me?"

"Your mother loves you very much, Grace," Leila said above the wail of an approaching ambulance. "Remember that before you do anything so foolish again."

"I will. But what about Mel? She doesn't think her parents care about her at all."

Leila wondered herself, but she tried to keep Grace's spirits up. "Maybe if we combine forces, we can get Mel to stop binging and—"

"No, she's not doing that anymore!" Grace interrupted. "Oh, Leila, Mel's been eating hardly anything, and she's been throwing that up."

"What?"

"There was this boy who broke up with her because of her food obsession. Mel was determined to get him back. I don't think he meant he wanted her to lose more weight, but she wouldn't listen to me."

"When did she stop eating?"

"Almost two weeks ago. I threatened to tell her mother. That's why she wouldn't talk to me."

Leila was thoughtful. Could Mel be developing an even more serious eating disorder, anorexia nervosa? If so...

"Mel could die," Grace said in a small voice, completing Leila's thought. "I don't want to be next."

Leila put an arm around the girl's shoulders and squeezed. "You won't be. I'll give you all the help and support you need. I promise. And, hopefully, Mel will come out of this all right, too."

With the new complications, Leila didn't know if she believed what she was saying, but she had to give Grace some hope for her friend.

Mrs. Vanos was the next person to come through the door into the waiting room. Grace tensed, but she faced her mother, and when Mrs. Vanos held out her arms, the girl sobbed and ran to her. Leila left mother and daughter alone. She approached the desk and asked the clerk on duty if there was someone who could tell her about Melanie Bricker's condition.

A few minutes later, Dr. Chavez came out of the emergency room to speak with her. Leila had no more than introduced herself before the Brickers arrived. The wealthy couple rushed through the crowded waiting room, ignoring everyone—even Leila—as they focused on the doctor.

"I'm Sandra Bricker, and this is my husband, John," she said, asserting herself as the spokesperson of the couple. "Where have you taken our daughter?"

Dr. Chavez raised his eyebrows. "Melanie is still in the emergency room, Mrs. Bricker. We're just about to transfer her to a ward."

"A ward!" the woman echoed, her tone horrified. "Don't be ridiculous. Melanie is not staying in a horrible place like this. She's coming home with us."

"That wouldn't be advisable," Dr. Chavez said. "Especially since we have her hooked up to an IV."

"An IV! What have you done to my little girl?" Mr. Bricker demanded to know.

"I've been trying to save her life." The doctor glared at the couple whose elegant clothes set them apart from everyone else in the room. "Right now we're pumping minerals into her, treating her for a nutrient deficiency. She has both potassium and electrolyte imbalances and arrhythmia—that means she has an irregular heartbeat. I'm afraid your daughter is in pretty serious shape."

Sandra Bricker clung to her husband's arm. "Oh, John, she must have some horrible disease."

Studying the woman's carefully made-up face and perfectly coiffed hair, realizing Mrs. Bricker had taken the time to perfect her appearance before coming to the hospital, Leila couldn't remain silent any longer.

She spoke to Dr. Chavez. "Melanie is bulimic, perhaps even anorexic."

"An eating disorder. That makes sense," the doctor said. "The signs are all there."

Mrs. Bricker gave Leila a furious glare. "There you go with that ridiculous nonsense again! How dare you lie to this man. I told you my daughter isn't some mental—"

Dr. Chavez interrupted her tirade. "Miss Forester here may be correct. In addition to the more serious problems I mentioned, your daughter's salivary glands are infected, and her gums are receding, both obvious symptoms of the disease caused by frequent purging."

"John, we can't let some poorly paid quack libel our daughter. Do something."

"I suggest you wait until morning," the doctor said coldly. "Your daughter is in no condition to be moved now. Tomorrow you can arrange for an ambulance and have her taken to the hospital of your choice, one where the quacks are better paid." He nodded to Leila. "Miss Forester."

With that, the doctor stalked off, disappearing into the emergency room.

"You!" Sandra Bricker shouted at Leila. "This is *your* fault."

Still holding on to her daughter, Mrs. Vanos stepped forward. "It's no such thing. Leila is the only one who noticed what was going on with *our* daughters. Put the blame where it belongs—on us."

WYNNE BROKE THE SPEED RECORDS getting to Cook County Hospital. He wanted to be there for Leila, to give her his support. If Mel didn't make it, Leila would go on blaming herself as she had that morning.

How he'd wanted to take her in his arms then and soothe her conscience, but he hadn't dared. It had been enough that she'd come to him for help. That revealed a giving of trust she herself probably hadn't analyzed. He would have to wait for the rest. But for how long?

The words echoed through his head as he parked the car and ran for the emergency-room doors. He spotted Leila immediately. She was surrounded by Grace and her mother and a couple who he assumed were Mel's parents. While Grace merely looked frightened, all four adults were tensed and apparently in the midst of an argument.

"How dare you blame us!" Mrs. Bricker was saying to Mrs. Vanos as Wynne approached. "Speak for yourself, but don't put words in my mouth!"

"Go ahead, keep hiding your head in the sand," Grace's mother replied. "You might not have a daughter who will upset your carefully planned life for very long."

"We'll take Melanie to our own doctor," Mr. Bricker stated. "He's one of the best in the city. He'll figure out what's really wrong with her."

Wynne stopped next to Leila. While she gave him a look that expressed her relief at seeing him, she addressed herself to the Brickers.

"What is the matter with you both?" she demanded. "Why can't you believe me?"

"Are you some kind of expert on eating disorders?" Mrs. Bricker asked.

Wynne thought her tone held a crow of triumph. Beside him, Leila tensed. He surreptitiously slid his hand to the middle of her back, the gesture intended to give her his support. She took a deep breath, and Wynne could feel her body's slight tremor under his palm.

"As a matter of fact, I am," Leila admitted. "I can't pinpoint exactly when Mel got desperate enough to go beyond safe dieting and exercise, but I can tell you what it was like for her once she let her desire for perfection get out of hand. She probably started by sneaking extra food once in a while—sweets, mostly, because sugar gives a dieter a rush. Then she would feel guilty because she was supposed to be losing weight. Somewhere she got the idea that she could get rid of the extra calories by going in the bathroom and sticking her fingers down her throat."

Mrs. Bricker made a choked sound and clutched at her husband's jacket sleeve. "Please, leave the disgusting details for someone who will believe this pap."

"What's disgusting," Leila responded, "is your continuing refusal to face up to your daughter's problem, one you probably helped create."

"How dare you!"

"I dare because of Mel, Mrs. Bricker. Because I can't stand the thought of what she's doing to herself. Unless you intervene and get her professional help, no matter how much weight she loses, she will never be satisfied because she will never be perfect. I wonder who gave her the idea that she could be.''

''There's nothing wrong with being the best.''

''There is if you're holding out your love to your daughter like some kind of a damn prize! Striving for an impossible goal is killing Melanie. Binging and purging has been a way of life for her for a long time. Now she's refusing to eat. She's lying in the next room hooked up to an intravenous feed, and still you refuse to admit that she needs help. Think about it, Mrs. Bricker. How many times did Melanie leave the table to head for the bathroom right after eating a large meal? When she came back out, was her face swollen, her eye makeup a mess?''

Wynne saw Leila's point hit home in John Bricker's expression. Guilt was etched on his features. Still, his wife wasn't ready to concede the argument.

''How do you know so much about this disgusting habit?'' Sandra Bricker demanded. ''You're an exercise instructor, not a physician.''

Again, Wynne felt Leila's tremor. He slipped his hand around her arm and squeezed. He could feel her pulse racing, could sense the effort it took her to explain.

''I know...because I've been there, Mrs. Bricker. I spent a year of my life doing exactly what your daughter does. I'm a recovered bulimic. I'm one of the lucky ones. But don't fool yourself—not everyone with an eating disorder recovers. Some don't live long enough. I was in a support group for three months. Betty had been anorexic for three years or so. One day she didn't show to a meeting. She couldn't. Nineteen years old and she was in a mortuary. Would you like me to describe the details of the wake? The funeral?''

Mrs. Bricker looked as if she were ready to faint. She leaned into her husband. ''John, make this woman stop telling us these awful things. Tell her they have nothing to do with our Melanie.''

''Leila isn't making up lies about Mel,'' Grace finally said. ''Mel's the one who taught me how to lose weight the easy way. Only it isn't easy, at all.''

''John...''

''Maybe we'd better discuss this later, at home.''

''No! There's nothing to discuss.''

Ignoring his wife for the moment, John Bricker spoke directly to Leila. ''Thank you for opening *my* eyes, at least.'' He pulled his wife toward the clerk. ''Let's find out what we have to do to get Melanie transferred to another hospital tomorrow. Then maybe we can see our daughter for a few minutes before we leave.''

Leila took a long shuddering gulp of air as she watched them walk away.

''Now what?'' Wynne asked.

''Now I guess we go home.''

''I don't know how to thank you,'' Mrs. Vanos said.

''You can thank me by praying for Mel. She's going to need all the help she can get.''

''Leila, I'm sorry about giving you a hard time when you were trying to help,'' Grace said from her mother's side.

''Why don't we talk about it tomorrow at the club,'' Leila suggested. ''Maybe I can convince you to take what you're learning in that nutrition class seriously.''

''Deal.''

Mrs. Vanos started to lead Grace away, but the girl pulled back long enough to add, "You know, for an adult, you're okay."

"Coming from a teenager, I guess that's a pretty big compliment," Leila murmured, her dark eyes following mother and daughter as they left hand in hand.

"I would say so," Wynne agreed. "Listen, I don't think there's much else you can do here tonight. Why not let me drive you home?"

"Thanks. I would appreciate that."

Wynne led Leila out to the parking lot. Her steps were deliberate but slow, indicating an exhaustion that probably went beyond the physical. He waited until they were in the car and driving away from the hospital before he looked over at the passenger seat. Leila's head was thrown back, her eyes closed. She might have been asleep.

Only he knew she wasn't. She was waiting for him to say something. Anything. He might as well oblige her.

Eyes on the road, Wynne said, "I sensed you were holding something back when you told me about Manley the other night. And yesterday morning when you were talking about catching Grace in the ladies' room, you made a comment about the two problems being inseparable."

Leila shifted position and sat up straight. A quick glance told him she was looking out the window.

"It's one of those things that isn't as simple as it sounds," she said with a deep sigh.

"Why not try me?"

For a moment he didn't think she would, but it seemed she was only gathering the right words.

"When I was able to put things in perspective, I realized how truly humiliating my life had become. I was doing everything in my power to hang on to Christian—even to the point of endangering my health—and all for a man who didn't deserve one tenth of what I gave him. Christian never truly cared for me. I was merely a valuable commodity. A human stock option."

"That would be difficult to talk about."

"I talked, but only to my therapist and the members of my support group. You were right when you said I should have told the people I cared about. I had myself fooled. I thought I was recovered, that the nightmare was over, but it wasn't, not while I kept secrets buried inside myself. I was so ashamed of what I'd done that I found it easier to push away anyone who came too close than to talk about the past."

"That makes your telling the Brickers what you did doubly courageous."

"Being in the waiting room, wondering if Mel would make it, made me realize keeping my deep dark secret was the most ludicrous thing in the world. What's a little soul-baring compared to saving another life? But that Mrs. Bricker is something else again. I only hope telling her what I did wasn't for nothing."

"Mrs. Bricker might want to keep her head buried in the sand, but her husband got the point. I think he'll see to it that Mel gets help."

"I hope you're right, that it's not too late."

Wynne heard a wistfulness in her words that made him think she wasn't just talking about Melanie. If she wanted *him* back in her life, why couldn't she just say so?

And why couldn't he ask?

Fear of rejection was a powerful emotion, Wynne suddenly realized. More powerful than love.

LEILA WAITED FOR WYNNE to say something personal to her, but he remained silent as they approached her building. When he pulled over to the curb, he acted as if he intended to get out and open her door.

"I can take it from here," Leila told him.

He didn't bother arguing.

Disappointed, she lifted the handle and opened the door. Before swinging her legs out and setting her feet on the pavement, however, she turned to him. She couldn't help wondering if this might not be the last chance she had to patch things up between them. But something held her back.

"Wynne, I want you to know how grateful I am."

"I didn't do anything."

"You were there when we needed you. Thanks...for everything."

Even to her own ears that sounded like a goodbye. Was it? Wynne didn't say anything to stop her from sliding out of the car. Either she had wounded him too deeply, or he just didn't love her the same way she loved him.

Whatever the reason, she came out the loser.

CHAPTER FIFTEEN

THE NEXT FEW WEEKS dragged for Leila. Other than having brunch with her parents, she had no interest in seeking out social activities. She tried to throw herself into her work, but some of her natural enthusiasm was lacking, and she couldn't seem to rally.

"You barely touched your lunch," Gail commented as they left Health Nuts to report for afternoon duties. "Are you sick or what?"

"Or what, I guess."

"You have a case of Wynne on the brain."

"More like the heart."

"So what are you going to do about it?"

"Nothing."

"You're not going to tell him you love him and miss him and want him back in your life?"

"Not unless he shows up on my doorstep." That he hadn't called once was a sure sign of his disinterest.

"You don't have a doorstep. You live in a high rise."

"Gail!"

"Leila! Honestly, you're too stubborn for your own good."

"Maybe."

"What are you afraid of?"

"Now you're starting to sound like Wynne. Does he give lessons?"

"Ask him."

They were still arguing good-naturedly when Leila spotted Grace hanging around outside her office. The teenager seemed to be waiting for her.

"I'll let you alone for now," Gail said. "But only because I've got an appointment in the lab in five minutes. You and I haven't finished this discussion."

"Catch you later."

Leila shook her head as the other woman veered off toward the cardiac rehabilitation lab. Gail was like a bulldog once she got hold of an idea. Leila would deal with her later, but right now she was anxious to talk to Grace.

"Hi, Leila. I was waiting for you."

"Hi, yourself." Leila raised her eyebrows. "Why haven't I seen you around the past couple of days?"

"Don't get all worried. I'm not trying to avoid this place or anything. I figured that with Mel home from the hospital and all, I should spend some time with her."

"Sounds reasonable. I'd like to hear all about it. Come on into my office."

Grace complied and made herself comfortable. Leila noticed some subtle changes about the teenager. She had a new stylish haircut and her workout clothes were jazzier than any she'd worn since she joined The Total You. And while her makeup was subtle and quite appropriate for a fifteen-year-old, it looked as if it had been applied by an expert hand. Leila had suggested Mrs. Vanos help Grace make some exterior changes while she was losing weight to give her self-confidence and make her feel good about herself. Obviously, Grace's mother had taken the advice.

Leila leaned back against the edge of her desk. "So, how is Mel doing?"

"She looks and feels better." Grace's forehead pulled into a frown. "But I'm not sure that she ever really will be better the way you mean. She has to want to be normal again first."

"We have to keep hoping that she will."

"That's what I told myself. Mel was so frightened in that terrible hotel room—and then again when she woke up in a hospital bed. I thought she would have learned her lesson from that scare, but not her. Instead, she has this crazy idea that whenever she gets really down she can just go to the hospital and get an IV for a nutrient pickup."

Leila's spirits sank. That was not what she'd been hoping to hear. "Is she seeing a therapist?"

"Her dad's going to make her go to some famous psychiatrist twice a week, but Mel told me she'll lie to the guy. So what good will it do?"

"A professional is trained to get past the lies, Grace. If only you could convince Mel to go to your support group with you. She might be able to open up to other young women with eating disorders."

"She says she won't, but I'm not giving up on her. I'm going to stand by her no matter what."

"No one could ask for a better friend."

"Listen, I'd better get going." Grace rose. "I told my mother I would have dinner waiting for her when she comes home tonight. I'm making grilled fish kabobs with fresh vegetables and rice."

"My mouth is already watering, and I just ate lunch."

Grace grinned. "I learned how to make that in the low-calorie cooking class you suggested I take. Dieting doesn't have to be boring."

"Your mother is lucky to have such a smart and terrific daughter. It sounds like you've got yourself together and are doing great. I'm so pleased."

"I did throw up once since that night in the hospital," Grace admitted.

"Once in two weeks is better than every day," Leila said encouragingly. "It took me a long time to stop completely. If I was under too much stress, I would overeat and then feel guilty. But eventually I learned to deal with my problems in other ways. Like exercising."

"I did it after I realized I gained five pounds from eating the way I'm supposed to. But I'm positive I'll lose the weight again. It'll be slower going, but I have half the summer left before school starts to reach my goal. And if I don't make it by then, I'll do it before Thanksgiving, for sure."

"I know you're going to succeed, Grace." Leila was glad the girl finally had developed some confidence in herself. "And if you ever need moral support, I'll be here for you."

"Thanks." Grace threw her arms around Leila's neck and gave her a warm hug. "Believe me, Leila, it helps having someone on my side who really knows what it's like."

Leila was thoughtful after the teenager left her office. While she'd devoted her professional life to guiding clients toward safe dieting and exercise, helping other young woman actually overcome eating disorders had never occurred to her before—undoubtedly because she'd been trying to ignore her past.

The more she thought about doing something positive, the more appealing the idea became. Heaven knew she could find time to spare for a good cause. Why not volunteer to work with an eating disorder clinic a few hours a week? If she could get through to just one person, she would consider that payment enough for sharing her story. Now that she'd brought the past out in the open, she had nothing to lose and everything to gain. It was an agreeable way of neutralizing the bitter memories and feelings.

Deciding to call one of the Chicago-area centers in the morning, Leila finished the afternoon's work in better spirits than she'd been in for weeks. The feeling stayed with her as she took the elevator down to the ground level. Before she could proceed to her apartment, the security guard stopped her.

"Miss Forester, I have a package here for you." The gray-haired man reached under the desk and pulled it out for her.

Taking it from him, Leila murmured, "I didn't order anything. I wonder what this could be."

"Don't know. The gentleman just said to be sure you got it in person."

"Gentleman?"

"Yeah, the guy with the mustache who used to leave his car parked out front."

Wynne. Excitement pulsed through her as she took the package and thanked the guard.

In the elevator, she opened the envelope attached to the outside of the package and read the enclosed note.

Dear Leila,
Sorry it has taken me so long to finish this, but

now it's yours. Do what you think is right. Only know I didn't mean to hurt you.

Love,
Wynne

The manuscript of *Hot Bodies*!

The package seemed to burn her hands before she got into her apartment and set it down on the coffee table. Leila slipped into a velour robe, fixed herself something to eat . . . anything to avoid the manuscript for the time being.

Finally, she could avoid it no longer. Even having admitted she'd been wrong about Wynne—to herself, if not to him—Leila opened the package with fear.

Her eyes widened when she saw the dedication. "To Leila. My heart is in your hands."

Her own heart thundering, she began to read.

Brenna's story began when she was seventeen, on the day her widowed mother remarried. Her stepfather barely waited for the ceremony to be over before he trapped Brenna and made sexual advances to her. When she tried to tell her mother, the older woman accused her daughter of lying, of trying to spoil her happiness. By the end of chapter 1, Brenna was in the streets. A runaway.

As she read further, Leila became absorbed in the plight of the heroine, who learned to survive by using her looks, if not her body, and consequently learned to distrust men, as well. A cross-country flight led her to Las Vegas and the scene Leila had read in Wynne's office.

That brought back disturbing memories of her argument with Wynne. Upset anew—this time at herself—Leila had to take a break. Leaving the manuscript sitting on the coffee table, she showered. That brought back poignant memories of the first time they made love.

She went back to *Hot Bodies* and once more got caught up in Brenna's life: her decision to go to school during the day while working in a Vegas show at night; her graduating and becoming a counselor for runaway kids; her distrust in men finally fading because of James.

Indeed, she found many similarities between herself and the heroine, but that no longer bothered her. Wynne's moving story was anything but exploitative, and he'd obviously based much of the story on his experience with runaway kids. As he had tried to tell her, it wasn't that simple.

Leila put the manuscript down only after reading the last page, where Brenna agreed to marry James. If only her own life could have such a happy ending. Right now she was feeling like Cinderella after the ball—an emotional scullery maid. Leila snorted at the analogy and wondered what Wynne would think of her creative metaphor.

Maybe she should ask him. After all, she was always telling her clients they were responsible for keeping themselves physically fit. She should apply that philosophy to herself in this case, because it was equally important to be emotionally healthy. It was time she took responsibility for her own happiness.

It was almost four in the morning, but Leila didn't let that daunt her. She got dressed, packed up the manuscript and called a taxi service. Within minutes she was on her way to Wynne's place.

Silently rehearsing what she was going to say when she got there, Leila grew more and more nervous as the taxi approached the Andersonville area. She wasn't ready. The driver stopped his vehicle in front of Wynne's darkened home. Panic almost made her ask the man to turn the cab around and take her back where she belonged.

But she didn't belong in the high rise alone. She belonged in a house filled with promise, one that might need to be patched and painted but would always be filled with love and warmth. Her life might not have been a fairy tale, but she deserved a happy ending.

She paid the driver and waved him off, then, facing the dark house, wondered what she would do if Wynne wasn't home. She hadn't thought of that. There was always the bench in the garden, she told herself. She could wait for him there. How ridiculous. She was already solving problems before she knew they existed. There was only one way to find out if Wynne was home.

Leila stalked up his steps and leaned on his doorbell. Literally. The quiet shattered, the house came to life. She could tell a light went on upstairs. And then she heard a male voice cursing. Smiling, Leila released the bell and waited. With fingers curled tightly around its edges, she hugged the manuscript to her chest.

Her pulse was racing far beyond the safe zone by the time the porch light went on and the front door opened. Wynne stood there looking as he had the morning she'd come to him for the girls' sake. Bare feet, bare chest, unruly hair and rumpled shorts. He was a mess . . . but a feast for her eyes.

"Who ran away from home this time?" he asked.

"I did." Leila took a deep breath. "I came to tell you I was wrong and I knew it and I was too stubborn to admit it. I'm sorry."

His cheek dimpled even as he grumbled, "Well, it certainly took you long enough."

"I may be a slow learner. But once I get something, I get it right. I should have apologized weeks ago, but I was afraid I had hurt you too badly and that you wouldn't want me anymore."

"Oh, I still want you, but only if I can have all of you this time."

"Then it's not too late?"

"Do you believe I love you?"

"All hundred thousand words' worth." Leila looked down at the manuscript and loosened her death grip. She held it out toward him. "Got any stamps? I think we should mail this to your agent immediately."

Wynne took the package from her and set it down inside the doorway. "That can wait until morning. I can't." When he pulled her into his arms, he murmured, "So fairy tales *can* come true."

"If you're young at heart," Leila added with a surge of happiness. "Say, you don't perchance have any extra happy endings around here?"

"If I can't find one, I'll write one," Wynne assured her, and concluded the first chapter of their lives with a kiss.

Author's Note

If someone you know or love has an eating disorder, you aren't alone. For information and help, contact:

ANAD
National Association of Anorexia Nervosa and
Associated Disorders
Box 7
Highland Park, IL 60035
(312) 831-3438

Harlequin Superromance

CALLOWAY CORNERS

Created by four outstanding Superromance authors, bonded by lifelong friendship and a love of their home state: Sandra Canfield, Tracy Hughes, Katherine Burton and Penny Richards.

CALLOWAY CORNERS

Home of four sisters as different as the seasons, as elusive as the elements; an undiscovered part of Louisiana where time stands still and passion lasts forever.

CALLOWAY CORNERS

Birthplace of the unforgettable Calloway women: *Mariah*, free as the wind, and untamed until she meets the preacher who claims her, body and soul; *Jo*, the fiery, feisty defender of lost causes who loses her heart to a rock and roll man; *Tess*, gentle as a placid lake but tormented by her longing for the town's bad boy and *Eden*, the earth mother who's been so busy giving love she doesn't know how much she needs it until she's awakened by a drifter's kiss...

CALLOWAY CORNERS

Coming from Superromance, in 1989:
Mariah, by Sandra Canfield, a January release
Jo, by Tracy Hughes, a February release
Tess, by Katherine Burton, a March release
Eden, by Penny Richards, an April release

CALL-1

Have You Ever Wondered If You Could Write A Harlequin Novel?

Here's great news—Harlequin is offering a series of cassette tapes to help you do just that. Written by Harlequin editors, these tapes give practical advice on how to make your characters—and your story— come alive. There's a tape for each contemporary romance series Harlequin publishes.

Mail order only

All sales final

Harlequin Romance Movie

TEARS IN THE RAIN

STARRING
CHRISTOPHER CAVZENOVE AND
SHARON STONE

BASED ON A NOVEL BY
PAMELA WALLACE

PREMIERING IN NOVEMBER

TITR-1